Forging On

D0347300

Catherine Robinson lives with her husband in Lancashire, where she has always lived, and where (when not teaching or writing) she has raised a son, farmed a small flock of Derbyshire Gritstone sheep, and bred horses. *Forging On* is her first novel.

Forging On

CATHERINE ROBINSON

An Orion paperback

First published in Great Britain in 2017 by Orion Books,
an imprint of The Orion Publishing Group Ltd
Carmelite House, 50 Victoria Embankment
London EC4Y 0DZ

An Hachette UK company

1 3 5 7 9 10 8 6 4 2

Copyright © Catherine Robinson 2017

Lyrics from 'Hot Stuff' © Casablanca Record and Film Works, Inc.

The moral right of Catherine Robinson to be identified as the
author of this work has been asserted in accordance with
the Copyright, Designs and Patents Act 1988.

All rights reserved. No part of this publication may be
reproduced, stored in a retrieval system, or transmitted,
in any form or by any means, electronic, mechanical,
photocopying, recording or otherwise, without the prior
permission of the copyright owner.

All the characters in this book are fictitious,
and any resemblance to actual persons, living
or dead, is purely coincidental.

A CIP catalogue record for this book
is available from the British Library.

ISBN 978 1 4091 6844 7

Typeset by Deltatype Ltd, Birkenhead, Merseyside

Printed and bound in Great Britain by
Clays Ltd, St Ives plc

MIX
Paper from
responsible sources
FSC® C104740

www.orionbooks.co.uk

For my son

STRATFORD COLLEGE OF AGRICULTURE:

FACULTY OF BLACKSMITHING AND FARRIERY

Apprenticeship Journal for the month of: September.

Comments: I have started my apprenticeship under the guidance of Mr Stanley Lampitt of Hathersage, North Yorkshire where I am the junior of Mr Lampitt's two apprentices.

Learning outcomes:

I am familiar with my new workplace and its health and safety procedures.

I am able to prepare, set and maintain a fire.

I can safely sharpen tools.

I can load and unload the vehicle prior to and following every job.

I can wire-brush feet.

Signed: William Harker. Sept 30th 2015   (Apprentice)

Signed: SL Sept 30th 2015   (Master)

Chapter 1

The Rottweiler was foaming at the chops; white slobber had pooled in the creases of its jaw and saliva was yo-yoing from its fangs. I turned to Stanley.'Why me?'

'Because you're the bloody apprentice and you do what I tell you, comprendo?'

'What if I get bitten?'

'I'll dock your bastard wages for being useless; now get out.' I touched the door handle. 'William, it's on a bloody chain!' Still, I didn't move. 'Go on! I'll count to three. One ...' I burst from the van. The dog's chain slithered on the stones. It launched. Surely, if it could reach the van its face would have smashed through the passenger window by now? Its massive head grew. *Stay calm*, I told myself, *stick close to the van.* A thunk. Stanley was right. It had reached the end of its chain. I breathed, gave him a thumbs up and took two strides towards the house – then an urgent rattle turned my head. It was coming again! How could it be coming again? In that nanosecond of paralysis, ten feet of snapped chain gave me my answer.

I'm not a sprinter, but eight stone of Rottweiler behind me unlocked my true potential and Usain Bolt would have had night sweats if he'd seen me cross that yard. I took a leap worthy of an Olympic pole-vaulter and grabbed the stables' overhanging roof. I could hear Stan roaring with laughter over Paloma Faith's 'Ready For the Good Life'. This was his best entertainment since leaving Fetch-It – his last but one apprentice – cleaning the coal all afternoon.

With one extra wild kick, I managed to swing my legs up and clamber onto the stable roof. I'd have enjoyed the view of the distant beck glittering its snail-trail over the surrounding purple moor, if I hadn't been gasping like a landed tench. Stanley wasn't admiring the view either. He was beating the steering wheel in glee. The Beast of Wharfedale was on two legs now, bouncing, bellowing and trailing its chain, and in the distance Old Pedley was ambling out of the squat stone farmhouse. Pedley only had one speed, and it was slower than the growth of the weeds that had reached the mullioned windows. Eventually he looked up through jam-jar lenses. 'Nah then, lad, what are you doing up theer?' I'd have thought it was obvious. 'Rosie, come here, lass.' The Beast dropped to four paws, waved her stump tail, lowered her teddy-bear head and wandered to Old Pedley.

Only now did Stan get out of the van: 'What a bloody chicken, eh, Mr Pedley? I told him Rosie wouldn't so much as knock the skin off a rice puddin'.' (He'd told me no such thing.)

'I hope he's less freetened o' me 'osses,' Pedley chunnered, taking a length of baling twine from his pocket and looping it round the dog's collar. Only when I could see that Rosie was compliant did I drop from the stable roof.

'He might be a poncey little flake, but there's nobody better wi' th'osses than our Will,' Stanley said, ruffling my hair like he'd paid me a compliment.

Pedley grunted.'You're on'y takin' t'shoes off 'em today, any road.' I groaned. Stanley wouldn't be taking the shoes off Pedley's six gigantic draught horses; I would. Shire feet are hard as rock and clamping your knees on massive hooves bruises the insides of them. They don't tell you that at college. They don't tell you that working over an anvil sends invisible shards of metal into your skin either.

'Put your face straight!' Stanley ordered. 'Grappling wi' nine tonne of horse flesh'll be right up your street after that little show of athletics.' He jumped into the van. 'Four o'clock. And mind yourself with Billy!'

Mind yourself with Billy is the sort of parting remark no farrier wants to hear. I pretended some confidence.

'Shall we get Billy over with first then, Mr Pedley?'

Mr Pedley hesitated. 'I reckon Billy's best left until you've speeded up a bit.' Was he leaving him until last so I'd done the bulk of the work before I was airlifted to Leeds General? Through the shoe-pulling and rasping of Dolly, Bessie, Sonny, Percy and Flower, my mind was only on Billy and when seventeen hands of sleek black muscle finally strolled out of the barn, it was with the assurance of a gang fighter. Mr Pedley tied Billy up, then sat on the low wall and folded his arms. That worried me too; he'd been filling hay nets, brewing up and mixing feeds when I'd been working on the others.

I walked to Billy's shoulder, talked softly to him then slid my hand down his left foreleg. Billy raised his foot with the same obliging courtesy that the other horses had shown. Relieved, I took the hoof pick from my belt. Whilst Billy gently mouthed the rope tying him to the stable wall, I scraped debris from his vast foot. I replaced the hoof pick, took my buffer from my chaps (farriers' chaps do the same job as builders' overalls) and began lifting the clenches on his near fore.

So there I am, bent under Billy's big belly, gradually growing in confidence, telling myself that it's all to do with your attitude, when a clatter is followed by a snort from Old Pedley. I look up and see my hoof pick six feet away on the cobbles. Billy has picked my pocket and lobbed it across the yard. I sigh, lower his foot, put my buffer in my chaps, cross the yard, collect the hoof pick, replace it, walk back, bend double and lift Billy's dinner-plate foot again. Within seconds Billy has repeated the trick.

'He's a bloody character!' Mr Pedley laughs as he crosses the yard to collect my hoof pick again. He puts it on the wall next to me and I take my shoe puller to Billy's foot. I've freed the first shoe when I feel a sudden tightness. Before I've registered the reason for it, my feet are off the floor and I'm dangling arse up, like a floating corpse. Pedley lets out a guffaw and Billy shakes me so that hoof pick, rasp and nails spill onto the cobbles – then he opens his mouth. A second after I've hit the cobbles, my chaps follow. Pedley is rocking with laughter. 'He pulled that stunt on t'vet! She damn near injected herself with her own ketamine!' I straighten up and stare at Billy who is rolling his eyes, like a bad actor in *Othello*. 'He ripped t'britches' arse right out of her jeans!'

I decide to forget my chaps and Pedley watches me as I align my tools on the wall instead. I start lifting the clenches on Billy's off-fore and gradually become aware of a gentle, slightly uncomfortable swaying. His attention span is obviously limited, but with the approach of four o'clock preying on my mind, I decide to press on.

'Hey up! That was your rasp!' My rasp is now in the field, ten feet away, and I can't hop over the wall as there's a six foot drop. So, I set off towards the gate and Pedley launches into a tale of Billy grabbing the judge's bowler hat at the Great Yorkshire Show. 'It was bloody hilarious! He was waving it at the crowd. He should have been a stand-up comic, should our Billy.'

Bloody hilarious, I think, and I remember my father's advice. *Go to university*, he'd said. *Get a degree and then decide if you want to work with horses*, he'd said. Ankle-deep in mud with a light drizzle on the back of my neck, it was an appealing alternative.

I am halfway across the stone-walled paddock when my hammer describes an arc through the air and thuds in the mud. Pedley is doubled over now. 'He's a bloody clown!' Billy is bending down for my shoe puller. 'Get it off him!' I yell, but the horse is like a shot putter building for his throw.

'What?' Billy's head is nodding in preparation.

'The puller! Get it off him!'

'The what?' Too late. It flies, handle over tip, and Pedley chuckles in delight. 'You have to laugh at him, haven't you!'

I'd just bent under Billy again when I heard Stanley's van draw into the yard. I knew I was for it. A time-wasting glance at any girl in jodhpurs earned me a clip round the ear. Now he was bawling over the noise of his engine. Not, 'Hi, Will,' or, 'How d'you get on, Will,' or 'Thanks for busting a gut and keeping me out of prison for animal cruelty, Will,' (which I had done, because as sure as God made little apples he would have walloped that stand-up-comic of a shire horse), but: 'Why is your arse still in the air, you bloody idle waster?'

'He's been a bit tricky, Stan.'

'I've driven to Eckersley, shod four ponies, and driven back again in the time you've been pissing about!'

'It were t'same when I worked at t'brewery,' Old Pedley piped up from his perch on the wall where he'd been sitting for the last hour. 'They're freetened o'graft, this generation.'

'He's only had to take their bloody shoes off!'

'I don't know how you've the patience with them, Stanley.'

Whilst I removed Billy's hind shoes and made two un-assisted trips into the field in fading light, Stanley and Pedley grumbled about the idleness of modern youth, the poverty of their childhoods and the corrupting influence of the Xbox. I gave Billy's foot one last rasp round and Pedley peeled off six twenty-pound notes and handed them over. 'It's a bloody good job it weren't piece work, in't it – eh?' I gathered up my tools, slung them in the van and pushed Stanley's Jack Russell terrier off the passenger seat.

When we'd waved our goodbyes Stanley turned to me, grinning.

'You knew full well I wouldn't have them done by four, didn't you?' I said, and he chuckled so that his massive shoulders shook in his checked shirt.

'Did Billy give you the runaround then?' I slung him a with-ering look, turned to the passenger window and insulted him under my breath. 'Did you just call me a bell-end?' I didn't answer. 'I'll have you know I'm a decent bloke, compared to most farriers!' I turned back. His bald head was gleaming.

'Try comparing yourself to most human beings!' Stanley fell silent as the cottages of Throstleden fast-forwarded past our windows.

'I should box your fucking ears,' he said at last. Then he turned up Radio 2.

Chapter 2

Only last week, I was filling up the van and the guy at the next pump asked why a young lad like me had become a farrier. Our ancient Ford Transit is heavy on diesel, but there still wouldn't have been time to explain it, so I offered him girls in jodhpurs.

The truth is that from the minute I was forced into a classroom I hated the clagged air of Beaumont College, thick with thought. Its windows taunted me with squares of sliding sky. Lesson after lesson, clouds morphed and bloomed, whilst I dreamt of sheep-splashed acres.

We had twelve acres at home and wind-scoured or mud-slicked, they were the fields of heaven to me. Every season had its adventures. In winter I smashed ice on the troughs with a spade; in spring I bottle-fed lambs; in summer I folded fleeces with Kiwi shearers who turned up full of stories like mediaeval journeymen. I watched skylarks hatch and rode home on top of the hay bales.

Twelve acres is too little to farm, but my mother – Lizzie Harker – ran The Lizzie Harker Natural Horsemanship Experience. She dropped me onto a Shetland pony as soon as I could sit upright, and then I progressed through Welsh Section A, Welsh Section B and Fell before I was big enough to ride her horses. Until I started working with them, I thought they could all be ridden without a saddle or a bridle.

By the time I reached year eleven, school still seemed a waste of youth and of Yorkshire. I remember Dad waving my report over my head and bellowing at me, 'You might as well stare out of Pickerscale Comp's windows instead!' It was water off a duck's back; I'd heard it all before – and Granddad didn't care so long as his twenty-three thousand pounds a year paid for him to sip Pimm's in Beaumont's cricket pavilion and point to his name on the roll of honour.

'Veterinary science?' Dad attempted, as my school career sputtered to an embarrassing halt.

'I won't get the grades, Dad.'

'I'll pay for you to repeat the year.'

'Just pay for me to go to Guantanamo and have done.'

'Land management, then?'

'They manage land from behind a desk.'

'What about the Household Cavalry?'

'And get shot at?'

It was only when my lousy A-level results confirmed their worst fears that Granddad strolled into the kitchen and announced he'd arranged a placement for me at Paul Dunster's racing yard. 'Only for a year, William; until you decide to stop playing at *Swallows and Amazons*.'

I loved that racing yard. I was outside all day, in all weathers. I loved the knife-edge exhilaration that plunges between ecstasy and fear. I loved the racehorse contradiction of fragility and power. I loved the craic with the lads. But even with my slight physique, staying under eight stone was torture and after six months I was longing for a meat pie and suspecting I'd end up one of the frail impoverished 'lads' still living in a tied cottage after forty years of riding work. Only the very best make the racetrack, let alone the winner's enclosure, and I wasn't looking like the next Frankie Dettori.

I was mulling this over whilst Paul Dunster's farrier shod a racehorse in front of me. I'd watched farriers at work all my life, but I'd never really paid attention before. Here was precision, concentration and horsemanship – and work under a wide grey sky. I slipped off the haylage bale and ambled over. 'Do you mind if I watch?' He shook his head and a trickle of sweat scampered down his neck and over his bulging bicep. 'How long did it take you to train, then?'

'Five years,' he answered, through a mouthful of nails.

'At college?'

'At the college of hard knocks and fresh air, mostly!' I watched him line up a nail. He re-angled it then banged it in with four hard raps. The horse raised its head. The farrier soothed him, then lined up another nail.

That evening Matty's voice thumped out of our shared hayloft bedsit before my second foot had crossed our threshold: 'Steak pudding, chips, mushy peas and gravy.' I was supposed to counter it with an equally appealing, but permitted, dish.

'Lemon sorbet and raspberry coulis.'

'No!' The jockey's voice rang with disdain. 'That's not a main course!' I could never understand why he tortured himself like this. The pinboard over my bed bore a picture of my mother with her horses, Granddad's postcard from St Lucia and a list of racing fixtures. Matty's board was covered in takeaway menus, magazine recipes and backed with a Pukka Pie poster. 'I like imagining,' he explained.

'I'll be ordering if my plan works out.'

'What's your plan? Bulimia?'

'Nope!' I placed my Pro-Crush whip on the chair. 'Farriery.'

'You?'

'Why not?'

'Because you're about the size of a rabbit.' I peeled off my Paul Dunster jacket. 'I've a plan of my own, as it goes.'

'Oh, yeah?'

'National Hunt racing.'

'How's that going to help?'

Matty sat up from his prone position on the bed. 'Are you joking? I'll have an extra stone to play with!'

11

'You'll get creamed.'

'And you won't? Banging nails into their feet!'

Within two weeks Matty had a trial in Lambourn which coincided with my one weekend off in four, so on Saturday morning he drove me the twenty-five miles from Paul Dunster's yard to my home at Mossthwaite, then continued on his four hour journey. I'd been researching into farriery courses, but had said nothing to my parents. The word 'college' might go some way to appeasing my father but it wasn't medicine, or law, or engineering so I needed to pick my moment – ideally when Dad had a glass of wine in his right hand and Mumma at his left. I was beginning to think I wouldn't find it, when Granddad passed me the gravy boat at Sunday lunch and asked if I'd thought any more about my future. There was no avoiding it now. I looked up, met his eye, and told him I had. I used the word 'college' three times during my enthusiastic exposition, in which Mumma smiled and Granddad nodded with interest. '... So it's an outdoor job that combines horsemanship with craftsmanship,' I concluded.

Granddad gave a final cheery nod then set about his Yorkshire pudding. Mumma looked satisfied and took the gravy boat, but my father didn't even pick up his knife and fork. Instead, he placed his elbows on the table and plaited his fingers.

'A tradesman?'

'Hardly!' Mumma exclaimed, but Dad was looking at me over the top of his glasses.

'You do know that Piers is applying for Oxford?'

Granddad spoke without looking up.'Don't make this into a competition between cousins, James.'

'And farriers aren't blacksmiths any more. They're specialists.' (Thank God for my mother!) 'They understand the biomechanics of foot flight and the stresses through the internal structures of the foot. A vet defers to a good farrier in matters below the fetlock.'

My father unplaited his fingers and picked up his cutlery. 'College, you say?'

'In Warwickshire – then a four-year apprenticeship.' He sawed at a piece of beef.

'Have you checked the entry requirements?'

'Yes, and I have them …'

'Let the boy make his choices, James.' (Thank you, Granddad!) 'He's wanted no more than to be outside in all weathers since he could walk.'

Still my father concentrated on his plate.

'Is it a good living?'

'At seventy pounds a set!' Mumma exclaimed. 'I should say it is!' Dad glanced at her in shock – he had obviously never realised how much of the family income our farrier took – then he turned back to me.

'If you're sure this is what you want, William, you'd better start making enquiries.'

'I have.' I smiled. 'I have an interview next Thursday.' Granddad patted me on the back, Mumma kissed me on the cheek and told me she was proud of me and Dad shuffled to the cellar for a bottle of champagne.

'To a decision,' he said, without smiling. 'Albeit an unconventional one!'

A year after my father had proposed that toast, I was knocking on Stanley's front door in Hathersage. Hathersage isn't fifteen miles from where I grew up, but I'd never been there before. It's a relic of the industrial revolution. Its factories have been converted to flats, its Methodist chapel is a furniture warehouse and the Cribbs Estate protrudes from its western edge like a 1960s' conservatory from a listed building.

My satnav brought my six-year-old Vauxhall Astra to a halt on the town's main road and, with my certificate of Pre-Farriery in a plastic wallet, I stepped onto the threshold of an alien world.

Six foot six of tattooed muscle opened the door and looked me up and down. 'You're not so bloody big, are you?' The opposite thought had just passed through my mind. Stanley was about forty-five, and his gleaming shaven head was the cheeriest thing about him.

He invited me into a flashy modern kitchen which unsettled me as much as his brusque greeting had. Even though we were in a 1930s detached on the town's main road, I'd expected a country cottage kitchen with a wood-burning stove. He indicated a chrome stool next to the granite worktop and completely ignored the CV which had taken me hours to write. Stanley folded his vast tattooed arms. 'What d'y'think o' me kitchen, then?' I probably looked a bit wild-eyed at his interview technique.

'It's very nice.' It must have been the right answer because Stanley nodded.

'It bloody is. It should be an' all. Do you know how much these worktops cost me?' My mouth had gone dry. The questions were getting harder. 'Five grand. Five bastard grand – and do you know why?' I gulped and shook my head. 'Because I like nice stuff.' I swallowed. 'Do you want to see my bathroom?' I didn't know the answer. Was I supposed to want to see the bathroom? Was it a job requirement?

'Would you like me to?'

'I would, lad, aye.' So I followed him down a shagpile lobby, past Farrow and Balled walls and up a marble staircase. The bathroom was the size of a small dance hall. In the centre was a deep, roll-topped bath, in the corner a double shower – 'It's remote-controlled, is that' – and in the opposite corner, a bidet. 'Do you know what that is?' I could answer this one, but it was best not to sound too cocky.

'Is it a bidet?'

'It is, posh lad! It is! It's what the French wash their arses in.' He was clearly delighted either with my knowledge, or the French habit, or his own bidet. Either way, I followed him back to the kitchen where he proceeded to demonstrate a coffee-making machine. 'Do you fancy a cap-oo-chee-noh?'

'No, thanks.' I wished we could talk farriery.

Stanley finally sat down with his cap-oo-chee-noh. 'This is how it is, Posh Lad.' (Why was I ' Posh Lad' when he had a kitchen worthy of the Beckhams? Was it my accent? Was it because I recognised a bidet?) 'I don't bugger abaht wi' CVs. I'm not interested in what you've done; I'm interested in what you're goin' to do. I don't stand for any pissin' abaht. I haven't got this swanky house o' mine wi' pissin' abaht. Graft. That's what got me this – and if you'll graft, same as me, you can have an 'ouse as nice as this one day. And if I don't like ya, you're down the road, laddo – comprendo? Nah, these are t'rules: no idling, no backchat, no thieving off me and no pissin' abaht. Can you manage that?' I was still nodding. 'Well, we'll see, won't we? Because I change my apprentices more often than other farriers change their socks. I won't have wasters!'

I later found out that Fetch-It had lasted six weeks with Stanley, and Fuckwit, before him, only a month. One other apprentice was currently surviving Stanley's regime and was within a year of qualifying. Ewan Grimshaw was soon to be my friend and ally, but to Stanley he was Dolloper.

Stanley picked up my carefully crafted CV and handed it back to me. 'You might want to keep that for when you're looking for your next job.'

I shook his hand, thanked him and headed for the back door, still unsure of whether or not I'd got the job. As I passed between the Doric columns of his back porch he spoke: 'Monday morning, eight o'clock.' I smiled. 'And if you're still as puny by Christmas, I'll sack you. No blacksmith has arms like bastard chopsticks.'

'Thanks. Thanks for the opportunity, Mr Lampitt.'

'Stanley!' he barked. 'It's Stanley, Posh Lad.'

*

When I arrived at eight o'clock sharp, Ewan was already un-packing boxes in the forge. The former garage's up-and-over door was up, so I was able to observe him as I walked down the drive. Ewan was taller than me – though as I barely scrape five foot five, most men don't find that difficult. He was wearing a red hoodie and faded jeans, his dark hair was in the short, neat style my granddad approves of, and he was moving with rhythmic fluidity. It wasn't until I drew nearer that I realised he'd been singing to himself.

'Will Harker,' I said, holding out my hand. Ewan hesitated. He glanced up with round brown eyes, wiped his hand on his jeans, shook mine awkwardly, then returned to unpacking. 'Both boxes?' I asked. Ewan nodded, and we fell into a rhythm.

The forge was behind Stanley's house – or Bling Manor, as we came to call it – and this functional building, in which I was supposed to acquire the physique of Sylvester Stallone, would be my refuge from the Yorkshire madness that Stanley's round was about to unleash on me.

By the time Stanley emerged scratching his chest, we'd man-aged a stilted conversation about my journey, stocked the van, watered his hanging baskets and fed his Jack Russell. Ewan silently handed Stanley his morning brew and sat down on a box of horseshoes with his own. Stanley raised his eyebrows at Ewan. 'Make a brew for Posh Lad!'

'He dun't want one.'

Stanley slowly turned his head and shoulders towards me and stared at me as if I'd just admitted to drinking the blood of babies. 'You have to have a brew, lad!'

I was about to make history as his shortest serving appren-tice. Fetch-It, six weeks; Fuckwit, one month; Posh Lad, one hour. 'Sorry, Mr— Stanley, I don't like it.'

Stanley stood in full open-mouthed incomprehension. 'Well, have coffee then!'

'I don't like coffee either.' The silence clanged like a dropped horseshoe. 'Sorry.'

Stanley was shaking his head in utter disbelief. 'Well what do you drink, when you're at home, like?'

I shrugged. 'Water?' It was another wrong answer.

'No! I mean for a brew – what do you drink for a brew?' I had been hoping to avoid this.

I swallowed. 'Earl Grey.'

Ewan spluttered then choked on his Yorkshire tea. Stanley narrowed his eyes and shook his head. He'd heard it but it wouldn't quite compute. 'Earl Grey?'

I nodded.

'Earl fucking Grey?'

Sod it, I thought, I've probably blown it now anyway. 'Twinings Earl Grey.'

Stan sighed and raised his mug. 'You want to get this down you, lad. You can't beat Yorkshire's own!'

It was Ewan's turn to take him on. 'It's not, though, is it? Not really.'

'Not what?'

'Yorkshire's own.'

'Course it bloody is. Why do you think they call it Yorkshire tea?'

'It's not grown in Yorkshire though, is it, Stan?'

'Course it bloody is! *Yorkshire* tea!' He was pointing at the words on the box.

'That's only its name though, in't it, Stan?'

'Is it bollocks! Why would they call it Yorkshire tea if it weren't grown in bloody Yorkshire?' He turned to me. 'Have you heard him? I'm supposed to get that bloody dolloper through his apprenticeship in the next twelve months.' I smiled weakly, hoping to keep out of it, but Ewan wasn't for dropping it.

'I'm right, aren't I? Tell him! You can't grow tea in Yorkshire!'

I cleared my throat. 'Well, I think it's grown in China, or India ... usually, but it'll be Yorkshire water.'

17

Ewan was triumphant. 'See! It's too bloody cold in Yorkshire.'

Stan's eyes darted between us for a second. 'I bloody know it's too cold in Yorkshire,' he announced. 'I am not bloody stupid, am I?' He took a big gulp of his tea. 'Obviously it needs a warmer climate.'

For a moment I thought he was conceding defeat. I had yet to learn that Stanley could never be wrong. 'They grow it under bastard glass, don't they.' Somehow he managed to say it like it was Ewan who had been stupid. 'Now swill the bloody cups out, Dolloper.'

Chapter 3

Stanley put his mug on the floor for Lucky who lapped the dregs of his brew then he swiped Ewan's mug from his hands. Ewan sat there, still holding his ghost mug, and sighed as Stan stood up. 'Right, Dolloper; you can do Worthington's donkeys while I show Posh Lad what's what.'

'Can't you do Worthington's donkeys while I show Posh Lad what's what?' It wasn't even a game try. Ewan's face was admitting defeat even before Stanley had opened his mouth.

'Why would I leave you to bad-mouth me while Worthington's donkeys are puncing me from here to Wakefield?' He slung him the van keys. 'Twelve o'clock sharp. Back here.' Ewan grunted and walked towards the bright yellow van. I remember making a mental note to strive for something more tasteful should I ever have DipWCF after my name.

DipWCF: Diploma of the Worshipful Company of Farriers. Throughout my year's pre-farriery course at Stratford the words had conjured an ancient trade, sweated out in village squares by honest yokels in breeches. This was no modern apprenticeship; the papers signed by apprentices are the same as those signed in 1356. I think the wages are the same as well.

Stanley's bright yellow van was signwritten with a grinning brown horse in a tweed jacket and – bizarrely, as our profession depends entirely on the fact that horses don't have opposable thumbs – giving the thumbs up, with *Get thy 'oss shod 'ere!* in a speech bubble.

Ewan sulked his way into the van and Stanley opened the

19

passenger door for the dog. Ewan pleaded, 'Do I have to take Lucky?' I wondered at his reluctance; Lucky was small enough to fit in a shoebox and her white satin pelt was splashed with two black patches; one on her right, and one on her left. The left-hand patch was shaped like Mickey Mouse, which added to her innocent appeal. Her foxy little face was brown, save for its dark widow's peak, and as Ewan and Stanley spoke her velvety ears were triangulating with interest.

'Don't be so bloody selfish; she doesn't want to be stuck in t'forge all morning!' She jumped in, stump-tail wagging.

As the van pulled onto Hathersage Road, Stan turned back to me. 'Right, a few dos and don'ts, and then a tour of my empire. Firstly – and this is very important, Posh Lad – never, ever lose your temper with a horse. If you think you might lose your rag, you just walk away for a minute. Nasty Neddy who's just punched you round the yard for an hour is her baby – com-prendo?' I nodded. My mother spent her days teaching patience around horses and losing your temper only makes matters worse. 'Secondly, always, always, always make time to *listen*. If she wants to blether on about a crack in its foot, or how many bloody ribbons it's won – you listen. What do you do?'

'I listen.'

'Exactamundo. I don't care how late we're running. No client, no business. She has to think you love that 'oss as much as she does.' I nodded. 'Good,' he stated, then he encompassed the forge with open arms. 'So, welcome to my empire!'

The up-and-over garage door was up and the concrete floor and breeze-block walls were as far from the romantic image of a forge as Stanley, in his padded shirt and jeans, was from the beaming leather-aproned craftsmen of yore. The curved brick front of the glowing coke forge crept closest to the traditional picture, so long as you ignored the aluminium chimney. Next to the brick forge was a bright red fire extinguisher. Stan pointed to it. 'Under no circumstances whatsoever must you use that fire extinguisher.'

I frowned. 'What if there's a fire?'

'You use a bucket of water.'

'But what if—'

'There is no what if! I don't care if my bastard house is burning down – you use buckets, you lazy sod – comprendo?' I nodded. 'It costs eighty bastard quid to refill one of them things!'

Stan named the tools on the wall aloud for me: 'Pritchel, nippers, hoof knives, soft-faced hammer, blemisher ...'

Blemisher?

' ... shoe spreader, clench cutter, shoe pullers, hoof testers, hot-fit tongs ...' He showed me the lengths of steel under the workbench; the sink, the kettle, the rows of boxes marked *5" fullered*, *5½" plain*, *eggbar*, the boxes of nails, the brush, the shovel, the pile of coke and a bin full of rusty horseshoes. 'Now, come wi' me,' Stan commanded.

I followed his hulking frame through the doorway and past the chicken run – where he pointed out his favourite hen, Aunty Dorothy – to the back of the forge where he stopped and folded his arms in fatherly pride. 'That,' he crowed, 'is what you could have if you're prepared to break sweat every day like I am.'

Before us, gleaming and slick as an ice sculpture, slept a long, white Porsche. I could almost hear its sleepy purring. Stanley had just given me the best possible reason to spend the next four years bent double under a horse for a hundred and fifty quid a week. I sighed in aching longing. I know cars are wrecking the planet. I know they cost a fortune – but I love them. 'Fancy a spin?' I looked at him bug-eyed. The car flashed its lights at me like a hooker and I dropped into the deep bucket seat beside Stanley. He fired the ignition and lowered the windows. The car growled like a disgruntled lion, then eased out of the drive as if its shoulder blades were rolling.

We turned onto Hathersage Road with the bass beat of Status Quo bouncing our bones. As we cruised to a growling halt between a white Transit van and a bus, every head on Hathersage Road turned. Stanley rested his tattooed arm on the lowered window and two girls in tight jeans turned and stared. They were nearer my age than Stan's but he winked. 'A'right, girls?' I might have smiled if I'd been with Ewan, but I kept my eyes front, hung my hand out of the car and tapped the metal to the beat; then I remembered I was tapping to Status Quo, and stopped. The lights changed; Stanley hit the gas pedal. The Porsche roared and the g-force pinned me like I'd been punched.

We sped between grimy grey walls, past the petrol station and the American Golf Store. The Wacky Warehouse and the garden centre were a blur, then, after three minutes of dangerously exceeding the speed limit in an urban area, we were roaring between drystone walls. Twisting Pennine roads flung me from window to gear lever and back again. I clung to the seat to avoid overfamiliarity. We lashed past country pubs, wind turbines, and sheep shelters. He didn't even slow down for the cattle grids. We were on the open moor which billows up above Hathersage's crenulated skyline; rolling purple acres where the only structures are the gritstone crags rising out of the heather. Even the sheep who casually stalk the tarmac dived for the ditches as we passed.

I was glad to be alive by the time we turned back into Hathersage Road and prowled up Stanley's drive. 'What do you reckon to that then?' I'd bitten my tongue at the second cattle grid and was nursing it behind my molars so it took me a moment to answer.

'Great.' The car was great, it was the driver I had doubts about. The Porsche's door thunked expensively as I closed it, and before I turned away I ran my hand lovingly down her wing as if she were a racehorse. Stanley lingered for one last glimpse like he was leaving a lover, then turned towards the forge.

He put the kettle on. 'Right. I think it's time I saw what you're made of; how's your telephone manner?'

'OK, I think.'

'Good. You can ring up Hobday's and order me a new blemisher belt.'

I gulped. 'A blemisher belt?' Was this his first piss-take? Would he be in the Fleece tonight, gasping with laughter at his own wit? 'Do you mean a linisher belt?'

'Oh, you're the bloody expert on farriers' tools, are you?'

I shook my head. 'Sorry, it's just that I've never heard of—'

'If I say I want a blemisher belt, I want a bastard blemisher belt. Comprendo?'

I decided I'd better go along with it. Perhaps it was a local name, so whilst Stanley clattered his way through his tools, looking for items I could sharpen, I picked up the phone and rang Hobday's. 'A blemisher belt,' I requested, cringing.

The voice on the other end was deadpan: 'Would that be for Mr Stanley Lampitt, by any chance?'

My relief must have been audible. 'Yes!'

'Tell him a belt for his *linisher* will be in the post today.' I hung up, grinning.

Stanley dropped half a dozen blunt hoof knives in front of me. 'See. Smart arse.'

I was relieved when I heard the handbrake of the van. There was a pause before the van door opened, then a yell, then a gnashing, then an airborne Jack Russell arrived arse first, shook itself and walked to its water bowl. Stanley addressed Ewan: 'What time do you call this, meladdo?'

'I know, I know. Mrs Worthington was worried about the thrush in her donkey's foot, so I was explaining to her—'

'And how much did you charge for that little consultation?'

Ewan strolled towards the kettle.

'I'm not running a bloody charity here! You can't stand about chewing the fat with every crackpot who wants to whinge about her horse. Do you want to finish at ten o'clock every night?'

Ewan ran the tap.

'Time is money, Dolloper! You're not wasting my time blethering with fuckwits about bastard donkeys! You can knock that twenty minutes off your lunch!'

Ewan shook his head in disbelief and Stanley flounced towards Bling Manor leaving us with our Tupperware and sandwiches.

I turned to Ewan. 'Do you know what he just told me—'

'I know, I know. Always make time for the clients.'

I glanced towards the house. 'You can't do right for doing wrong, can you?'

'Don't worry about me!' Ewan grinned. 'I've just had a swift half in the Fleece. You've got to get one over on Stanley when you can.'

'So you mean …?'

'I made it up.' I bit into my soggy tuna sandwich. 'Let me guess, he's shown you his Porsche, he's introduced you to Aunty Dorothy, he's had you sharpening his tools and he's told you to "never ever use that bastard fire extinguisher"?' Ewan could have been a clairvoyant.

'Correctamundo!' He grinned at my imitation. 'And he got me to order him a blemisher belt!' A jet of half-chewed Cornish pasty shot across the forge and I knew then that we were going to get on. Ewan had worked for Stanley since he was fifteen and he regaled me with four years' worth of Stan stories over lunch. When Stan strolled in, replete, Ewan turned to him grinning.

'I'm glad you've ordered a new blemisher belt. That old one just wasn't blemishing, was it?' Stanley shot Ewan a sideways glance. He knew something was going on, he just didn't know what. 'We'll be able to give them heels a right good blemishing now, won't we?'

'Just get in the fucking van,' he ordered.

Chapter 4

Ewan's roots on Cribbs Estate had inured him to Stanley's murderous outbursts. Furniture bursting though bedroom windows and the casual violence of his neighbours' drunken weekends rendered Stanley as no more than a nuisance to Ewan.

'Late night?' I'd ask at the sight of his red-rimmed eyes.

'Oh, Chantelle stabbed Dwayne's leg with the bread knife last night so it was like Brixton riots out there till gone three.' I thought he was making it up at first. My experience of domestic violence was my mum closing her laptop on my dad's fingers.

'What did you do?'

'I turned the bloody telly up,' Ewan answered, with the patience of a nursery nurse.

Ewan was the second of two brothers raised by their single, randomly employed dad. His mam had walked out when Ewan was two – at about the same time that the chemical works that had employed his father, uncles and grandfather for a hundred years closed down. The whole family were tipped onto the dole queue, with all the rest of Hathersage's able-bodied men who'd known no other life.

I was uncomfortable when I first drove between the shit-spattered pavements, huddles of hoodies and loose Staffies on Ewan's estate. I'd pulled my six-year-old Astra onto Ewan's drive behind a rusted white van on bricks, then paid an eight-year-old bully a fiver to 'guard it'. Lee – Ewan's older brother – had the money off the kid within ten minutes, but not before his mate had pissed all over Lee's work shoes. All the while a German shepherd was booming at me from the other side of a slobber-smeared window. I had to step over two discarded tyres and a broken pram to reach the front door.

Within a minute I was ashamed of my preconceptions. The hearty handshake from Ewan's dad and the smell of frying bacon were as welcoming as an open fireside. Even Ricky – the dog – was not what he seemed. The carpets were threadbare and the armchairs mismatched but I gradually came to recognise Ewan's dad as a hero. He's been mother and father to his sons; he's worked on supermarket checkouts, motorway services and the council tip, juggling his hours to fit round school. Lee and Ewan were expected to earn; university hadn't even been an option, let alone an expectation. Lee had trained as a motor mechanic, and a Saturday job cleaning Stanley's forge had evolved into an apprenticeship for Ewan. I'd bristled at being called Posh Lad, but Cribbs Estate showed me that everything's relative.

That first morning we squashed into the front of Stanley's Transit van. The front seat was made for three, but Stan seemed to take up half the width so I was squashed between them and had to negotiate with Ewan if I wanted to scratch my nose. Lucky balanced herself on Ewan's lap, back feet on his thighs, front feet on the dashboard in her Jack Russell driving position. 'It'll be reyt when I get another van,' Stanley announced. 'You can go off and do some trims on your own then, Dolloper.'

'Will you have it painted up like this van?' I asked, hoping he wouldn't.

'Nah, we're going to be "Professional Western Farriers", aren't we?' He drew a window-wiping arc with his arm, as if the words were emblazoned on the windscreen. 'That's reyt, in't it, Ewan?' Ewan wasn't capable of speaking.

'Why Western?' I asked. Ewan dug me in the ribs. His flesh was trembling, and he'd started to bite on a knuckle.

26

'Well we couldn't say Eastern, could we? I mean, we don't sell bastard Turkish Delight!' It was too much for Ewan whose laughter erupted as a wail of agony. Stanley was very pleased with his joke.

Lucky commented on passing sheep, whilst the landscape piled its hills in the windscreen like overlaid acetates: emerald, on olive, on gauzy grey. Ewan found his composure and spoke over the dog's yapping: 'I'm not taking Lucky out in my van, Stan.'

'You bastard are, lad.'

'She's your dog!' I glanced at her, all bright eyes and pricked ears.

'You'll do as you're told while you're working for me.'

'Why don't you leave her at the forge if you don't want her in your van?'

'Look at her!' Stanley gestured at the dog's intent gaze and gently waving stump of a tail. 'She loves coming out!'

'I don't want her in my van.'

'I don't believe you sometimes, Dolloper. You call yourself an animal lover.'

It was the equivalent of a magician's rope trick. You gave Stanley a straightforward statement and with a flick and a shake, it came back to you in knots. I lifted the maligned dog onto my lap and there she stayed, a parcel of packed muscle, until we pulled into Rodrigo's yard.

Stanley parked up and switched off the engine, but nobody moved. I felt Lucky stiffen. Her eyes were darting like wasps in a beer garden. Stan and Ewan looked at one another. 'We can't!' Ewan said. His voice was half glee and half horror. Stanley was grinning from ear to ear though.

'It's our ONE chance, Dolloper ...' The dog was shaking now.

'What?' I was genuinely puzzled.

'Go on then!' Ewan said. 'Count of three!' I was clueless. 'One! Two!'

'Will somebody tell me what's going on?'

'Three!'

Stanley leapt out. Ewan clambered after him and the doors slammed. Suddenly Lucky was a writhing fiend. The guttural gnashing erupting between her clashing teeth was the stuff of horror movies. I grabbed her scruff but six kilograms of muscle was twisting and whipping in my hands like uncurling wire. She swung, snarling and snapping at my wrists. Her teeth were bared, her nose was concertinaed, her eyes were bulging and now her incisors were splitting my skin. Dimly aware of Stan and Ewan doubled over in laughter in the outside world I was grappling one-handed with the door catch.

'Chuck her!' Ewan shouted through the glass.

Where? She'd be on me again before I could get out. Just before major bloodshed occurred, Ewan opened the door and I did chuck her – right past his ear. She continued her expert twisting, landed on all four feet, shook herself and toddled off with her stump-tail wagging.

'Sorry, mate,' he gasped. He didn't look sorry. 'Too good a chance to pass up.' He didn't sound sorry. He was laughing.

Stanley was still bent double with his hands on his knees. 'She's a bloody one, that Lucky. Can't stand anybody getting out of the van!'

'Well, thanks for warning me.'

'Oh! Where's your sense of fun, Posh Lad?' It was leaking out, along with my Type A Rhesus positive.

Stanley was good-humoured about the waste of antiseptic. He didn't even begrudge the plasters from his first aid kit, but as he was tending my wounds I noticed the nicks and scars all over his own hands. 'That's why it's called Lucky. It's Lucky to be bastard alive!' I winced at a fresh trickle of TCP. 'Oh, don't be so bastard soft. You'll get your own chance to shut somebody in the van with her! Now put your face straight and do some graft.'

Ewan was already bent double under a grey polo pony.

You'd be right in having failed to identify Yorkshire as polo country, but Rodrigo Rodriguez was making a tidy penny from it. His name in Buenos Aires had the same clout as Ryan Giggs' would in Manchester. He'd been a high goal polo player. He'd played with Prince Charles, and rumour had it that he'd taught Prince William to ride. Now in retirement, he was sourcing failed racehorses, retraining them as polo ponies and shipping them to Argentina.

'Why in Yorkshire though?'

Stanley nodded to where a slender goddess was watering a hanging basket on tiptoe. Her sleek black hair rippled down her back and every sweep of her wavy body was hugged by a white T-shirt and canary-yellow jodhpurs. She dropped to her heels and swayed across the yard with the grace of a young deer. Chelsea Rodriguez. Formerly Chelsea Feathers of Slack Bottom Farm. (I have not made that up.) Her plump pout parted, and she spoke.

'A'reyt, Stanley?'

'Aye, champion.'

She pulled at her top. 'That bloody water's dripped all dahn me tits. Milk and two sugars?'

'Aye, ta.'

'What about t' new lad?'

'Nah; he on'y drinks Earl Grey.' She must have looked me up and down but I was busy avoiding her eyes – and her tits.

'Cute, in't he?'

'Posh Lad?'

'Aye. Small, but perfectly formed.' Stanley didn't look up.

'Put your tongue back in, Chelsea, he's a job o'work to do!' She laughed and sashayed across the yard. I, meanwhile, was wire-brushing a hoof to the point of combustion. Ewan watched Chelsea until she disappeared into the farmhouse.

'Must be your sparkly blue eyes.'

'Piss off, Ewan.'

'Or your baby blond hair.'

'It's mousy.'

'She was in our Lee's year at school,' he mused, resuming work with his paring knife. 'So I'd say she's landed on her feet.'

'Aye, she has,' Stanley remarked. 'Which is a miracle when you look at the size of them tits.'

I made sure I was swapping ponies in the barn when Chelsea returned with the brews. By the time I'd fetched a skittish chestnut out, Ewan was bent under his grey again. I handed him a nail and moved the conversation on: 'What's this Professional Western Farriery then?'

Ewan nodded towards Stanley. 'Look at him! He's the biggest cowboy this side of York.' I laughed out loud.

'What's so bastard funny?' Stanley shouted from under a chestnut gelding thirty feet away.

'We were thinking Wild Bill Hickok for the new van,' Ewan answered. Stanley stood up. He knew he was missing a trick again. 'Or else Davy Crockett.' He reached for the rasp, his brow still creasing. Then his jaw slackened. Ewan was already halfway across the manège by the time Stanley had vaulted the rails. He flung his rasp at Ewan who dodged it, then, defeated by youth, Stanley slunk back to his brew.

'Have I ever done a bad job for you, Chelsea?' he shouted towards the flower beds, but before her plump pout could form itself round an answer her husband had shouted from the barn.

'I lend you Stetson, Stanley!'

'Oi! I do a bloody good job for you, you cheeky dago!'

'And you charge me ten pound more for it!' There was a glimmer of panic in Stanley's eye but it was gone in a millisecond.

'Polo ponies take longer!' Even at this point in my career, I knew they didn't.

I watched a central ribbon of clover disappear between the wheels of the van before the track ended and the moor soared skyward, starred with sheep and striped with drystone walls. 'It's like a map of the night sky,' I remarked. Stanley gave me a sideways glance of incredulity and Ewan burst into song.

> *'Stars shining bright above you,*
> *Night breezes seem to whisper, "I love you ..."'*

'Now look what you've started!' Stanley grumbled as the van pulled onto the main road. I was yet to learn that Ewan needed little provocation for a song. His voice was infectious, though, and by *'Say nighty-night and kiss me ...'* Stanley had joined in. I blew him a kiss and made Ewan stutter. It was looking like I could enjoy this job; I just had to learn the words.

Back at Bling Manor, Stanley explained the procedure for exiting the van, hitherto withheld. One: engine off. Two: immobilise terrier. Three: door handles primed. Four: standby. Five: fling terrier over centre seat. Six: exit. In practice, five and six were conducted simultaneously and the result was no more than one mauling a week – on average.

STRATFORD COLLEGE OF AGRICULTURE:

FACULTY OF BLACKSMITHING AND FARRIERY

Apprenticeship Journal for the month of: October.

Comments: This month I have witnessed the efficient deployment of the forge's health and safety procedure. There were no serious injuries, though we were made aware of the financial implications of the incident. I am becoming familiar with the expectations of Mr Lampitt and his varied client base and he commented on my positive interaction with a client.

Learning outcomes:

I can remove worn shoes under supervision.

I understand the procedures for handling untouched youngstock.

I understand the necessity of a correct hoof/pastern axis.

Signed: William Harker. Oct 31st 2015   (Apprentice)

Signed: SL Oct 31st 2015   (Master)

Chapter 5

About a month into my apprenticeship I was dipping a crust into my egg yolk at Ewan's kitchen table when he randomly observed that a fancy dress and joke shop had opened on Eckersley High Street. 'They sell smoke bombs,' he said. I looked up; Ewan's face was grinning back at mine. Result.

The timing was everything. We'd know our moment when it arrived, but it hadn't arrived when Ewan was called away on two weeks' block release. 'Don't use it while I'm at college,' he warned, but I wouldn't have dreamed of it. This was a pleasure best shared.

I spent the first week of Ewan's block release bent double over a coke forge with Stanley. By the end of the week we'd made a set of tongs, a pritchel and a bob punch, and I'd been called a gormless gobshite, a dithering dickhead and a cackhanded cockhead. In the second week I was used as bait for Pedley's Rottweiler, entertainment for his shire horse and amusement for Stanley. Stanley dropped soapflakes in the cooling bucket, asked me to retrieve the soaking shoe then laughed himself sore when I yelped and flung it across the yard. Soapflakes, it turns out, stop the water from cooling the shoe. I told myself he wouldn't have done it had Ewan been there, but the following week I caught Ewan approaching the cooling bucket with a box of Lux.

'Too late,' I said, 'I've been had,' and I held up my still-seared fingertips. Ewan burst into laughter.

'You're not a sulker, are you!' he said.

'I'll tell you what!' Stanley exclaimed. 'He's a pleasure to maim, is this lad. Remember how personal Fuckwit used to take it?'

'The thing is,' Ewan continued later over his cheese and pickle sandwiches, 'Stanley can dish it out, but he can't take it.'

'Is the smoke bomb such a good idea then?'

'It's a bloody genius idea,' he grinned as he wiped a dribble of pickle from his chin.

Our opportunity to use the smoke bomb finally came on a Friday afternoon. I'll let you picture it:

Stan draws up in his Porsche but instead of walking into the forge, he dashes straight into the house. Ewan and I lock eyes. This is our moment. I down my tools, run to the Astra, shoot down the side of Bling Manor and shove the smoke bomb under the Porsche. We've not said a word, but Ewan's right behind me with a taper. In seconds blue smoke is boiling from under the Porsche and I'm banging on the kitchen door. 'Stanley! Stanley! There's smoke coming from your car!'

Stanley doesn't wait for me to repeat it. The door bangs back and even though he's still pulling up his jeans, he leaps the three steps like 007. He collides with my right shoulder and blasts towards the plumes, stones spitting from under his feet. He flings the bonnet up and smoke spews out. 'Jesus Christ!' he screams, with his hands in his hair. 'Don't just fucking stand there!' (We weren't standing. We were buckling at the knees, but we were behind him.) 'Oh fuck!' His hands are over his face. 'Go and get the fire extinguisher!'

'But, Stan, you said—'

'FETCH THE FUCKING FIRE EXTINGUISHER! You gobshites!'

Ewan can hardly stand, let alone move, but somehow he shambles to the forge whilst Stanley ricochets between anger and despair. 'Bastard heap of German crap! They should have stuck to making Stukas.' He kicks a tyre and walks a circle. 'It's not even fucking paid for. Bastard pile of bastard crap!'

The fire extinguisher turns the corner before Ewan does, its nozzle pointing at the car. Ewan elbows Stanley out of the way and nearly falls into the engine cavity as with theatrical urgency he empties all eighty pounds' worth of foam on the engine. When the hissing has stopped, the canister's empty and the smoke bomb's spent, Stanley turns to where we should be. Except we aren't. We're on our backs on the drive, holding our guts in writhing agony.

Understanding slowly dawns on him. He pushes a foot under the car and our smoke canister rolls out. That erupts an explosion from Ewan and me. He drops the bonnet of the foam-filled Porsche. 'Oh, ha fucking ha.' We're rolling on the gravel like a pair of upturned beetles. 'Oh, very fucking droll.' He picks up the spent smoke bomb. 'Your tomfoolery has just cost me eighty quid.' There's a squeal of undisguised joy from Ewan now. 'Funny, is it? Well let's see how funny it is when I dock your wages forty quid apiece.'

I manage to struggle upright. 'Come on, Stanley, you have to admit it was funny.' Ewan is still rolling in ecstasy.

'It's one thing you taking the piss, it's another when I have to pay for the bastard privilege!' I can feel my face creasing again. Stanley addresses the dog: 'See that.' He points at us. 'That's what eighty quid's worth of fun looks like.' I loll back and join Ewan on the gravel again.

'Worth every penny, Stan,' he rasps. 'Worth every single penny!'

Chapter 6

I was lacing up my work boots when a missile thunked against my scalp then hit the floor with a wallop. I picked up a box of eighty Earl Grey tea bags with a newly blunted corner. I was genuinely touched. 'Thanks, Stanley.'

'Don't drink 'em so bastard fast. They were four ninety-nine.'

'Thanks.'

He grunted his way to the kettle. 'Nah, I'll tell you t'job for this mornin'. We're off to Lord Hathersage's. He takes a keen interest in his 'osses. He doesn't leave it to some lackey groom – he likes to be in on t'job. So if he's there, you don't piss about – do you hear me?' I was aware of Ewan raising his eyes to the heavens whilst I poured milk into three cracked mugs. Stanley saw it too. 'Listen here, Dolloper, he's the Queen's fucking cousin, so he deserves some respect.'

'More respect than Old Pedley, or Rodrigo or Robert Jennings?'

'Of course more respect than Old Pedley, or Rodrigo or Robert Jennings!'

'Why?'

'I've just bastard told you why, you dolloping little commie pinko. Were you not listening?' Ewan shrugged. The only thing that delighted him more than winding Stanley up was being traduced for his left-wing leanings. 'So,' Stanley had turned his back on Ewan, 'you don't speak to him unless he speaks to you, and if you do have to speak to him, you call him

38

"sir" – and you take that bastard beanie hat off!' Ewan let out a roar of mirth.

'And Mao Tse Tung can stop here and muck out them 'ens!'

'It's better than watching you wringing your cap all morning,' Ewan shot.

'Be grateful I'm not sending you to the bastard gulags. Posh Lad here won't show me up, will you?'

I didn't speak.

Ewan slopped his mug down with an ill grace; mucking out hens wasn't in his job description. I managed to mouth a cringing apology to him whilst Stanley knocked back his brew.

We climbed into the van and Stanley slammed his door just as Lucky reached the footplate. He wound down the window. 'Keep an eye on the dog, Dolloper!'

'Are you not taking her with you?' But Stanley had raised the window.

The drive down to Hathersage Hall swept us between rolling sheep-grazed pastures, and past a lake that lay like a coin in the valley – just as Capability Brown had intended. We entered through wrought-iron gates the height of most Yorkshire houses and were waved on by the man in a car-park kiosk. The vast Georgian pile loomed before us and as we crunched onto a gravelled forecourt Stanley slowed, so I could take in the architecture. We passed under an imposing stone arch which delivered us onto the most impressive stable yard I have ever seen. To our left were the steps, French windows, porticos, columns and sashes of the east elevation of Hathersage Hall, and to our right, the old coach house, each bay of which housed a classic car. I wanted to pore over every one of them, but a middle-aged countryman in a tweed shooting jacket and expensive wellington boots appeared from the Georgian stable block. He looked like someone I might meet at a point-to-point. Stanley jumped out of the van and shook the man's hand. I noticed his stance become less upright, more crouchy. I climbed out and began readying the portable forge and arranging our tools, aware of a vague braying from the gentleman and lots of 'Yes, sir; yes, sir. I understand, sir' from Stanley. The gentleman then called for Whisper to be fetched out and he walked to the side of the van to watch his groom trot his horse up. It was there he encountered me. Stanley was quick to intervene: 'Sorry, sir, I should have said, sir. This is Will, he'll be working with me until he qualifies.'

I did what I always do. I held out my hand, looked him in the eye and said, 'How do you do, nice to meet you.'

'And you, Will; I'm James.' Lord Hathersage shook my hand firmly then turned to watch his impressive hunter.

It was an interesting morning. The hunter was long in the pastern and Stanley had to address the problems of its hoof to pastern axis. As he laboured, James chatted to me about his racehorses. I'd seen two of them race at Ripon, so we exchanged racing stories, tips and observations. The next two horses were more straightforward to shoe and James stood shoulder to shoulder with Stanley as I removed their old shoes. 'Young Will here seems to have a way with horses,' he observed.

'Yes, yes, sir. He's very calm.'

'Is he going to have the chance to shoe racehorses whilst he's working for you, Stanley?'

'Yes, sir. I'm hoping so, sir,' Stanley stammered. If he'd been wearing a cap, he'd have doffed it.

'Splendid. I'd say that's where the young man's passions lie, wouldn't you?'

When we climbed back into the van two hours later Stanley was grim-faced. 'You little bastard snake!'

'What?'

He set about a poor mimicry of me: '"Oh, James, did you see Polar Advantage's finish at Kempton?" "Thank you, James." "You're quite right, James." "Ho, ho, James."' I stared at him. 'Twenty-two years I've been shoeing for Lord Hathersage.

Twenty-two years of bowing and scraping and tugging my bastard forelock. Twenty-two years of being tret like stable staff and calling him sir. You're here ten minutes and it's *James* this and *James* that and *James* the jeffing other!'

I dug a sandwich out of the Tesco bag at my feet. 'Stanley,' I said, at last, 'if you act like a peasant, you'll get treated like a peasant.'

He started the engine. 'You're a little clever dick, you are.'

Back at the forge Ewan had cleaned out the hens and walked the dog. 'Mandy rang for you.' Stanley grunted. 'She said it were personal, not professional.' There was still no reaction from Stanley. 'And a bloke we haven't shod for before, over Throstleden way.'

'So, have you booked him in?'

'No.'

'I left the diary here!'

'Stanley, I've never been able to tell from that if a job's in Skipton or in Scarborough.'

'Are you daft, or what?' Stanley opened the diary at a random page and pointed to three ovals of decreasing size. 'Scorthwaite livery yard.'

Ewan's brow creased. 'How is that Scorthwaite livery yard?'

'Dogs' doings! It's a picture of dogs' doings! There's always dogs' doings on the yard.' Stanley was chopping with his hand as you do when you're explaining the self-evident to a complete dope. 'Think, lad!' He flicked to another page on which he'd drawn a dome shape with two dots three quarters of the way up it and a wavy line across its lower edge. Ewan shrugged. Stanley sighed, exasperated. 'Higher Friar Farm with the haunted barn.'

'Well why don't you just write Higher Friar Farm, like any normal person, instead of making it into a fucking puzzle!'

Stanley opened the diary again at a page on which he'd drawn an approximation of a wasp.

'Manor Farm?'

'Yes! You're getting the hang of it now! What do you think I put for Hathersage Hall?'

'A crown?'

'Yes! See, it's not hard, is it, when you think. Old Pedley's?'

'A beer keg?'

'A beer keg? Have you heard him? Don't be so bloody stupid. What's a beer keg to do wi' t'job? It's a dinner plate!'

Ewan's brow creased. 'When have we ever had our dinner at Old Pedley's?'

'Are you thick or what?' Stanley looked at me for confirmation of Ewan's utter stupidity. 'Shire's feet are like dinner plates!' He shook his head. 'I give up with you, I really do.'

'*Why can't you just write the names and addresses in the bloody diary, Stanley?*'

'You know, Ewan, you're just bone idle sometimes.' He slammed the diary shut. 'I'm trying to teach you a very simple code and you just can't arse yourself with learning it.'

'But, Stanley – a simple code already exists. It's called *writing*.'

I volunteered a solution. 'I know, why don't I do a key in the back of the diary?'

It took me weeks and I never really cracked it. There were new symbols for new clients and some clients whose symbol never settled. My favourites were Mandy's – which was a picture of breasts – and Ralph Mattison's, which was a coffin. (I never asked.)

Ewan was utterly flummoxed when he found a visit designated by a horseshoe shape. 'Bloody genius that, Stan!' he raged down the speaker phone from the New Van.

'Lofthouse Riding School!'

'How am I supposed to know that?'

'It's their logo, you dolloper.'

Chapter 7

The New Van, when it turned up, only advantaged Stanley. Ewan had looked forward to escaping him but Stanley gave him all the dirty jobs and all the dangerous jobs, and sent Lucky with him so Ewan took a daily mauling. I'd been in the habit of collecting Ewan every morning and enjoying his dad's bacon butties. There was no need now that Ewan had the New Van, but his dad insisted I still come once a week. 'Don't be a stranger,' he said, patting me on the back.

The New Van, which had been presented with predictable pomp, was a rusting white Berlingo with no rear bumper and a red driver's door. Ewan looked at Stanley. 'I thought you said you'd make it smart?'

'I did. Then I remembered it would be parked on Cribbs Estate every night.'

'Are those tyres legal?'

'Listen, Dolloper, if I'd put decent tyres on it you'd be coming down in the morning and finding it on bastard bricks.' Ewan sighed the sigh of one who knows his station in life. 'Any road up, first job in t' New Van is one for the two of you.'

We exchanged glances. Why would Stanley be sending us out together? *Divide and conquer*, he'd said. 'It's only trims, so it'll let me crack on at Mandy's.'

'Where?' There was darkness in Ewan's voice.

Stanley grinned.

'It's at Loddenden Top, isn't it?'

Stanley's grin widened. 'You'll be reyt. You 'ave the horse whisperer with you this year.'

'Oh bloody hell, Stanley! Aren't you coming?'

Stanley put his hands on Ewan's shoulders. 'I would rather set fire to my own hair and put it out with a shovel than go to Loddenden Top.'

Ewan didn't point out that Stanley had no hair, instead he refused to take Lucky. 'We'll have enough on without getting mauled into the bargain.'

Stanley shrugged. 'I suppose it won't kill her to stop in t'forge for an afternoon.'

The New Van's engine started with the rattle of a lawn-mower and the door closed on the third slam. Ewan spoke as he eased off the drive. 'You watch,' he observed, 'he'll never take either of us to Mandy's. He has something going on with her.'

The thought of Stanley with a girlfriend was as absurd as it was revolting. The only woman I'd ever seen at Bling Manor was Sandra, his cleaner. She did his laundry, left his evening meal under cling film and was about as welcoming as a komodo dragon.

'Have you seen her, this Mandy?'

'Not since his wife left him.' My head ratcheted a full 180 degrees.

'He was married?'

'Yes. To Lynne.' Tumbling realisations clattered down the chutes of my brain.

'What happened?'

'She got sick of him.' Ewan shrugged. 'Took the kids and walked out.'

'Kids!'

'Well, teenagers. Katie and Jonathan. Took him months to get his shit together.'

We were silent as the van trundled between bare hawthorns, twisted like battlefield wire. I'd never thought of Stanley as a family man. Ewan switched on the radio and started singing along to Ed Sheeran.

'So, is Sandra a recent employee?'

'She's his next-door neighbour. She started coming in to make sure he ate up.'

'I thought she was his cleaner.'

'She is now.'

The Berlingo rattled past five sheep advancing on the carriageway then grumbled through Loddenden village, and on up the fell road towards the distant communication mast. It seemed not to have low enough gears to tackle the gradient, and Ewan broke off his singing now and then to cajole or abuse it.

We climbed out of the New Van onto a yard of limestone chippings before a farmhouse that could have been Wuthering Heights. Despite my efforts, he still refused to explain what we were to face, except to admit that it was only Stanley's brute brawn that had saved them last time and we'd be lucky if we escaped without multiple fractures, what with me being such a streak of piss. Loddenden village had been still, but here our waterproof jackets cracked against us like sails and the moor circled us, its contours dipping and rising like a buttoned cushion. Pinprick sheep were grazing under a boiling sky, and I was calculating the likelihood of rain when a woman in her forties emerged from the farmhouse, attempting to zip her jacket, close the door and hold on her headscarf all at once. 'All right, lads?' We nodded. 'I've got them in the round pen.' My stomach was waterfalling inside me as we followed her round the back of the house to where twenty Welsh ponies were wheeling and churning round the perimeter of a ranch-style corral. Their heads were up and one or two were screaming for the wilderness with ear-splitting whinnies. 'Is Stanley not with you?'

Ewan shook his head. 'He had another job on.'

The woman looked me up and down. 'Well, good luck,

then, because the muscles on him look like peas on a knife.'

'Don't underestimate him, Mrs Collinge. He has a way with him.'

She folded her arms. 'Has he really? He'd better mind himself with that chestnut, all the same.' They all looked as wild as the Yorkshire wind.

'Which ones are we doing?' I asked.

She addressed Ewan. 'You haven't told him, have you?'

'I'd never have got him here.'

She gave a sardonic laugh and turned for the house. My eyes were streaming with the wind when I looked at Ewan.

'We're doing the lot, aren't we?' Ewan nodded. 'What are they? Three-year-olds?'

'Mostly, there'll be some four-year-olds she couldn't catch last year.'

I watched them wheel round like swarming starlings. 'Have they ever been touched?'

'Nope. She runs a stallion with twenty mares on the moor and rounds her youngstock up once a year.'

My stomach lurched. 'What's the technique, then?'

'Throw yourself in the mud, grab a passing foreleg and whatever happens, you don't let go.' That didn't sound like much of a technique. 'You twitch it and I'll trim its feet as quick as I can.' My mother would have been horrified. I looked at the ponies, galloping and screaming. Twenty minutes with her and each one would be safe enough to handle.

'Can't we separate them?' Ewan shook his head. 'It's just that, if I had half an hour or so with each one ...'

'We'd finish about midnight!' I put on my gloves and walked into the pen feeling sick to my stomach. I was colluding in an avoidable act that would stress the ponies and put us in danger. I stood in the centre of the corral like a doomed gladiator.

'It gets easier as the pen empties,' Ewan said.

The ponies huddled, they hesitated, they rolled their eyes and bunched with their backsides to me. I approached twenty

46

rumps quietly, eyes down, like my mother would, but like a shoal of fish they stirred, plaited in and out then wheeled away. The centre of the pen was clear. 'Pick one out and grab it!' Ewan yelled over the wind. Looking at it would cause it to panic more, but I had to. How else would I catch one?

I eyeballed a weedy-looking grey and attempted to draw level but it turned its backside to me and set off in the opposite direction. 'Don't send it a bloody email!' Ewan shouted. I locked on to a chestnut instead, then remembered her gypsy's warning and changed my mind. 'You bloody flake!' I tried the grey again. I jogged level with it. 'Just grab it!'

I heard my mother's voice: *Close hands slowly, open hands quickly.* How could I grab with slow hands?

Three failures later I just flung myself in the dirt and seized a bay leg. 'You'll lose your bloody hands doing it that way, you berk!' The owner of the leg was rearing and twisting and ponies' feet were stamping inches from my ears. My nerve broke and I let go. Ewan was halfway across the corral. 'You had that!'

'This is bloody ridiculous!' I protested, crawling to my knees.

'Watch and learn,' Ewan said, rolling his sleeves up.

He stood in the middle of the corral intent as a hawk, then he blasted into action and landed slap on his belly with the foreleg of a dun colt in his right hand. The colt reared and twisted. I was so lost in awe that I'd forgotten to move. 'NOW!' Ewan yelled. I ran across and somehow I got a rope collar on the thrashing beast. 'Twitch!' Ewan was yelling. 'Twitch it!' I groped in my muddied chaps for the twitch, grabbed the pony's nose and clamped it on. It often takes a couple of minutes for the horse's endorphins to get into its bloodstream but this pony stopped struggling straight away. Ewan was able to trim all four feet, pausing now and then for the occasional tantrum, then we opened the corral gate and released the pony into the yard. Ewan looked at his watch. 'If every one takes us thirty-five minutes, we'll finish at eleven thirty tonight, so long as we don't stop for dinner.' I could have wept. He handed me the gloves. 'Your turn.'

I decided not to think. I threw myself at the first leg that passed me, then opened my eyes and saw it was a chestnut. 'Pick it right up!' Ewan yelled. The pony reared but I held on and Ewan was quicker with the rope halter and twitch than I had been. The chestnut exploded more frequently than the bay, but we had it done in twenty minutes. By the time we'd done the fifth pony we still had all our fingers and had it down to ten minutes. My confidence was up now and we rattled on without a hitch. At two o'clock I mentioned that I was starving. 'Let's just keep going,' Ewan said. 'We can eat later.'

When we released the final pony – a strapping grey mare – it was twenty past six. At half past six the phone rang. 'Are you done?'

'We're on our way now.'

'To Leeds General?'

'To the forge.'

'I don't suppose that tight-fisted besom fed you?'

'Not so much as a brew all day.'

'Grab yourself a curry and a pint at the Taj Mahal. I've paid you on.'

I took the phone from my ear and stared at it. 'Ewan, there's a bloke on the phone saying he's paid us on at the Taj Mahal.'

Ewan shouted at the phone. 'We're all shit-up, Stanley – but ta!'

'I've left you some clean clothes with Nadeem.'

I put the phone back to my ear. 'Thanks, Stan.'

'You've earned it, Posh Lad.'

Ewan grinned. 'He must have got his leg over at Mandy's.'

As the New Van dropped into Loddenden, the setting sun spilled its light on the valley floor. A diamond glinted off a distant skylight, the slate roofs of the Legohouses gleamed and the carpet of the Dales was backlit like a stage set.

I raised my water bottle. 'Thanks, Mandy.'

Chapter 8

We were farriers to two racehorse trainers, one of whom was Richard Jennings who ran a slick operation on the other side of Eckersley. He had thirty top class horses in training, a horse-walker, solarium, circular all-weather gallop and ninety acres of post-and-railed paddocks. His horses were mainly flat runners, though he also trained half a dozen hurdlers. The joy of Richard Jennings' yard for Ewan and me was his daughter, and stable jockey, Pippa. Pippa's jodhpurs coated her like a film of oil, and she wore them with black leather knee-length boots. Her straw-coloured hair poured down her back like slithering honey, and on a horse she was a centaur, absorbing its movements with fluid hips and a straight back.

Stanley watched Ewan's mouth drop open and his hammer still as his eyes followed Pippa across the yard. 'You've no bastard chance, mate.'

'I can look, can't I?'

'Not on my time you can't. No!'

During tea break, I had the chance to lean on the van and chat to her about her coming rides and their prospects. I tried to include Ewan, but he blushed and stammered and looked at his shoes. Pippa was confident and cheerful and asked me where I went out at weekends. The truth was that since starting my apprenticeship I'd been more interested in sleeping at weekends, but I mentioned some clubs and wine bars she knew and my spirits soared when she said, 'I might see you around, then.' Ewan was already back at work when Pippa sauntered towards the tack room.

'You could be in there, Posh Lad,' Stanley said. I thought so too. 'I'll lend you a box to stand on if she cops on.' Then he and Ewan folded in laughter under their respective horses.

They were laughing so hard, they had failed to notice a white Range Rover glide into the yard. A uniformed chauffeur stepped out, walked to the passenger door and graciously swung it open for a short dapper man who was dressed from head to foot in white; his suit, shoes and tie were white. The only darkness about him was in his close-cropped black beard and his dusky skin. He was unearthly, as if he belonged to another world. Even when a man the size of a bus shelter stepped out of the car with him, I could barely take my eyes from the little man who moved with the poise of a dancer. Behaving as if he were utterly alone, he strolled to where I was tying up a sixteen-hand white-grey in preparation for removing its racing plates. 'Ah!' he exclaimed. 'You have my Princess Noor.' His English was heavily accented and I would have proffered my hand had he not been so clean, but he was already proffering his. 'Sheikh Abdul Al'Amiry,' he said, baring a row of ice-white teeth. I rubbed my hands on my chaps and gingerly offered my fingertips, which he took and shook generously. He indicated the mare. 'She is good girl for you?'

'She's a real lady,' I answered truthfully. He ran his hand down her back and along her flank, then turned to the bus shelter and held out his hand. In it was placed a single white polo mint which the sheikh pushed at the horse's nose, exposing a glinting gold Rolex as he did so.

At that moment Richard Jennings scurried up looking more flustered than I'd ever seen him. 'Your Highness! I hadn't known you were coming.'

That got Stanley's attention. The sheikh raised an impervious palm at Jennings. 'I prefer to call unexpectedly. Tell me, are my horses well?'

'Tip-top, Your Highness. Tip-top. All of them ...' And his

voice faded away as he led the sheikh to see his other horses. I wondered if all of them were white.

'He's a bullshitter,' Stanley observed. 'The Sheikh of Arabeek would be better off putting his 'osses with Mervyn Slack.'

I smiled at the thought; Mervyn Slack's yard was as different from Richard Jennings' as Bradford is from Henley-on-Thames. Mervyn had been a famous footballer in the 1970s – partly because he nutted the opposition's centre forward during an international at Wembley. On retiring from football he'd inherited the family farm at High Scorthwaite and combined his knowledge of fitness training with his lifelong love of horses. He was already in his seventies when I met the gruff, hard Yorkshireman whose name was known by everyone's mum and dad, including mine.

After twenty minutes Jennings and the sheikh reappeared and even though Jennings' leather boots were dusted with shavings, the sheikh was as pristine as when he'd stepped out of the Range Rover. He had walked in and out of seven stables without any mark besmirching his whiteness. I was removing the final racing plate from his grey mare when he approached me again. 'You like my Princess Noor?'

'I do,' I said. 'She's a lovely filly.'

'You look after her well?'

Stanley spoke up for me: 'Oh aye. He's a way with horses, has our Will. He'll look after your filly.'

The sheikh patted me on the back then reached inside his jacket. 'For you,' he said. He removed a note from his wallet and thrust it into the pocket of my chaps. His lackey opened the door of his Range Rover for him and the sheikh stepped in. He seemed to me to be poised on an edge between the mortal and the mystical. I watched his car glide out of the yard with barely a purr.

Stanley broke my wonder. 'Did he just give you some money, you little creep?' He pointed at Ewan with his hammer.

'Ewan, have you ever been given money by an Arab sheikh?'
Ewan laughed and Stanley straightened. 'Ewan here's lived on
Cribbs Estate all his bastard life. The first car he's ever had is
that skip I bought him last week.'

Ewan's brow furrowed. 'What're you on about, Stan?'

'Injustice, Dolloper! I'm on about injustice! You've been
shoeing with me for nigh on four years and Lord Hathersage
doesn't even know your bastard name! Posh Lad turns up here
and a lass you've fancied for years starts tossing her hair about,
and a bastard Ay-rab gives him money – for nowt!' That was a
long speech for Stanley.

I walked to the back of the van, bulging with guilt and
hoping that Pippa was out of earshot.

'Ignore him,' Ewan muttered. 'It's not your fault.' Injustice
to Ewan was as immutable as the weather. I dragged the
sheikh's note out of my chaps, and in my hand, bold, brazen
and red, was a fifty pound note. Ewan's face was frozen in
shock. I stared at it. 'Bloody hell, mate. You could take Pippa
to the Taj Mahal with that.'

I looked to where she was reaching up to bridle a fine black
colt. It would take more than a trip to the Loddenden curry
house to impress Pippa; I wasn't even sure that its namesake
would cut the mustard.

'I could …' I said. 'Or else you and me could go to the Taj
Mahal after work …'

Ewan grinned. We high-fived and I returned to work.

STRATFORD COLLEGE OF AGRICULTURE:

FACULTY OF BLACKSMITHING AND FARRIERY

Apprenticeship Journal for the month of: November.

Comment: I have witnessed the consequences of hoof neglect. (The neglect had not occurred at the hands of our client who had purchased the animal unaware of the seriousness of its condition.) Foot reshaping and consequent limb realignment will be undertaken following the sedation and/or gelding of the animal to prevent injury to its handlers.

Learning Outcomes:

I can confidently use the first aid training learnt at college.

I understand the difference in foot conformation between a donkey and a horse.

I understand the idiosyncrasies of blood supply to the donkey's foot.

I understand the appointment system used by my ATF.

Signed: William Harker. Nov. 30th 2015   (Apprentice)

Signed: SL Nov. 30th 2015   (Master)

Chapter 9

If it was swanky or shiny, Stanley had to have it, but user manuals were an insult to his manhood. He rarely had the first concept of how to operate the things he bought. 'This,' he'd announce, opening the latest box to be delivered, 'is state-of-the-bastard-art!' But within weeks he would always be able to piss faster, shit sharper or crap quicker than the electronic device could calculate/navigate/entertain or fry chips.

Two days before a memorable visit to Mervyn Slack's, Stanley had walked into the forge carrying a package and grinning from ear to ear. 'Wait while we get this goin' then!' he announced, ripping at the paper like a child on Christmas Day.

'What is it?'

'What is it? It's state-of-the-bastard-art, this is, lad!' Ewan groaned. 'It'll solve all our problems will this.' He held it aloft. 'It's the latest iPhone. You just have to talk at it, and it'll book all your appointments in.'

'How?' Ewan asked.

'What do you mean "how"? I've bought it, not bastard invented it!'

'It'll be a useless pile of fucking foreign faff next week, like the deep-fat fryer, the ash vacuum, the bread maker ...'

'Oh, just get in the van, Dolloper, or we'll be late for Mervyn's.'

Shoeing racehorses sounds glamorous, but they'll kick you in the kidneys sharper than a carthorse. There's nothing more sobering than a shaking, shivering, sweating three-year-old next in the queue. Ewan took it in his stride though, like he took the wild ponies at Loddenden Top, my comparative success with Pippa Jennings and the day-to-day dramas of the Cribbs Estate. He sang our way to High Scorthwaite word perfect through 'Dream a Little Dream of Me'. Swing was his chosen karaoke genre, and our journeys were rehearsals for his Saturday night appearances at the Cribbs Social Club. He was halfway through 'Fly Me to the Moon' when we pulled up on Mervyn's yard.

'Right,' Stanley announced, 'I'll shoe Mister Manners, Michael Bublé here can sort out the sand crack on the chestnut filly, and you can start on Earthquake.' I groaned. Earthquake was a seventeen-hand beast of a horse. 'No point hiding our talents!' Stanley chuckled. 'Dolloper can serenade while you soothe the savage beast.'

Roofing work on Mervyn's forge meant we were temporarily relocated to a narrow alley between outbuildings. It wasn't an ideal location but Mervyn Slack had converted every shed, garage, piggery and shippon into a stable, such was the demand for his services, and at least it was quiet. I was only removing worn shoes, but Earthquake was in a particularly bad mood. No amount of steady breathing, slow gripping or passive resistance was having the slightest effect. He was putting enough power behind every kick to do serious damage to a farrier's kneecap.

To avert a blow, it's best to hang on to the leg and keep hold. If there's no fresh air between hoof and farrier, it limits the damage. Twenty minutes of piston-pumping a hind leg tires most horses, but to this Trojan it was an irritation. Three times it lifted me off my feet and launched me across the alley. Stanley ignored my maiden flight. He tutted and shook his head at my second. At the third he addressed the horse: 'You could have somebody's eye out with that.' At the fourth he finally spoke to me. 'Come here. You're about as much use as a blancmange hammer.'

Relieved, I took over his work on his mannerly gelding. Stanley took off his shirt, bent down and grappled Earthquake's leg. He meant business. The horse tried the same trick, but Stanley hung on. It fought him on and off for a further few minutes, then sighed and took a mouthful of hay. 'You see?' Stan panted. 'It helps if you're not made of pipe cleaners.' Stanley reached for the shoe pullers, and winked at me. 'It knows it's beat now.' But, as I suspected, the beast had been biding its time. In one super-equine thrust it flung all seventeen stone of Stanley Lampitt through the air.

Ewan and I watched his expressions change through shock, horror and anticipation as clearly as if a film roll had been slowed down. His trajectory was as slow as a pebble through treacle. Only when he smashed through the outhouse door opposite did sound return to the world and life pick up its regular pace. His bulk had splintered the wood as perfectly as a police battering ram and now he was on his backside with his four legs in the air. I looked again. Somebody was underneath him.

'What the fuck!' The voice was shocked; muffled.

'Sorry!'

'You've knocked me clean off the fucking lair.'

Ewan's face ripped to a grin.

'I know. I'm sorry.'

'Look at the fucking door!'

'Sorry, Mervyn.'

Ewan had been suppressing his mirth to save their embarrassment but when Mervyn emerged hauling up his trousers it was too much. Ewan let out a wail of agony and my own composure cracked. Mervyn turned away, retrieved his newspaper from the lavatory floor, and shambled down the alley chunnering about not being able to have a shit in peace. Stanley watched him go. 'Why's the silly old sod having a crap in the outside lavvy anyway?' Neither of us dared answer. He reached for his shirt and I attempted to return to work but

I caught sight of Ewan. His eyes were scrunched to slits and his mouth was stretched to his ears. 'I mean, you can't just have a crap where it's convenient, like they do in them foreign places.' Ewan let out another wail and dropped the foot he was holding.

Throughout the morning we took it in turns to shake with the suppressed memory. Stanley gave us his death glare – but by the time Jay, the Head Lad, arrived to pay us even he was beginning to see the humour in it. 'I were groping for a purchase for a good five seconds before I knew where I wa'. God alone knows what I've had a hold of!'

'And Mervyn.' Jay grinned, writing out the cheque.

'You what?'

'God and Mervyn know what you've had hold of.' Stanley wiped his hands on his jeans and shuddered.

Now that Ewan had his van, I arrived at the forge before him each morning, and Stanley would drop a pile of envelopes in front of me and ask me to have a look for anything urgent. 'Sandra will see to them when she's back from New Zealand.' I'd sift the business from the personal and identify what needed paying whilst he made me an Earl Grey in the kitchen. Gradually, however, the personal pile was growing taller and taller. 'Have a look at them, would you? Not my thing, paperwork.' There were letters stamped NHS and letters with a solicitor's frank on them.

'I think you should do it, Stanley; it looks like there's private stuff here.'

'Why? Are you going to put it in the Eckersley *Gazette*?'

'No ... but, surely Sandra's due back. She's been gone ages.'

'Just bastard open them, lad.' He tore at a slice of toast with his teeth whilst I read the words of Messrs Rigby, Draper and Shaw regarding their client Mrs Lynne Lampitt.

'Lynne's solicitors say you've to either give her two hundred grand or else sell the house.'

'They can fuck off. Next.'

I stared at him. 'You need to respond.'

'If I respond it'll be with a brick through their bastard window. Next.'

I tore open an envelope marked NHS and read: 'As you failed to attend your appointment at the gastroenterology clinic on 11 October we regret that your name has been removed from the waiting list in accordance with the policy of the North Yorkshire Hospital Trust.'

Stanley halted his toast on its journey to his mouth. 'What appointment? I never knew I had a bastard appointment.' By now I had opened an earlier letter informing him of an appointment at gastroenterology on 11 October. 'Why don't they use the bastard phone? They've got my phone number!' He flung the toast down and stalked to the sink.

'They probably expected you to read your letter.'

He was seething. 'I'll let them bloody pen-pushers have it later.'

By the time I'd sorted the household bills from the flyers and a new tax code, Ewan had clattered the New Van onto the yard. I walked down the back steps of Bling Manor with a steaming cup of coffee and a warning: 'He's in a foul mood. Lynne wants him to sell the house and there's something up with his guts.'

'There's been something up with his guts for years. He only has half a bowel or something. That's why he never comes to the Taj Mahal.'

'Is that why he can't hold his drink?'

'Nah. That's cos he's a lightweight flake.'

Stanley's hens had escaped from their run so I edged past them to open up the forge. Hens have always revolted me. I hate the red fleshy bits on their necks and heads. I hate their neck-poking strut. I hate their scaly feet and the way they poise a wizened claw above the dirt. So far, I had managed to disguise this aversion from Stanley and Ewan. It hadn't been easy, but it had been necessary; any weakness would be exploited mercilessly. You'd be surprised how many stables have half a dozen Rhode Island Reds stalking the yard, but I kept a weather eye on them from under my horse and only crossed a yard when there were none in my path. I was a bit too obvious this morning though.

'What's up wi' you?'

'Nothing.'

'They're hens, not American pit bulls.'

I shrugged carelessly. 'I just don't like them.' Ewan called me a big wussie and started flinging stock into the van. At least it wasn't Stanley.

'Right, lads. First job: them donkeys at Throstleden. It's a new client.'

Ewan and I exchanged glances.'How many donkeys?'

'Two.'

'What's the catch?'

'There is no catch. I need to ring the hospital. That's all.'

'Are you using your new iPhone?'

'I'm still fathoming it.'

'Read the instructions!'

'Just go and trim your donkeys, Smart Arse.'

Ewan was chuckling as he closed the van door. 'It's typical of him, this, you know. He'll be raging about it in a week.'

'I'll set it up for him.'

'Don't do that!'

'It's no sweat; my dad has the same one.'

'You do that and you'll end up as Keeper of the iPhone. Every missed appointment, every double-booking and every twelve-mile trek between appointments will be your fault!' He was right. I was already acting as Stanley's PA. I decided to leave him to it.

The owner of the donkeys was a very genial man in his fifties who had bought them for 'a bit o' company'.

'Great,' I said. 'Where are the head collars?'

He looked blankly at me. 'Head collars?'

'To hold them.' He shrugged. I looked at Ewan. Ewan sighed. The spare head collar was in the Old Van, so we plaited two makeshift versions from baling twine and gave thanks that the donkeys were among the more cooperative of their species. The naivety of their owner made for a testing morning but he was grateful for our tuition in donkey care – as I dare say the donkeys were – and gave us twenty pounds more than the bill. Stanley wasn't seeing the colour of it; we agreed on that without discussion.

We were trying to figure out the meaning of Stanley's next symbol in the diary (a bath) when my phone rang. 'Get your arses over here, now.'

My stomach lurched. 'What's up, Stanley?' I put him on speakerphone.

'Just do as you're told.'

Ewan shouted at the phone: 'There's two more jobs yet, Stanley.'

'I've cancelled them. I want you back at the forge.'

'Righto,' I said, trying to sound unconcerned, and hung up. Ewan turned to me.'"Righto"?'

'It was my unconcerned voice.'

'Well I'm bloody concerned.'

'So am I.'

He must have been, because there was no singing. We drove the ten miles to the forge in silence save for a brief conflab in which we agreed that Hangdog might serve us better than Unconcerned, until we got to the source of the summons. We shuffled into the forge heads down, hands in pockets.

'Oh, bloody hell. Have you had a bad mornin' an' all?' Neither of us knew the right answer. 'Cos I've had a shit morning. Lynne wants to clean me out and the hospital wants to cut me up.' I was preparing to commiserate. 'So, stuff it. I've decided we're going go-karting, and then to the chippy!' Ewan and I looked at one another, incredulous. Stanley slapped me on the back. 'There's no point being your own boss if you can't give yourself a half-holiday when you're pissed off, is there!'

Stanley eased his Porsche off the drive, and with me scrunched in the back, we headed for Eckersley.

We had such a good laugh that afternoon that Ewan and I had to actively remind one another that Stanley is no more than evenly split between a decent bloke and a wanker. We were wise enough to lose to him twice each, and to accept his advice about how to take the top corner, but it was on our way back over Eckersley Moor that the action really started.

The road back to Hathersage climbs steeply over cobbles, past a mill reincarnated as a gym, between Farrow-and-Balled cottages originally meant for mill hands, and past the long lawns of Eckersley's modern afterthoughts. The housing halts where the road levels off, as if the developers lost their nerve on being faced with so much sky. My Astra crests that rise every morning, and on some mornings I can see the silvered River Lodden, snaking past Hathersage and Loddenden through the folds of the hills as far as Ripon. I've made myself so late on such mornings I've forgone my bacon sandwich at Ewan's – but it's been worth it to step out of my car and feed on the vastness of Yorkshire.

This was a bright autumn afternoon, the open moor was smouldering orange with fading bracken and the whole of Loddendale was laid out like a market stall below us.

Despite his enjoyment of the Porsche, the adrenalin of the go-karting and the open road ahead, Stanley was doing no more than sixty. We were having a good laugh about Stanley taking the last corner so fast he'd nearly rolled his go-kart when we heard a siren. Stanley slowed. I turned and saw a police car behind us with its STOP sign illuminated. Stanley groaned and pulled over and I watched three policemen jump out of their Range Rover – yes, jump – and run over to the Porsche carrying semi-automatics.

Baffling tornadoes of confusion had become commonplace whilst working for Stanley. His world had rules, expectations and givens that were utterly alien to me. Surely one police officer should have been striding to the driver's window carrying a notebook?

'Get out,' commanded the officer on Stanley's side as he gestured with his gun. Surely, he should have been leaning on the lowered window saying, 'Good afternoon, sir, do you know what speed you were doing?'

'Fuck me,' said Stanley. 'Have I landed up in Detroit? I was only in Eckersley ten bastard minutes since,' but he gets out, as does Ewan.

I'm crouched in the back, dumbfounded. What have we done? How the hell will I explain this to my father? Is crouching in the back of a Porsche illegal? The semi-automatic seems excessive. Ewan orders me out. I shake myself to life. My foot touches tarmac and an officer grabs my arm. He shoves it up my back and slams me against the bonnet of the Porsche. I am too frightened to speak. My face is pressed on hot metal. Will they put me in a cell? Ewan and Stanley are receiving the same treatment across the boot and a drystone wall respectively. Will I get to make a phone call? I hear Ewan's voice. He isn't fazed. Being raised on Cribbs Estate means he knows the rules.

Stanley shouts across: 'Is he touching your arse, Will? Don't let him touch your arse! You'd better not touch our arses, you dirty bastards!' I'm willing him to shut up.

The police officers are firing questions. *Where have we been? Where are we going?* Su Lin's chip shop in Fowlden isn't the right answer. My arm is shoved higher up my back. A radio starts to crackle. The officer with Ewan speaks to it. Suddenly I'm standing upright and a policeman is apologising. Ewan rants about police harassment and threatens to write to his MP. I climb into the Porsche.

Just as Stanley starts the engine an officer leans in. 'One final piece of advice, sir. Next time someone has a semi-automatic pointed at your head, don't imply he's a homosexual.'

It was only in the queue at Su Lin's that I grasped what Ewan and Stanley had computed at the side of the road: following an armed robbery in Leeds, three white males had escaped over Eckersley Moor in a white Porsche. Whilst we'd been bent double with semi-automatics at our heads, another squad had been catching the real robbers in Throstleden.

Stanley handed me a bag of chips, but I shook my head. 'What's to do wi' 'em?'

'Nothing,' I said. 'I've just lost my appetite.'

'Give 'em here,' Ewan ordered, and tipped them over his steak pudding. 'You'd starve to death on t' Cribbs Estate with that attitude.'

Chapter 10

Stanley's parsimony was unpredictable. He was as tight as a sausage skin one minute and recklessly generous the next. We were still paying for the fire extinguisher in monthly instalments when Stanley announced he'd bought us tickets for the hunt ball. It was a notoriously good do. The Yorkshire farriers had their own table and tales of hunt balls past had regularly been regaled to us in the forge. Ewan didn't look up from his anvil. 'What's to do wi' you, Face Ache? I thought you'd be chuffed.'

'It's not just the ticket price, is it?'

'I'm in t'chair! We'll have a proper neet!'

'I'm not buying a dinner suit for one "proper neet".'

'Bloody hell, Dolloper! I've bought your ticket. I'm not buying you a bastard dinner suit an' all!'

'My dad's will fit you,' I said. Ewan hesitated.

'Put his dad's suit on, you bloody killjoy!'

His eyes darted between us. 'To be honest, I don't think it's my thing, Stan.'

Stanley looked at me nonplussed, then turned back to Ewan. 'How is a free piss-up not your thing?'

Ewan had returned to hammering hot metal. 'I dunno … The folk there. They're not my type.'

Stanley pointed at me. 'Bertie Wooster there's not your type but you're as thick as bastard thieves!'

'Oh, come on, Ewan,' I begged. 'This could be my big chance with Pippa Jennings!'

He was defeated. 'Go on then; if I can borrow that suit.'

We'd had a slack morning. Ewan and I were getting shoe-making practice in before the end of term exams and Stanley was sorting the stock when the iPhone rang. Stanley glared at it like it was challenging him to a fist fight; then he glared at us. 'Are you two bastard deaf or something?'

Ewan glared back. 'It's your phone.'

'It could be a bastard client.'

'They're your bastard clients.'

'We could be losing business here, Dolloper.'

'Well answer the bloody thing then.'

In desperation Stanley grabbed the device and dabbed at it with massive paws. It was like watching a bear trying to ring for a pizza – except Stanley was shouting, 'Hello! Hello!' as he prodded. It stopped ringing. 'Hello!' He took it away from his ear and eyeballed it. 'There's nobody there.'

'You took too long,' Ewan said.

Stanley stared menacingly at the black pad in his paw. 'Useless foreign fart!' he shouted, and lobbed it at the opposite wall. It struck a breeze block then clattered to the concrete floor. Under Stanley's gaze, I walked over and picked it up. The screen was cracked but it sprang back to life at my touch. I retrieved the last number and spoke to the donkey man (now designated in the diary by a dunce's cap). 'They won't need trimming again,' I said, raising my eyes to Stanley, then I explained as slowly as I could that their feet would only need trimming about four times a year.

'No,' he said. 'I've bought another. And a llama.'

An hour later Ewan and I had been dispatched and found ourselves in a barn with a sixteen-hand-high Andalusian mule. We stared at it. This was no Bridlington donkey. 'What did you buy that for?' I asked.

Donkey Man was sheepish. 'I dunno, really.'

'You do know it's entire?' Ewan added.

'It's what?'

'It still has its meat and two veg.'

'Should it not have?'

I put my head in my hands.

Ewan took over. 'The first thing you need to do with that, is get it gelded.'

'Can you not do it?'

'No, we bloody can't!'

'So, can you not do its feet if it has its balls on?'

Its feet were curling like a pair of Arabian slippers, which suggested that no one had succeeded before us, but Ewan turned to me. 'We can't leave it like that, Will.' I glared at him in silent protest. 'Look at it! We'll have to give it a go.' I was beaten. Ewan turned to fetch his tools and Donkey Man shouted after him.

'Mind that llama! Don't turn your back on it!' Ewan scanned the paddock then dashed to the van. 'The thing is,' Donkey Man was explaining, 'I think the woman I bought them off must have been a witch.' He was grinding a toe into the dirt of the barn floor. 'I'd gone to buy some hay, but when I got home I had a llama and a giant donkey in t' trailer.' I watched the six loose bantams pecking about in the straw until Ewan returned and haltered the stallion.

Between us we managed to take some length off its front feet, but it was too quick with its back feet, so we told Donkey Man to ring us after he'd had it gelded. 'Fair enough,' he said. 'Do you fancy a bacon butty?' We'd earned it, so Ewan packed his toolbox and I waited for the bantams to clear the door before I followed them into a blowing drizzle. It swarmed like a shoal of invisible fish and in the half-hour we'd been in the barn it had puddled and squelched the paddock. I was examining the beads of rain bobbling my sleeve when a movement in my peripheral vision made me turn. The llama was bounding towards us at a determined canter. My mind snapped with Donkey Man's warning – *Don't turn your back on it* – but Ewan and Donkey Man were a good twenty yards ahead of me. 'Llama!' I shouted. In the time it took for them to react, the llama had covered ten yards. Donkey Man turned to face it and as if in slow-mo, his expression turned to terror as the great shaggy beast reared up. It dangled its feet above him then brought down its skull like a demolition ball. By the time Donkey Man had hit the grass the llama was rearing for Ewan but I caught its flank with a sliding kick from behind. It gave a lolloping plunge and cantered to the gate.

'Thanks,' Ewan breathed. He straightened his fleece jacket and we looked down at the motionless body at our feet.

'Do you think he's dead?' I asked. Ewan shook his head.

'He's breathing.'

We had to act fast. Donkey Man was a funny colour and the mud was chilling him. I put him in the recovery position and Ewan rang 999, then Stanley.

He was all heart. 'Bloody hell, Dolloper! We're supposed to be at Pedley's at twelve!'

'We can't leave him! He's unconscious!'

'Well he'll still be there when the bastard ambulance arrives then, won't he!'

Fortunately, the bastard ambulance arrived pretty promptly but the moment the first paramedic put her hand on the gate, the llama's attitude changed. It pricked its ears, tensed its muscles and by the time the gate was open it was cantering at her. Ewan jumped and roared. I whipped my damp sweatshirt off and waved it wildly. The llama slowed to an affronted trot, then stopped. The paramedics dashed in. Now and then the llama attempted another line of approach, making us dart and semicircle, but the trusting paramedics worked on, injecting, immobilising and strapping. When I heard Donkey Man groan a rush of relief warmed me. 'Right then, Christopher, we're just going to take you to Leeds ...' a paramedic was saying. I hadn't known he was called Christopher. Gently they raised the stretcher and we guarded the gate until they'd manoeuvred Christopher safely into the ambulance. We made good our own escape by backing out of the field.

'She was bonny, wasn't she?' Ewan said as we set off in the van.

'Who?'

'The one with the ponytail.' I'd been too preoccupied with the killer llama. 'Do you think she's out of my league?'

'Why would she be?'

'It's a good job that; paramedic.'

'You should have spoken to her.' He gave me a sardonic look and I shivered in my damp sweatshirt as the New Van laboured out of Throstleden towards a dove-grey sky, shot through with iron and slate.

Old Pedley was shouting across the yard at us before I'd shut the van door. 'He's been having a laugh with your boss, has our Billy, hasn't he, Stanley?' Stanley managed to disguise a snarl as a smile. He'd doubtless planned this job for me, but our Donkey Man emergency had spoiled his plans. 'He's just lobbed his knife in t' field, hasn't he?' Stanley was silent. 'And he's been scratching his bald head with his front teeth. Then he picked his teacup up off the wall and he poured it all down Stanley's back! He didn't even break the cup! He put it down again!'

Stanley stood up. 'I'll tell you what, Mr Pedley, why don't you go an' make me another brew? It's thirsty work is this.' Old Pedley turned to the house with Rosie the Rottweiler at his heels, and Stanley addressed us as he picked up Billy's foreleg: 'You two can get some bastard work done instead of lolling about like a pair of condoms in a convent.' I decided not to ask why condoms would be lolling about in a convent. Instead I tried a genial smile. 'There's two youngsters in that barn want trimming.'

At that moment Billy dropped his one and a half ton of

horse flesh onto the foreleg Stanley was holding. Soaked, bitten and covered in tea, this was the last straw for Stanley. He dropped the leg, straightened up, took back his fist, and swung a strong side-cut towards Billy's mouth, but while his hand was arcing through the air, Billy drew back his lips and bared his teeth. When Stanley's fist impacted, it was with three portcullis inches of equine incisor.

Stanley was still groaning and clutching his knuckles when Pedley shuffled out with two cups of tea. 'Nah, then what's he bin doin'?' he enquired as he handed a mug to Ewan.

'Oh, he's just hurt his hand,' Ewan said, vaguely.

'Oh, aye? Try to slug Billy in t' gob, did he? Because he doesn't want to be doing that. Chap at t' brewery broke his knuckles doin' that.'

Stanley nursed his bleeding knuckles all the way to the Old Van where he sat sucking them and squeezing them whilst Ewan patiently finished Billy then trimmed the two massive fillies.

When we'd done, I opened the Old Van to climb in with Stanley, who'd been consoling himself by sucking polo mints. Now he shouted across the yard, 'Oi! Dolloper! Where do you think you're going?'

'Home!' Ewan answered from the New Van.

'You've not given me the cash from this morning's job!'

'He was unconscious!'

'Oh, champion! You spend all bastard morning on a job that's not booked in. You're so late that I get injured – and then you tell me we've done it all for free!'

'What did you want me to do, Stanley? Frisk him?'

Stanley fired the ignition. 'He's not getting away with it.'

'It was only a tenner,' I said, as we pulled away.

'A TENNER!' I hadn't helped. 'You were gone three bastard hours! What did you do? Plait its fucking mane and tail?'

'It was a stallion. We could only trim its fronts.'

'You're supposed to be a bastard horse whisperer!'

'That's my mother.'

'This was a bastard donkey! Three-year-olds handle donkeys at Bridlington!' He grimaced as he flexed his knuckles over the gear lever and we drove on.

I watched wordlessly as the evening sun sank behind the moor. It poured a pale peach glow on the fading slopes, blinked, and was gone.

At Bling Manor Lucky was helped into a double tsukahara with half pike twist before she hit the lawn. As she toddled off with her tail held high Stanley turned to me. 'I know you think I'm tight, Posh Lad, but you've to watch every penny when you're in business. I'm still chasing Birdie for those two hundred notes he owes me.'

I hadn't a clue what he was talking about.

Chapter 11

Stanley was still grumpy the following morning. We sipped tea in silence then I decided to stock the van just to get away from him. It was a job I usually did with Ewan but he hadn't yet arrived. At eight fifteen I rang him, but he didn't pick up.

At eight twenty he rang me, urgency subduing his voice. 'Will, I've bumped the New Van.'

Stanley had appeared at my shoulder, so I tried to be nonchalant so as not to arouse his interest. 'Oh, never mind. Just get here when you can.' Stanley snatched the phone.

'Get here in ten minutes or I'll dock your bastard wages!'

I heard the tinny scratch of Ewan's voice but before I could reclaim my phone Stanley had roared into the receiver: 'I WILL DOCK THEM SOME BASTARD MORE THEN!' I took the telephone.

'How bad is it?' I asked, assuming Ewan had confessed. 'Is it driveable?'

Stanley snatched it back. 'What the fuck have you done?' There was another tinny scratching, then Stanley sighed. 'Right, right.' He was surprisingly calm over the chipmunk tinniness of Ewan's desperate tones. 'Who won't?' The tinniness scratched on in his ear. 'Ten minutes,' he said, then walked to the Old Van, flung open the door and commanded me in. 'Not you!' he yelled at the dog. 'There'll be carnage enough when I get my hands on the Dolloper, without you getting stuck in.' Lucky slunk through the dog flap and into the kitchen.

In the seven minutes it took to drive from the forge to the top of Hathersage Road, I had received five frantic texts from Ewan. Stanley was slapping the steering wheel with the heel of his palm. 'Tell him I'm going to rip his bastard head off,' he said when he saw me tapping in my answer. I didn't. I tried to reassure him.

At the top of Hathersage Road a queue of traffic was snaking past the New Van which was in the middle of the road with its front bumper jammed under the bumper of a 1970s Skoda. We pulled up beside it. The Skoda's driver was bullying an Asian newsagent. 'You see him, yes? You are witness, yes?'

Stanley walked past him and addressed Ewan. 'Get in your van.'

Ewan looked at him. '"Are you all right, Ewan?" "Have you injured yourself, Ewan?" "You must be shaken up, Ewan."'

'Get in your van, or I'll bloody injure you.'

The Skoda driver swung round. 'He not drive van! He take my fender!' A group of schoolkids had wandered out of the newsagents and were now a flump-sucking audience.

'See!' Ewan shouted. 'He's been saying this since ten to eight.'

'Just drive the bastard van, Dolloper.' Shaking his head, Ewan climbed in the New Van but the Skoda driver ran into the road and stood behind it.

Ewan lowered the window. 'He's been doing this for nearly an hour, Stanley. He says he wants four hundred and fifty pounds before I can move the van!'

At first Stanley chuckled, then he threw back his head and guffawed. It started as a theatrical laugh but he was soon genuinely convulsed. The newsagent, Skoda driver and schoolkids stared at him, bewildered. 'Four hundred and fifty notes?' he repeated. 'For that?'

The Skoda driver was offended. 'Is classic car!'

Stanley clapped his massive paws on either side of the Skoda driver's arms. 'Listen here, my comrade. His van and your pile of Czechoslovakian scrap aren't worth four hundred and fifty quid put together!' He took out a fifty pound note and snapped it in front of the driver's face. 'This will buy you a brand new Skoda with a full tank of premium four star. Now, get off the bastard road and let the boy move his van.' Stanley pushed the note in the driver's top pocket, replaced his hands on his upper arms and lifted him as if he were a garden gnome. He then deposited him on the pavement, took his hands from his shoulders and patted the driver's cheeks, all to the delight of the watching schoolchildren.

Ewan started the engine and put the van into reverse. For two feet the Skoda followed and then, with a metallic grinding and splitting, it divorced itself from its bumper. The driver howled and covered his eyes. The bumper clattered to the tarmac and the schoolkids laughed.

'Thanks, Stanley,' Ewan said through his open window, and the newsagent walked into the road and picked up the bumper.

'That fifty quid's coming out of your wages, Dolloper.'

Ewan blanched. 'I'm still paying for the fire extinguisher!'

'So you are. Looks like you'll be paying me next week then.' Ewan stared, incredulous. Stanley turned away and jumped in the van.

With Stanley furious and Ewan sulking, the day's jobs seemed to creak along and I could see no improvement in Ewan's mood when I called for my weekly breakfast the following morning. I enjoyed the predictable routine of the Grimshaws' kitchen. Steve – Ewan's dad – was always at the stove in his stockinged feet, Ricky was always stretched by the radiator and Lee always shambled in in his boxers and bashed the radio from Eddie Mair to Chris Evans. Steve never reacted. He would fire me a list of questions he knew the answers to: *smoked or unsmoked? brown or white? toasted or fried?* The plates were plonked on the table and Ricky would stretch, yawn and lollop to Steve's elbow in the expectation of bacon rind.

'Right,' Steve said as he picked up his fork, 'I'm doing eleven till seven at Morrison's then nine till twelve at the Esso station, so I can either walk the dog or do us a casserole – which is it?'

'Casserole,' Lee stated. 'Ewan'll walk the dog after work.'

'You'd better save me some bloody casserole then,' Ewan said.

'And me.' Steve pointed his knife at his eldest son. 'This greedy sod necked the last one down.'

'What, a whole casserole?'

'I thought they'd had theirs,' Lee was protesting, thrilled at his own gluttony.

'You're an animal,' Ewan stated, sliding his plate into the sink. 'And you can wash the breakfast stuff.'

'Why?'

'Because Dad's making a casserole and I'm walking the dog!'

Lee dragged at his fried bread. 'I'm buying a dishwasher when my Land Rover's paid off.'

Ewan grinned. 'In't it great now we're all working?'

'You never fetch a full pay packet home,' Lee shot. 'I'll buy you some rubber gloves.'

I loved their sibling banter. I was going to describe it as a pleasure I'd been denied, but I couldn't in all conscience use the word when comparing myself to Ewan; a cleaner carried out my domestic duties, and I kept all I earned.

Our next job was on Sylvia's yard. If there had been no hens, Sylvia's yard would have been paradise. It was nestled in a little wooded hollow, and today branches of ash and beech, oak and elder were splaying fretwork patterns on a white sky. The hot drinks overlapped and she'd always baked us a cake. The price I had to pay was her shameless adoration and her wittering on about her show ponies. Her ponies were pampered, cosseted and clean and the only thing she loved better than squeezing my cheeks was talking of their successes in the show ring. Stanley humoured her for the sake of his wallet, but a legal battle with his ex-wife, a flaring digestive disorder, grazed knuckles and a dented van had all conspired to sour him of late.

The first pony she brought out was Poppy. 'Look at this one, William! What do you think?'

'She reminds me of my second pony,' I said, patting the filly on the neck.

'I paid a lot for her. She's out of the Bryn Barrych line. Her great-grandmother is a Horse of the Year Show champion.'

Without a word of appreciation, Stanley set to work on Poppy, whilst Ewan started the trimming of Sylvia's gentle broodmare. Sylvia served us steaming mugs of hot chocolate and home-made fruit cake as spongy as a mattress, then she called across to Stanley. 'The judge at Boulder Vale said she'd never seen better conformation than on our Poppy.'

Mercifully, Stanley was holding a nail between his teeth when he told her that he didn't care if it had the conformation of a fucking hippopotamus. Sylvia looked at me with a furrowed brow. 'Did he say hippopotamus?'

Ewan was quicker off the mark. 'Lot of us! He said her conformation's wasted on the lot of us!'

'Oh.' She didn't look convinced. 'Only, I was hoping to qualify it for the Horse of the Year Show.'

'It's a better chance of winning Crufts,' Stanley snarled from underneath her pride and joy.

'He's in a bad mood,' I whispered. It seemed to reassure her, and, ever understanding, she took him another slice of cake.

'Oh! Poppy came with a companion!' she exclaimed as if she'd just remembered. 'It's the cleverest pony I've ever had. Do you want to see it?' Given that I see ponies every hour of my working life I wasn't especially interested, but I was courteous, so she returned with a Shetland pony the same colour as my long-dead Thimble. 'This is Teddy!' Teddy was aptly named; it had more in common with a cuddly toy than it did with another equine. The sound of Stanley's hammer blows rang from the anvil and Ewan wasn't looking up from where clouds of smoke were engulfing his burning-on, so admiration of Teddy was down to me.

'He's very cute.'

'Isn't he just! I think his feet need trimming but I don't know how he'll be, so it might be better if Stanley does him.'

It might be better if Stanley doesn't, I thought. Shetlands are surprisingly lethal. If you can imagine a twenty stone Labrador with its paws on your chest, you've grasped the effect of a rearing Shetland. Their short legs spit out in all directions, their low centre of gravity makes them hard to unbalance and you've to bend so low, you can't dive away. 'You're all right, Sylvia,' I said. 'I'll hold him and Ewan'll trim his feet – won't you, Ewan?'

'I wouldn't want you getting hurt, love.'

'He won't get hurt!' Stanley shouted. 'He's like Doctor bastard Dolittle.'

Ewan launched into a chorus of 'Talk to the Animals', but Sylvia talked over him.

'I wouldn't want to be responsible, Stan.'

Stanley straightened. 'It's all reyt for me to take a thrashin' though, is it?' I exchanged worried glances with Ewan. This wasn't looking good for Teddy.

Sylvia was stroking Teddy's nose. 'He can tell the time,' she said, changing the subject, then she handed me his rope and rolled up her sleeve.

Ewan tried to lift the mood. 'Come on, Stan. You've got to see this.'

Sylvia stood in front of the pony and pointed to her watch. 'Have a look at this, Stanley!'

Stanley sighed, straightened and folded his arms.

'Teddy, what time is dinner time?' Sylvia asked, as if she were addressing a nursery class. She clapped once and Teddy stamped a front foot.

I laughed out loud and Ewan made another attempt to engage Stanley: 'Did you see that, Stan? It's a clever little sod!' Stanley ignored him.

'Teddy, what time is stable time?' Sylvia asked. She clapped twice and Teddy stamped twice.

'What the hell's stable time?' Stanley asked.

'Teddy knows what it is!'

'What time is hay time?' She clapped three times, and Teddy stamped three times.

'What time is bedtime?' Four claps, four stamps.

'Who goes to bed at four o'clock?'

'Oh, come on, Stanley!' Ewan protested. 'You've got to admit it's clever.'

'It has nowt to do wi' t'watch!' Then he unfolded his arms, took Teddy's lead rope and tied him to a ring on the wall. Sylvia looked crestfallen and I prayed that Teddy would behave himself.

He didn't. All Stanley did was lift the pony's back foot. I know because my eyes hadn't left the equine fluff ball in the ten seconds that had passed since Stanley took the rope. That's all he did, he just lifted a back foot and in one movement the pony swung round and barrelled the side of Stanley's knee with such force it looked like Stanley's leg had bent sideways. A sickening groan crawled out of his throat, he staggered, then in a burst of temper he threw a right hook at Teddy. The pony saw it coming. It ducked away and Stanley's knuckles hit the breeze-block stable wall, reopening the wounds inflicted by Billy. It was Teddy's cleverest move so far.

Sylvia saw the blood. Her expression froze between horror and anguish. 'Oh, you barbaric man!' she blurted, slapping her palm across her lips.

'Barbaric? You want to see me when I'm drowning kittens on a Sunday afternoon!' It was too much for Sylvia. She ran for the house, tears streaming down her face.

'He missed,' I consoled her in the kitchen. 'He split his

78

knuckles on the wall.' I was still pleading Stanley's ill health, marital breakdown and smashed van when he walked into the kitchen with his hands in his pockets. Ewan had assumed a similar pose behind him, though I could see a wriggle at the corners of his lips.

'I don't know what came over me,' Stanley was saying in a voice a bit too dramatic to be convincing. 'He's a lovely pony, that Teddy. Ewan, go and get Teddy some Polo mints.' Then, in a bid to convince her he was Yorkshire's answer to St Francis of Assisi, he over-egged it with, 'I always have Polo mints for the horses.'

'You ate them,' Ewan said, deadpan.

'Oh yes.' And with a stretch-eyed glare he handed Ewan a fiver. 'Nip to the paper shop and fetch a few packets for Teddy, would you?' Stanley followed Sylvia's eyes to his blood-ied knuckles. 'Oh no!' he said, covering them with his other hand. 'I did that yesterday, on a Shire!' There's no helping some people.

STRATFORD COLLEGE OF AGRICULTURE:

FACULTY OF BLACKSMITHING AND FARRIERY

Apprenticeship Journal for the month of: December.

Comments: A varied month: I have volunteered my services to a local racehorse trainer to further develop my horse-handling skills. I have socialised with other Yorkshire farriers and have been impressed by the mutual support offered within our small profession. I have received Christmas thank you gifts from clients – a gesture indicative of my progress in client relations and noted by my ATF.

Learning Outcomes:

Improved anvil technique.

Gauging of the temperature of metal from its colour – (though both skills need further development).

Signed: William Harker. December 31st 2015   (Apprentice)

Signed: SL December 31st 2015   (Master)

Chapter 12

It's impossible to dress for the weather when you're standing upright over a fire one minute and bent double under a horse the next. Scarves dangle in your way, hats drop off, hoods obscure your vision and gloves impair your dexterity. We'd placed a folded cardboard box next to the forge as temporary foot insulation, and a pair of tongs was nestled in the fire. Ten seconds in the fire turns their handles to hand-warmers; twenty seconds turns them into skin removers. Ewan has the scars. Sleet-numbed flesh has cooked before you've registered the pain. Today, though, I'd timed it right. I cupped my hands round them gratefully and stamped my feet on the flattened cardboard box. If I'd been bashing at the anvil or hammering in a nail I might have generated enough heat to keep my blood from sludging, but a first-year apprentice does a lot of standing about. I watched as the clouds swallowed the distant bulge of Eckersley Moor and the sleet stiffened into snow. 'It's sticking,' I observed as it furred the edge of my cardboard square.

Soon Stanley was cooling the newly forged shoes by sizzling them in the snow and Ewan was crooning 'White Christmas' through the nails he held between his teeth. 'I'm just wondering if I'll get home ...'

'It won't as bad t'other side of Eckersley.'

'I've to *get* to the other side of Eckersley!'

Snowflakes were falling fast now, festooning Ewan's shoulders like confetti. I blinked them off my eyelashes and followed Stanley's gaze to where pale grey clouds were edged with yellow. 'We'd better make these the last set,' he said to Ewan. 'There's more up there.' By the time we climbed into the Old Van, Scorthwaite Moor had disappeared. Stanley let off the handbrake and we began the perilous slither down Fowlden Fell. Determined snowflakes raced at the windscreen. 'We'll be reyt when we get t'bypass.'

'Our Lee has a Land Rover,' Ewan mused.

Stanley was focused on descending a steep incline in a heavily laden Transit van, but he recognised a slur. 'Useless!'

'It gets over snowdrifts, bogs, the lot!'

Stanley changed gear to take a bend but the wheels didn't follow the steering and we took it in a half-pass. He was unconcerned.

'It doesn't get over the silly bastards who've abandoned their cars all over Yorkshire, though, does it? It's not Chitty bastard Bang Bang.' I couldn't take my eyes off the road. Every twist and gradient gathered new significance. 'Looks like you're in my spare room tonight, Posh Lad.' I groaned. Stanley was affronted. 'Hey! It has remote control curtains!'

Parallel ribbons of black tarmac tramlined us slowly into Fowlden, along Cribbs Road, through Hathersage and onto the drive of Bling Manor. Only then did Stanley slacken his grip on the steering wheel, and drop his shoulders.

That evening I sat in front of nose-to-tail *Top Gear* in a white leather armchair whilst Stanley nursed a can of Carlsberg and kept an eye on where I was putting my feet. After the third can, he spoke: 'That's where Lynne used to sit.' I didn't know what to say. 'Katie sat there, and Jonathan sat there.'

I swallowed. 'Do you miss them?'

He took a slug of his Carlsberg. 'The dog does.' He ruffled her ears. 'She still looks for them coming home from school.' He let Richard Hammond's voice fill the room for a minute then crushed his can in his fist like it was a crisp packet. 'Anyway, she can leave her bastard nail clippings on somebody else's Italianate bedside table with feather detailing.'

'Will anyone else have an Italianate bedside table with feather detailing?'

'Fucking Gary won't; that's for sure.' I decided not to ask about Fucking Gary.

'Do you still see your kids?'

'They're in Surrey.'

'You could Skype?'

He cracked open another can, then roared with laughter at James May spinning a Range Rover on a racetrack.

'That's a good job, that is! Driving fast cars for the telly!'

The next morning Ewan announced his arrival by bursting a snowball on the back of my neck. It splattered over my shoulders and hissed on the coals I was stoking. He laughed and came to warm his hands at the forge. Snow from his boots puddled on the concrete.

'Did you walk?'

'I enjoyed it. It's given Cribbs Road a makeover.'

I knew what he meant. It was as if Hathersage was in the middle of an unmade bed with the moors bulging above the gently rumpled town, like pillows. We wouldn't be driving up there today.

Stanley swaggered in with a brew warming his hands. 'Right,' he announced, and pointed at me. 'You can get some anvil practice in, and you,' he meant Ewan, 'can mend the weather vane that's been in t'shed for twelve months.'

'I need practice with a gas forge, Stan.'

'You need to do as you're told, lad!' Ewan stomped towards the shed and hefted a shower of virgin snow skywards with his foot. Lucky jumped at the snow shower, yapping. 'I don't pay you to play with the bastard dog!'

'You don't pay me to mend weather vanes either. I'm not a fucking blacksmith.'

Stanley slammed down his brew, dashed out, neck-locked

Ewan and rubbed a handful of snow in his face. Ewan squirmed and yelled, and the second Stanley let go he bent for a revenge armful, but Stanley tackled him at the knees. Ewan fell to the marshmallow lawn and Stanley dropped on him like lumber. He rolled him over and over, piling on more snow whilst Lucky circled and barked and dived in for the occasional nip. Ewan finally sat up, gasping for breath. 'I'm soaked, you berk!' Stanley flung a final fistful in Ewan's face.

'I suppose I'm mending my own bastard weather vane, then?' Ewan was wise enough not to answer and whilst Stanley dusted off his jeans, Ewan opened up the rear doors of the Old Van and fired up the gas forge.

I spent the first half of the morning trying to heat a shoe in the same fire Stanley was using. 'Not yet,' he'd shout when I saw a clear path to the fire. Then, when he was waving a white hot rod over it, 'Now, Posh Lad! Now!' I was relieved when he paraded a twisted metal spike about the forge, pronounced on his own brilliance and announced he was leaving us to it.

Ewan joined me by the coke forge and flicked on the kettle. 'Test me,' he said, and handed me a chart.

'Red.'

'Six hundred.'

'Yellow.'

'One thousand and fifty.'

'Pale yellow.'

Ewan furrowed his brow and took back the chart. 'You'll need to learn these, you know. You'll be using temperature gauges at college – not Stanley's guesswork.' I followed his eyes to the half-finished shoe I'd left dangling on the anvil. He picked it up. 'You're not holding your hammer right,' he said and threw the shoe back in the flames. When it was hot enough I lifted it out and dropped it on the anvil. I dealt it two blows but as I raised my arm for the third Ewan stopped me. He re-angled my wrist and pulled the shaft of the hammer through by an inch. When I next hit the shoe I felt the effect.

Stanley was a natural farrier but his teaching style was demonstration followed by abuse. Ewan was a natural teacher. He watched, analysed and communicated. He'd learnt through an observation more intent than I could manage; I needed showing.

The back door of Bling Manor clicked. It was a tiny sound and our nerves knew it before our ears did. 'Right,' Stanley announced, rubbing his hands. 'Time for a pint.'

The town was silent but for the crunch of our boots. A single pair of tyre tracks had striped Hathersage Road with polished snow. Parked cars were wearing it. The telegraph pole was white on the left, black on the right.

The Fleece was empty apart from Bob Entwistle, nursing a half pint. Stanley glanced at him. 'A'reyt, Bob? Fancy another?'

'I'm all right with this, thanks, Stan.'

The landlord thrust a glass under the pump. 'He's like one of the bloody fixtures and fittings,' he grumbled. 'You know why he won't have one, don't you?' Stanley didn't answer, but the landlord raised his voice. 'Because he's too bloody tight to buy you one back!' He levered the pump handle down gently. 'He was on the doorstep at eleven because it's cheaper nursing half o'bitter than it is paying for his bloody heating. He thinks I'm running a bloody care home.'

'Pull him another half,' Ewan said, rooting in his pocket, but Stanley indicated that he'd pay for it, then changed the subject. 'Has Birdie been in?'

The landlord plonked Bob's half on the bar. 'Have you seen t'roads? He can't bloody fly!' I carried our drinks to Bob's table.

'That's very civil of you.' Bob smiled.

'We're only having the one,' Stanley explained and Bob brightened further. He grilled us for racing tips, then moved on to another of his favourite topics: bantams.

'I'll tell you what you want to be givin' 'em this weather – suet.'

Ewan leaned back so the landlord could slam a steak pie in front of him. He looked up. 'I said steak pudding.'

'You've got what'll go in a microwave.' He slammed two more down and walked off.

'Just sprinkle a few flakes on their feed,' Bob was saying, 'and it'll be as good as wrapping 'em in red flannel.' I pushed my fork into my pie. It took surprising force. 'Do you have a lamp in?' Stanley couldn't answer. His jaw was working overtime on the brickwork pastry. Bob turned to me. 'Does he have a lamp in?'

'I don't know. I hate the things.'

'He's frightened of 'em,' Ewan added.

Bob cracked a laugh. 'How can he be freetned of 'em when he works with 'osses?'

'I'm not frightened of them. I just don't like them.'

'You shit yourself,' Stanley said as he pushed his plate away. Bob eyed the remaining half of pie with interest. 'I've done wi' that, Bob; if you can stomach it.' Despite his eighty-year-old teeth Bob tucked into it then set about Ewan's. I was determined to finish mine. I didn't want another night of *Top Gear* reruns and if it took two hours to get home, I'd need a full belly. Stanley zipped up his coat and flicked his head at Ewan. 'Come on, Dolloper. We'll get t'forge warmed up while he's breakin' his teeth.'

The landlord raised a tea towel. 'You've not paid for your food, Stan!'

'That weren't food, Trevor.'

Trevor gulped like a codfish. 'Be fair, Stan – my kitchen staff haven't turned up!'

'You shouldn't have bloody winged it then, should you?'

Trevor pointed a shaking finger at Stanley's receding shape. 'You!' His whole arm trembled. 'You're barred!'

'Am I buggery,' Stanley laughed. 'I keep this place going,' and he let the door drop into place behind him.

Trevor threw the tea towel on the bar and turned to me. 'Is there owt wrong with that pie?' Bob kissed a joined thumb and forefinger in answer. Trevor glanced at the door. 'I should bar him.'

Bob Entwistle bothered me. I knew that some older people weren't well off. I'd seen a *Panorama* about it. But the pensioners I knew flew to Tenerife when the temperature dropped below ten degrees. Wasn't there a winter fuel allowance for people like Bob? He was the same age as my granddad, give or take a year or two. Granddad drove a Lexus.

Back at the forge, Stanley was standing next to the Old Van. I couldn't see why. We weren't going anywhere. 'Come here,' he commanded, 'I've summat to show you.' Expecting a problem with the iPhone, or a dent in the driver's door, I walked over. The next thing I knew there were feathers in my face. I was gasping, screaming and spitting them out. Wings were on my head. Quills were on my lips. Scales were on my neck. I couldn't breathe. I was windmilling my arms against the squawking, chukkering and flapping. I staggered backwards. A wattle brushed my hand. I gasped for air. A beak banged my knee. Claws clicked my boots. It landed and scuttered away, flicking sparks of snow.

I bent over my knees, gasping. Slowly, my heartbeat steadied, the world stopped swimming and I lifted my head. Ewan and Stanley were leaning on the van, rocking with laughter. Twenty seconds' worth of redundant adrenalin was still coursing my veins. I let out a roar and ran at them. Stanley bolted for the door, but Ewan ran round the van. He slipped, caught the wing mirror to save himself and whilst he was dangling there I booted him up the arse. He clutched the seat of his jeans. 'It was Stan's idea!' Practical jokes were always Ewan's idea.

Chapter 13

I had never been so delighted to see rain. It punctured the snow; cratered it and swilled its grey globs into drains and gutters. I could go home. Stanley's house rules had been unpredictable and unsettling: *don't charge your phone in the kitchen, align the television controls with the edge of the armchair, always leave dirty boots on a black tile.* The forty-five minute detour to avoid the drifts on Eckersley Moor seemed a small price to pay for my mother's one rule: *don't let the cat upstairs.*

Intermittent drizzle dampened the whole weekend and by Monday morning Eckersley Moor was passable again, but only by the width of a single car. My forty-minute journey took me an hour so I was expecting a blasting but I found Stanley storming about the kitchen with a single boot in his hand.

'It must be the bastard fox!'

'Why would a fox take a boot?' He broke off to glare at me.

'Well, who do you think took it? A one-legged bastard housebreaker?' I shrugged. 'Go and make yourself useful! Search the bastard garden!'

I was peering under a hydrangea bush when Ewan killed the New Van's engine and climbed out.

'You won't find it there!' he chuckled. One boot was a taunt, a tease, a frustrating reminder of the pair. Ewan's work!

It was another twenty minutes before Stanley admitted defeat and stuffed his feet into a pair of wellies.

*

Christmas was approaching, and quite a few clients gave us Christmas gifts or tips. The words *This is for Ewan and Will* often accompanied an extra tenner or a box of chocolates or, on one rare occasion, a crate of Stella Artois.

'You're a smarmy bastard,' Stanley complained to me as Ewan and I divided our spoils at the end of the day.

I looked up at him, nonplussed.

'Have we ever had this before, Ewan?'

'I'm not complaining!'

'Well, it sickens me off. "Ooh what a nice lad","Ooh, hasn't he got lovely manners", "Ooh, what a lovely smile!"'

Ewan folded his arms. 'It's your clients he's smarming, you silly sod.' But Stanley shuffled off, muttering to himself.

My popularity should have enabled a more lavish Christmas than usual in the Grimshaw household, but on Friday 15 December Ewan opened his pay packet, then looked up at Stanley open-mouthed. 'There's nowt in it.'

'You're lucky there's not a bastard bill in it.'

Ewan blinked. Stanley counted on his fingers. 'Fifty quid for the Skoda, your final instalment on the fire extinguisher and the tenner you never had off Donkey Man makes sixty-five quid. Then there's a hundred and five pounds and fifty pence for the new boots I had to buy.' Ewan gawped at him. 'Oh, did I not mention that? Mary at number seventeen found my boot in her garden. It turns out the fox who lobbed it in there was wearing a red hoodie at the time.' He followed his observation with a delayed smack round the ear for Ewan. 'So by my reckoning *you* owe *me* twenty-five pounds and fifty pence which will be coming out of your next pay packet.' Ewan held his ear and protested the injustice.

'But you've paid for two pairs of boots and you've *got* two pairs of boots, now!' When that failed to appeal to Stanley's sense of honour, Ewan stormed off and began flinging tools in the back of the van with so much force I thought they'd burst through the side. Lucky belted for cover but Stanley was calm in his victory. He instructed him to make a pair of egg bars for Pedley's shire and told me to get in the van.

At a scrapyard on fifty acres of Scorthwaite Moor, Stanley and I were greeted by a stocky, florid-faced Irishman in his forties. His hair was styled in a long curly mullet and a gold hoop earring glinted in his left ear. His fellow travellers occupied the land sporadically, and when they did, they called on Stanley to shoe their horses.

'All right there, Stanley!' Flashman Freddie said, and offered his hand with a bent elbow, as if he planned to arm-wrestle rather than greet.

Stanley slapped his paw into Flashman Freddie's then introduced me. 'This is Posh Lad; Posh Lad, Flashman Freddie.'

Flashman offered his hand to me in the conventional way but when I took it, he crushed my bones to powder. Still gripping the remains of my hand he addressed Stanley: 'Is he sound?'

'Oh aye!' Stanley reassured him. 'He's reyt enough, is Posh Lad. What's job then?'

Flashman Freddie released my paralysed mitt and gestured that I should follow him. The second he turned his back I grimaced in agony and nursed my crippled fingers. I shook them, blew on them and tried to coax the blood back. Stanley glared at me. 'I'll be no use to you without a right hand!' I hissed.

'You won't have a right eye if Flashman Freddie sees you being a soft lad!'

Flashman Freddie led us across an expanse of gravel scoured by the moorland wind and prowled by two aloof German shepherds and into a vast modern barn. An articulated lorry with a smashed driver's window dominated the space. Flashman Freddie strode past it towards a row of stalls along the short end.

'Hey up, Fred, what's wi' th'artic?' Stanley's tone was studiously casual.

'Full of fucking bathrooms!' Flashman raged. 'What the fuck do I want with twenty fucking bathrooms? I've told them and told them to check what's in the back *before*, not after.' I gulped, but Stanley was unruffled. 'Both colts are racing on Sunday so they need road studs,' Flashman stated as we reached the end of the barn.

Stanley nodded his understanding and threw me a head collar as Flashman Freddie disappeared through a back door of the barn.

I looked at the hairy black cob on the end of my lead rope. 'Racing?'

'They race them on the bypass.'

'In all the traffic?'

'No, you crate egg! They shut the road!'

'Who does?'

'The travellers!'

'Is that legal?'

Stanley sighed at my stupidity. 'It's about as legal as stealing articulated lorries.' I led my colt out of the barn in silence whilst Stanley read my mind. 'Look; all we're doing is putting the bastard shoes on the horses. That's not illegal. He'll pay us upfront, and I guarantee these colts won't be a bit o' bother.'

The colts stood like a pair of rocking horses throughout the whole procedure, but my conscience was bucking and rearing like a mustang. Weren't we accessories? Wasn't our payment the profits of crime?

I was keen to leave when the colts were shod, but Flashman Freddie offered us 'a nice bit o' rabbit stew' he had bubbling over an open fire. There was horizontal drizzle but Stanley was as thrilled as a twelve-year-old boy scout when he was invited to sit on a straw bale and handed a tin mug of stew. He took a mouthful. 'Grand! You can't beat fresh-caught meat, Freddie!'

Flashman Freddie winked. 'Finest in Yorkshire.'

As I pushed the grey slop about and steeled myself for a mouthful, a sleek brindled whippet slipped down the steps of Flashman Freddie's caravan and insinuated itself under his armpit. 'Here she is!' He ruffled the dog's ears. 'The best little lurcher in Europe! That wee rabbit was dead before it knew there was a dog on the moor.' I looked into the grey gloop. I reckoned twenty mouthfuls would shift it. I closed my eyes and took a gulp. I was ready to fight a retch, but it was good. 'So then,' Flashman Freddie was looking at me when I opened my eyes, 'what do you do with your spare time, Posh Lad?'

It was one thing Stanley calling me Posh Lad, but this seemed a bit of a liberty. 'I like racing,' I confessed.

'You want to get yourself down the Fowlden bypass on Sunday morning, so you do. That'll be a spectacle for ye.'

I smiled weakly over my rabbit stew and was wondering if I should explain that I meant thoroughbreds not trotters when Stanley came to my rescue. 'It's the hunt ball tonight. It'll take him two days to recover.' I laughed wanly. Despite the hot food I was cold and damp, I wanted to go. Stanley, however, was in his element. He was settling to a second mug full of stew when two young men blasted towards us across the gravel. I couldn't imagine where they'd come from. There was nothing but moorland and drizzle between us and the horizon.

'Dad! Dad!' Flashman Freddie looked up. 'They're after us!' They were gasping for breath. One propped himself against the caravan and the other doubled over. Between their rasping breaths I heard the distant wail of a police siren.

'Oh, bloody hell, lads! Not again!' Flashman Freddie seemed more resigned than concerned. He stood and flung open the rear doors of a nearby Transit. 'Get in!' he commanded, then he turned to us. 'Excuse me, gents. I'll be back in a jiffy.' He jumped into the van and drove off. I looked at Stanley.

'Can we go now?'

'When I've finished my stew.' I stood up. 'Don't go poking about. Charmaine will be watching.' I looked blank. 'His wife.' I sat down again. 'Calm down, Posh Lad. Freddie's all right if you're on the right side of him. He's an old-fashioned criminal.' He chuckled to himself. 'A chap tried to rob him at Appleby and d'you know what he did? He looked the chap up and down, batted his gun on one side, kneed him in the groin, and grabbed it!' Stanley's voice rose to a crescendo. 'Then he breaks the gun, tips the bullets out, and pockets it! "That's how you rob somebody," he says.' Stanley was shaking his head in affectionate wonderment. 'He makes you proud to be a traveller.'

'Makes who proud to be a traveller?'

'Me!'

'You live on Hathersage Road!'

'I do *now*!' I furrowed my brow. 'My mam and dad went in brick when I was four. My dad never settled.' I wanted to know more, but Freddie's van growled onto the gravel.

'Sorry about that, gents. Do you fancy a cuppa?'

Stanley would have accepted it were it not for my pleading eyes and chattering teeth. Instead he promised he'd be back before Appleby Fair and we set off down the lane. A police car passed us at speed, and Stanley chuckled openly: 'Good luck wi' that, lads!' Cloud was boiling beyond the hills. Layer upon layer of it, from white through lilac to gunmetal grey crowded the windscreen.

'What do you think he did with that gun?' I asked as the van hissed through a puddle.

'What gun?'

'The gun he took off the lad.'

Stanley turned to me. 'Have you missed the entire point of that story, Posh Lad?'

I hadn't. I just wondered if Flashman Freddie had a gun.

Back at the forge, Ewan had finished the egg bars. 'Have you had any dinner, Dolloper?'

'How can I have any dinner if I haven't any money?'

Stanley blew out his cheeks. 'Put your bastard coat on and I'll buy you a pie in the Fleece.'

I stood by the fire to warm up a bit whilst Stanley went to change his boots. 'He can't smarm his way out of this with a pie,' Ewan mumbled as he pushed his arm into his jacket.

'To be fair, Ewan, it's a pie, an eighty quid ticket to the hunt ball, all our drinks tonight and an afternoon's go-karting. And you did drive his van into the back of that Skoda.'

'Whose fucking side are you on?'

'I'm just saying. That's all.'

Ewan checked over his shoulder then went in his pocket and showed me a twenty pound note. I looked at him, nonplussed. 'Joan Mitchell rang to book a trim in, so I've been and done it.'

I shook my head. 'You'll regret it.'

'Why?'

'He'll find out.'

'How?'

'Because he's Stanley!' I said.

Even before he ordered our drinks, Stanley had asked the landlord if Birdie had been in.

'Birdie? Not since Tuesday.'

'Have you told him I've been asking for him?'

'Aye.'

'Well, next time, tell him to walk across Hathersage Road and put his debts through my letterbox – comprendo?'

'I'm running a pub here, Stanley. Not a debt-collecting agency.'

Ewan sat with the Fleece's oldest regular again. 'A'reyt, Bob?' Stanley said as he put two pints on the table.

'He slips out the back when he sees you.'

'Who does?'

'Birdie. I've seen him slip out back twice when you've come in.'

Stanley took a gulp of his beer. 'Don't you worry, Bob; I'll have my money off him.'

Ewan brightened with a meat and potato pie inside him, so when Bob went to play dominoes, Ewan proposed a game of our own. 'I'll need two pound coins,' he said, 'and obviously, I've not got them.' Stanley obligingly fished out two pound coins. 'Right,' Ewan said, 'I'm going to put these pound coins on the table and you have to cover them with your hands.' Stanley followed instructions. 'Now, in a minute you've got to pick the coins up, and if you can do it, you can have them.'

'They're my bastard coins!'

Ewan ignored him, picked up my pint in his left hand and his own in his right, and placed each of the brimming glasses on the backs of Stanley's hands. 'Right then,' he said, getting to his feet. 'We'll leave you to fathom that out.'

'You what?'

'We're off now, me and Will. We'll see you at the Richmond Arms tonight – if you've fathomed it out.' He took a long gulp of Stanley's pint before picking up his coat and striding for the door.

'Oi!'

I followed Ewan.

'Oi!'

We didn't look round, but I could hear Bob Entwistle's laughter following us towards the door.

'Oi!' A note of panic had risen in Stanley's voice. 'Where the fuck are you going?'

I shoved through the glass doors behind Ewan. 'Are we leaving him?'

Ewan was wiping his eyes. 'Course we fucking are! And I'll get him with the spoons tonight!'

'The what?'

On the walk back to the forge Ewan explained the spoons to me, and the twist he planned to put on it. I shook my head. 'He won't fall for it. Not after what we've just done in the pub.'

'He will, because he'll be hammered!' I raised my eyebrows sceptically; Stanley wasn't drinking much these days. 'Trust me. I know Stanley Lampitt better than my own armpit.'

Chapter 14

When we arrived at the hunt ball, Stanley was already at the farriers' table, arms folded, face beaming, the elder statesman of the Richmond Arms. 'Dolloper! Posh Lad! Over here!' I had expected some reference to his abandonment in the Fleece but he seemed to have forgotten all about it and introduced us to the other Yorkshire farriers as if we were a pair of prize pigs. 'They're a right good pair o'lads, these two. This one,' he was referring to me, 'Looked like he were made o'pipe cleaners in September!' He took my developing bicep between thumb and forefinger! 'We have a right laugh, don't we – eh?' We nodded agreeably. 'So I thought I'd treat them tonight. Bit of a Christmas bonus, you know.' He had to show off – especially to Moneybags Morrison who pissed him off by getting all the veterinary referrals.

Moneybags looked me up and down. 'You're Lizzie Harker's lad, aren't you?' I nodded and turned away quickly. I didn't want Stanley suspecting a conflict of interests – Michael Morrison had been my mother's farrier for as long as I could remember; I'd have applied for an apprenticeship with him, had there been a vacancy

Stanley was fishing in his pocket for a wad of notes. 'Go on, Posh Lad. I'm in t'chair. Sort us out with ale till that lot runs out.'

I walked to the bar, and would have been distracted by Pippa Jennings in a red backless dress had Ewan not come up behind me, rubbing his hands. 'What did I tell you? It's all going according to plan.'

'Is it?'

'Yes! He's playing the big man. Flashing the cash. He's putty in our hands.' I'd ordered the drinks when Ewan added a vodka chaser to the list. 'All part of the plan,' he assured me with his hand on my shoulder.

Ewan plonked the chaser next to Stanley's pint. 'We've all had a shot at the bar, Stanley, so I've fetched yours over then you don't miss out.'

'See what I mean?' Stanley grinned at Moneybags. 'They're thoughtful lads, are these.' Then he downed it.

Ewan repeated that stunt three more times, and rather than be outdrunk by the younger men, Stanley knocked the vodkas back, even though it was against his better judgement. By the time his sticky toffee pudding arrived, Stanley was struggling to focus, but Ewan was on a mission. He coaxed an Irish coffee down him and then suggested that we play spoons.

One after another, each farrier put his pudding spoon into his mouth, handle first, then turned to the man on his left and tapped him on the head with the bowl. When it was my turn to tap Stanley, I put my spoon in my mouth and turned as if to hit him, but as Stanley cringed in readiness Ewan on his other side thwacked him roundly on his bald patch with the ball of his own spoon held in his fist.

After his second bashing Stanley was nursing his scalp. 'Bloody hell, Will, you're good at this.' He could hardly grip the spoon in his mouth, never mind inflict his blow on Ewan. The table was roaring with laughter and, of course, Ewan was enjoying every thwack he gave more than the last one. Stanley sucked his teeth at what he thought was my expertise but, true to form, he refused to surrender. On the sixth round, Ewan left his seat, took a run up and landed the spoon with such a force that, wasted as he was, Stanley knew that it hadn't been inflicted by a spoon between my teeth. He jumped up, swung round, shouted, 'Oi, you bastard!' then fell face first, scattering chairs and dragging the tablecloth with him. He groaned into the carpet, then lay still. Four farriers shook their heads good-humouredly then dug him from under used crockery. They lugged his lolling carcass to the street where Moneybags Morrison hailed a taxi and stuffed Stanley into it.

I spent the rest of the evening getting to know Pippa Jennings. I remembered her older brother from Beaumont's rugby team three years above me and we'd both jumped for our pony clubs. 'Did you ride a grey?' I nodded. 'I remember you! Didn't we beat you at Stonefold?'

'You did – but one of your team took a ducking at the water.'

'That was Pongo's fault,' she laughed.

'It was you!'

'We still beat you!' Ewan brought us more drinks and he blushed when she told him he looked smart. 'Do you still ride?' she asked, stirring her mojito with a straw.

'When I can.'

'Fancy a breeze up the gallops tomorrow?' I couldn't believe my luck. 'Report to my dad at about ten?'

It was a double success. I was to ride top-class racehorses and get another glimpse of a beautiful girl. I was still smiling when I climbed out of my taxi at one o'clock.

I arrived at the Jennings' on Saturday, hoping to put Pippa in mind of Poldark in my breeches and boots, but she just waved at me from fifty yards away. My disappointment puddled and might have drenched me, had not Richard Jennings legged me up onto last year's Triumph Hurdle winner. I felt like I'd met a celebrity and his head lad, Zach, laughed when I took a mounted selfie.

It was over a year since I'd balanced that knife edge between exhilaration and terror but the moment we picked up canter my limbs shifted, my muscles shuffled, then they settled like shaken sugar. I was home. The wind bit my face. Hoof beats matched heartbeats and my bones remembered the rhythm. We consumed the winter gallop in minutes, and as we walked our horses down the slope on a loose rein, my eyes followed Zach's finger round the estate. He pointed out the hurdle track, the summer gallop and the solarium – then it snagged on a horse being dragged about the small sand paddock. 'Precipitant,' Zach explained. 'She won't go in the starting stalls.' The horse was as far away from the four rusting starting stalls as she could put herself and her handler was cracking the whip.

'He won't get her in that way,' I said flatly. I felt Zach turn to me, rank and experience drawing out his spine.

'How would *you* do it then?'

'I'd get her to trust me.' He laughed out loud at that, but I'd seen my mother unruffled by the sneers of old horsemen who'd ended up eating their words. Shouts from the paddock grew louder as we approached, and Precipitant leapt from the sound of a lunge whip lashing the ground. 'If she goes in now, it'll be because she's more frightened of the handler than of the stalls,' I said. Zach shrugged. We were riding past the paddock now. The filly's flanks were frothed with sweat and her sides were heaving like bellows. The last time I'd seen a horse so stressed it was in the corral at Loddenden Top, and I was still ashamed of my involvement.

'No luck then,' Zach observed.

'It's going in if it takes me all day,' the handler growled.

'Do you want me to have a go?' I offered.

'You?' The handler's voice dripped with disdain.

'Lizzie Harker's son,' Zach explained with a flick of his head.

'Be my guest,' the handler said.

'Great!' I answered, ignoring the sarcasm snaking his voice. 'I'll have a word with Mr Jennings.'

*

'And what makes you sure you can do all this?' Richard Jennings asked after listening to me with his head on one side. I cut to the chase.

'My mother's Lizzie Harker.' I hated cashing in on her reputation.

'I didn't know that. I've tried to get her up here but she can never fit me in!'

'She's booked solid for eighteen months.'

'So, you're the next best thing, eh?'

'I wouldn't say that ...'

'I've been to a couple of her demos ...' and he enthused about my mother's skills all the way to the sand paddock.

Precipitant's handler had been joined by Zach and the filly was no nearer to the stalls. She was lathered in sweat now and spinning on the end of Zach's rope, first one way, then the other. 'She must be tired now,' Jennings shouted. Her breathing was fast and laboured.

'I don't think you'll get her in today,' I said.

'We bloody will!' her handler answered and cracked the whip on the ground behind her. She leapt forward, striking Zach's shoulder and knocking him to the ground. Free at last, she dashed to the fence and, desperate for an escape, she started high-trotting the perimeter.

'Drop your eyes!' I commanded. My authority shocked me but if she jumped from a standstill she could spear herself on the fence. 'Don't look at her!' With no eyes boring her, the mare's step slowed and she stood. Her head was up, her eyes were wild, but she was no longer panicking. Zach started to uncurl. 'Not yet!' I hissed.

It took over three minutes for the mare to sigh and lower her head. 'Should I catch her?' Jennings whispered.

I nodded. 'Don't look at her though; approach her shoulder at forty-five degrees.' He did as he was told. 'Don't touch the rope.'

'How will I lead her back?' Jennings whispered. He was stroking the mare's neck.

'Take your right shoulder past her nose and walk towards her tail.' To my relief, the mare followed him. 'Now your other shoulder ...' She followed him back. 'OK, just set off slowly towards the stables.' In the face of Jennings' wonderment, she followed him. 'Why wouldn't she?' I asked, sounding more certain than I felt. 'She was being hunted and you offered safety.'

'No one was bloody hunting!' Zach grumbled behind me, dusting off his jacket.

'You were staring at her; you were grabbing with your claws and you were trying to corner her.'

'I was trying to train her!'

'Train yourself! She's a prey animal with a brain the size of a walnut!'

Jennings opened Precipitant's stable door and she followed him in. 'What now?' he asked, easing her bridle over her ears.

'Can I work with her over the next few weeks?' Jennings agreed and Zach rolled his eyes.

Monday arrived too quickly. 'How many feet does a horse have, Dolloper?'

Ewan raised his eyes from the anvil. 'What are you on about?'

'I'm on about the number of feet on a horse. Have you not done that yet, at college?'

'Are you trying to be funny?'

'Just give me a ballpark figure if you're not sure.'

'Four!'

'Four! See, you have done it at college!' His face darkened. 'So why did you only trim three on Joan Mitchell's cob?' Ewan blanched. 'I'll tell you why, Dolloper: because you were in such a bastard hurry to get back here with my twenty quid in your pocket that you rushed the job, didn't you?' I raised my eyebrows at Ewan as a reminder that I'd told him so. 'Now get in that bastard van, and finish the job off.' Ewan sighed. 'And that makes £35.50 out of your next pay packet.'

Grudgingly, Ewan headed for the door and was just about to climb into the New Van when he turned, revenge glinting in his eye.

'What have you done to your head, Stan?' I focused my concentration on the mug I was washing up, but from the corner of my eye I saw Stanley touch the egg-sized lump.

'Fuck knows. I woke up with it Sat'day morning.'

Ewan jumped in the van with a satisfied grin. He was just about to slam the door when Stanley shouted: 'Dog!'

'Oh, hell, Stanley!'

'Have it!' Stanley growled, presenting Lucky by the scruff. Ewan grudgingly opened the door, Stanley threw her in and Ewan drove off. 'Right, Posh Lad. I've a job for you.'

I followed Stanley through the kitchen door of Bling Manor where he indicated I should sit on a bar stool. He rummaged behind the coffee canister and presented me with three letters. 'Read these.' I took one from its envelope, unfolded it and cast my eyes down the page. I was registering it as a CV when Stanley spoke again. 'Go on. Read it!'

I looked up. 'Out loud?'

'Aye.' He'd turned his back on me and was fussing with a tea towel.

'You want me to read this out loud to you?'

Still he didn't turn round. 'That's what I said, in't it?' His voice was tight. He sprayed cleaning fluid on a gleaming kitchen surface and swiped at it with a cloth. I felt like I was back in year six. I was just about to refuse when realisation began snapping like bubble wrap: his missed appointment; the symbols in the diary; the unread instruction manuals. His broad back and muscled shoulders looked suddenly vulnerable. Adult illiteracy had been a statistic, like the budget deficit and old-age poverty. I knew it was real, but not real like an anvil or

105

a mug of Earl Grey. Except now it was shuffling uneasily on the other side of the kitchen.

'How've you done it, Stan?' He turned from the sink.

'What?'

'Built up this business when you can't read?' He turned back to the sink.

'I can bastard count, Posh Lad!'

The first letter was an application for the post of *Temporary full-time farrier to oversee the running of a successful and varied practice including the tuition of two apprentices; accommodation available.* That made two shocks in as many minutes. The letter was from Dirk Koetzee, a South African who'd been practising on the Western Cape and would *welcome a few months employment in the UK, prior to returning to South Africa.*

I lowered the paper. 'What's going on, Stanley?'

He sighed. 'How can I leave you two feckless arse-wipes in charge while I'm in hospital?'

'We'd manage.'

'No. I've thought about it. I need a qualified bloke.' The second letter was from Robert Finley who *entered the profession late, following redundancy from McVities.*

A stone settled at the pit of my stomach. The third was from James Price, who was barely older than Ewan.

Stanley considered. He pulled his lip and rubbed his chin. 'I'll look at Finley and the South African.' He turned away and started refolding the dishcloth. 'Don't say owt to Ewan, will you?' I knew he wasn't talking about the farrier's job.

Chapter 15

Christmas caught me unawares. Until two years ago, Beaumont College had wassailed and carolled me through the first week in December, then tumbled me into a luxuriant four-week school holiday. In those days I'd perused the shops in festive anticipation – in between decking the halls and hunting with the Mossthwaite pack. I'd lingered by log fires smelling of cinnamon and wood smoke until Twelfth Night, when the new term had swallowed me again.

This year we drudged through drizzle until Christmas Eve then Stanley fumbled a tenner each into our hands and wished us Merry Christmas. 'Thank your mam for that whisky, Posh Lad. Tell her I've not bothered with cards this year; Lynne's department.' I nodded my understanding.

'Where are you going for Christmas dinner?' Ewan asked him.

'Sandra's.' I was relieved. We shuffled on the drive a while, back-patting without eye contact before I followed Ewan to Cribbs Estate.

I'd bought the Grimshaws a slow cooker as thanks for three months of bacon butties; that was Mum's idea too. Steve was embarrassingly grateful. His six 'You shouldn't have's were more excruciating than Stanley's three 'All the best's. He pushed a Morrison's mince pie in my hand and led me to the kitchen. 'Look what our Lee's got us.'

There, gleaming white and draped in torn polythene, was a Philips dishwasher.

'He's bought it for himself!' Ewan sneered just as Lee walked in, in his boxer shorts.

'Too right!' Lee said, and handed Ewan a packet. 'Happy Christmas.' Within a nanosecond a Marigold glove had licked Lee's bare thigh. He yelped and lunged for the stairs as another rubbery crack whacked his skin.

'Get some bloody clothes on!' Steve shouted as thundering feet boomed the stairs and smacks and profanities shook the semi. 'Twenty-one and twenty-four they're supposed to be.' He laughed, filling the kettle. 'Off out tonight?'

'Annual drinks and nibbles at Granddad's,' I said.

'Drinks and nibbles, eh?'

'How about you?'

'There's a karaoke on at the social.' It sounded more fun.

Christmas came and went like a cheap firework in a Bradford backyard. We were back at Mervyn's and Jennings' the day after Boxing Day. The following morning Ewan was dispatched to the wholesalers for extra racehorse nails and Stanley was explaining the difference between a cob nail and a racehorse nail when his iPhone rang. He stepped back as if affronted, then went through his usual screen-dabbing pantomime. Despite his thick paw, it connected. Ewan was already gabbling. Now and then Stanley stuttered as if he intended to speak but Ewan wasn't stopping. 'All right! All right!' Stanley finally managed. He was rummaging in the drawer now. 'Which A and E?' He came up with spare keys, went for the door and signalled that I should follow. In the forge he picked up a toolbox then jumped in the van: 'Yes, yes,' he was saying. 'Depends on the traffic.' Then he hung up and threw me the iPhone. 'You'd better start cancelling this afternoon's visits.'

'What's happened?'

'Dolloper's happened. We're going to Hawkins' Motor Spares, then Eckersley Accident and Emergency; in that order.' He fired the engine.

I was desperate to know what was going on but we had three small yards booked in and I was on the phone rearranging our visits whilst Stanley was purchasing a clutch cable from Hawkins' Motor Spares. I'd only just finished the last call when we pulled up behind the New Van, which was slewed to the side of Scorthwaite Road in front of a row of shops. Lucky was ping-ponging from window to window and yapping like a toddler's toy and there was no sign of Ewan. 'Are you going to tell me what's going on?' I asked, but Stanley just opened the New Van, grabbed the dog and held her at head height. 'You are a shit!' he announced as she wagged her stump-tail in glee. She was still wagging it when he flung her in the Old Van.

Stanley then proceeded to fit the clutch cable to the New Van, and whilst lying on the wet tarmac of Scorthwaite Road he explained that the RAC man who should have been fitting the clutch had jumped in the van to fire the ignition, 'but he had to get out again, hadn't he?' I winced. 'Lost the use of his bastard arm.'

I drove the New Van to Accident and Emergency where Stanley set about grovelling to a heavily bandaged RAC mechanic: Stanley was absolutely dumbfounded, astonished. Lucky had never done anything of the sort before. He was going to take the dog to see an animal behaviourist. He couldn't believe it. And of course he'd pay for his taxi, no problem.

The RAC mechanic accepted a twenty pound note in his polar bear paw and when he was out of sight Stanley cuffed Ewan round the back of his head with such force I thought they'd have to find him a bed. Ewan nursed his scalp. 'That's out of your bloody wages, Dolloper!'

A hectic racing calendar and family duty had kept me away from Jennings' yard over Christmas, but on New Year's Eve I began my work with Precipitant. I'd taken advice from the expert, who'd told me to build up the mare's trust then introduce her to other tight spaces. I pictured Pippa's awestruck wonder at my skills of horsemanship. I imagined her bewilderment when the mare walked between jump wings at a mere signal from me. I heard her gasp when the horse followed me about the school like an obedient dog.

I worked with the mare for two hours. Pippa never so much as passed the door.

STRATFORD COLLEGE OF AGRICULTURE:

FACULTY OF BLACKSMITHING AND FARRIERY

Apprenticeship Journal for the month of: January.

Comments: My ATF seems to be taking my opinions more seriously. This month he has solicited my views, and those of the senior apprentice, regarding his employment of a temporary farrier to cover his coming sick leave. I believe we influenced the outcome.

Learning Outcomes:

I have recognised that there may be more than one possible solution to a foot problem.

I understand the paradox surrounding the shoeing of brittle hooves.

Signed: William Harker. January 31st 2016   (Apprentice)

Signed: SL January 31st 2016   (Master)

Chapter 16

Robert Finley looked ten years younger than the thirty-six he claimed to be. He spent the first half an hour in the house with Stanley and emerged through the patio doors nodding at Stanley's pronouncements on shoeing style. 'Short and tight,' he was saying as they walked into the forge. 'In't that right, lads?'

Ewan pretended stupidity. 'I'd have said you're more *fat* and tight.'

Stanley was deadpan. 'He thinks he's a comedian.' Finley didn't smile.

Ewan stocked the vans and Stanley suggested I show Finley round the forge – which now had the addition of a horse poster with four numbered legs. Finley looked at it, but said nothing. He asked to see the chickens though, so I led him across the soggy lawn and pointed to the coop at the bottom of the garden. Whilst he was admiring Aunty Dorothy, I wandered to the border opposite the forge. It was barren now, save for six-inch rose stems and brown stalks. In summer it had swelled with roses, hollyhocks and hydrangeas. I picked up Lucky's ball – an action which ignited a volley of yapping – and Ewan sidled over.

'What d'ya reckon?' he asked, over the racket.

I pocketed the ball. Finley was stooped over the chicken coop; I sized him up. 'Like a telegraph pole, but with less conversation.'

Ewan nodded. 'Stanley'll like him though. He's putty.'

Stanley was on the drive now, holding the door of the Old Van open for Finley.

'Aren't you taking the dog?' Ewan asked brightly.

Stanley glared a warning but Finley showed a spark of enthusiasm.'Oh great! Does the dog come?'

'Yes! She loves it!' Ewan said, even though Stanley was making a threatening portcullis of his teeth behind Finley's back.

'What's it called?'

'Lucky.'

'Come on then, Lucky!'

But before the expectant terrier could bounce into the van Stanley had slammed Finley's door. 'They don't want dogs on the yard we're going to,' he lied. 'It's better if the lads take her to Mervyn's.' I could see that Ewan was preparing to gainsay him but Stanley had slammed his own door and was off.

Mervyn ambled from the house wearing the battered flat cap and the ancient Barbour jacket he fastened with baling twine. 'No Stanley today?'

'He reckoned we could manage a couple of trims without him.'

Mervyn watched me buckle on my chaps. 'I can't remember the last time he touched one of the youngsters.'

'He's not so well these days.' (God knows why I defended him.)

'Oh aye?'

'It's his guts.'

'Pity. I wanted a word.' Mervyn was chewing on a blade of hay. 'They keep losing their front shoes.'

Ewan put down his toolbox. 'If we shoe them any shorter they won't have any heel support.'

Mervyn was nodding. 'Aye, but you could put another nail in.'

Even I knew that was ridiculous, but Ewan folded his arms

114

the better to peruse the fool in front of him. 'And you think that'll do it, do you, Mervyn?'

'It should do.'

'Have a think about it.' He took a nail from the magnetic patch on his chaps and held it in front of Mervyn's face. 'Three quarters of a ton of horse flesh, versus one nail?'

For a moment Mervyn just stared. I thought he'd seen sense, but like Stanley, Mervyn could never be wrong. 'It's not just one nail though, is it? It's one *extra* nail.'

'Have you never heard of the straw that broke the camel's back? Well this will be the nail that smashed the horse's foot!'

Mervyn cast the blade of hay to the gravel. 'Forget it! I'll talk to th'organ grinder; you're nobbut his monkey.' For safety's sake, I took the rasp from Ewan's hand and steered the conversation to Mervyn's double at Sedgefield the previous Sunday whilst Jay tied up two thoroughbreds.

'I hear you've been doing riding work for Richard Jennings,' Jay said. I nodded as I appraised the foot balance of a beautiful iron-grey colt. 'We're always short of a work jockey or two here, you know.' I looked up.

'Are you serious?' Mervyn Slack had horses worth hundreds of thousands of pounds.

'We could do with him, couldn't we, Mervyn?'

Mervyn slung his answer over his departing shoulder. 'Aye, if he's any good.'

Back at Bling Manor Finley was on the wet lawn, throwing a ball for Lucky, and Stanley was brewing up in the forge. 'Well?' Ewan ventured.

'Good farrier. Tidy job.' My heart groaned. 'He'd rather be with the bastard dog though.' The three of us stared at the lanky farrier and the excited stump-wagging terrier. 'Which, I see, you left behind.'

'*We* have to get on with the new bloke as well though, haven't we, Stanley?'

He stilled his stirring spoon. 'Why? I don't get on with you, Dolloper.' He handed Ewan his brew. 'I thought I'd start him the week before I go into hospital, so we'd all be working together for a week.' He shouted to Finley through the open door: 'Brew!'

'No, thanks.'

'Jeez!' I muttered.

'Oi, Posh Lad! We had to train you to drink brews.'

We sat in silence, brews in hands, each of us brooding on the consequences of Finley as a colleague. 'You've still got the South African to see,' I reminded him.

Stanley sucked his teeth. 'I can't see me getting on with a foreigner.' Neither could I, but I couldn't see us getting on with Finley. 'Why don't you two take him out this afternoon and see how you get on?'

I felt, rather than saw, Ewan's smile at my shoulder.

There were three ponies to shoe that afternoon, at the Riding for the Disabled centre on the other side of Scorthwaite. Ewan was uncharacteristically keen to fetch Lucky but Stanley wouldn't have it. Just before we pulled off the drive, Stanley stuck his head through the van's open window and addressed Finley: 'Just make sure Dolloper here counts the horses' feet, will you, Robert? He's apt to get confused when he goes above three.' Ewan rolled his eyes and Finley looked perplexed, but neither spoke.

I did my best. I contrasted Scorthwaite's bleak wilderness with Eckersley's dark drama. I pointed out the changing colours of the moor. I noted the peat bogs, scree slopes and limestone pavements for him. I named the River Throstle and showed him where the kingfishers nest. By the time I stopped talking I felt stupid. I was grateful when Ewan flicked on Radio 1.

'What's Stanley like to work for then?' We were so startled by Finley's voice that both of us turned to him, and in the action Ewan caught my eye.

'Well … we think we should tell you something, don't we, Will?' I played along. 'We've been chewing it over all morning, and we think it's only fair to put you in the picture.'

'What picture?' I could hear the trepidation in Finley's voice.

'You might have worked it out for yourself, by now … but, Stanley's gay.'

Finley let out an audible sigh of relief. 'Blimey, you had me worried then. I'm fine with that – so long as he doesn't try it on with me!' He laughed, but Ewan didn't join in and when he'd stopped Ewan let the silence hang in the van like smoke. Finley took a breath. 'He doesn't, does he?'

By the time Ewan spoke again, the quiet was rotting the upholstery.

'Only the once.'

'You what?' Finley's eyes had locked on Ewan's face.

Ewan took a theatrical grip of the steering wheel. 'If he's going to take you on – he asks you to do him … a favour.' Finley's eyes were like wheel hubs. 'He leaves you alone after that though! That's right, isn't it, Will?'

I took my cue. 'Oh yeah; he never bothers you again.'

Finley turned to the window and Ewan let the silence seethe a while longer before he spoke again. 'When you get back he'll ask you to go in the kitchen, and that's when you'll have to do it.'

Finley turned back. 'You're winding me up?' I heard more hope than conviction in his tone.

'We just thought we should warn you.' Ewan's delivery was breezy. 'It's not as bad as you think, to be honest, and it's soon over with.' The silence was thick enough to butcher.

Finley was preoccupied as he silently shod three RDA ponies and all the way back to the forge Ewan reassured him that he'd be fine and it really was nowt.

Stanley warmly welcomed Finley's return. Lucky dashed to

greet her new friend. I put the kettle on and Stanley turned to his would-be employee. 'Reyt then, Robert, do you want to come into the kitchen to finalise t'details?' Ewan winked at him. Stanley took a stride towards the door, but Finley stayed exactly where he was.

'Can't we finalise stuff here?'

Stanley turned to face him. 'All the paperwork's in t'kitchen.'

'Can't you fetch it out?'

'What's to do with you?'

Finley looked at his boots. 'I don't want to go in the kitchen.'

'Have you a phobia of white goods or summat?'

I had to walk out for fear of giving the game away. Ewan followed me and we were still clutching our bellies to hold in the laughter when an engine started. We walked round the corner to see Stanley standing on the drive gazing at a departing tailgate. 'Funny bugger,' he remarked. We kept a few feet behind him as he folded his arms. 'You hear about it, don't you? Folk frightened of dishwashers and fridges and what have you.' Ewan clapped his hand over his mouth and I doubled over in silent mirth. 'Fancy, getting a job then refusing to sign the bastard papers.' Ewan was hanging on to my shoulder as his only means of keeping upright when Stanley turned round. His realisation was as violent and instantaneous as a gunshot. 'What've you said? You little shites!' He chased us up the garden and, ill as he was, we only escaped by vaulting the fence and legging it through his neighbour's shrubbery. It was an hour before we dared sneak back for our cars.

Chapter 17

The following morning Stanley's face was as black as the forge back. He didn't even put the radio on during the drive to Mervyn's and neither of us dared ask. When we arrived he deliberately parked the van as close to a group of scrabbling hens as he could. Ewan and I did our best to perform our Oblivious Workforce routine, but it was wearing.

'Did t'lads tell you they've been pulling their shoes off?' Mervyn asked, as he leant on the van.

Stanley grunted an answer that Mervyn didn't catch. 'I said, I don't tell you how to do your job, do I?' He slid the anvil from the van.

'I'm telling you nowt! I'm just asking what you reckon t' t'job!'

'Well, I don't reckon another nail'll stop it.'

Mervyn turned away. 'Another bloody farrier might though!'

'Suit yourself, but if another nail goes in them feet, they'll drop to bits.'

Mervyn turned back. 'I'm the bloody customer here, Stan!'

'And I'm the bloody farrier!'

Mervyn took two paces towards Stanley. 'Don't you pull rank on me, you clever Dick. I were messing with 'osses when you were still in short pants.'

Stanley swung round and pulled a box of horseshoe nails from the van. 'Here! Here's me nails, and here's me bastard hammer. Knock the bastard nails in yoursen, if you know so much, 'cause I aren't doing it!'

Stanley stood, proffering his tools, and Mervyn stood glaring at him. Neither would lose face but neither would back down. With his eyes still on Stanley, Mervyn snatched the hammer from his hand. Ewan must have feared he'd use it on him, because he walked behind Mervyn and grabbed it from his grip. Mervyn swung round.

'Gimme that back!'

'How old are you?' Ewan scolded.

'I could still knock his bloody block off!'

'Go on then! Go on!' Stanley was yelling. 'I'd like to see you try!'

'You're acting like a pair o'schoolkids!' Ewan shouted.

'Plant me one! Go on!' Stanley was staring down on Mervyn's flat cap now. 'Go on! Try it! You knock me out and you get to decide how many nails!' He took another step, but Mervyn stood firm so his nose was pressed into Stanley's Adam's apple. 'I'm waiting!' Stanley yelled. They stood there, backs tensed, breathing like a pair of aging apes, then, without moving an unnecessary muscle – Mervyn's right arm swung up and thumped Stanley a wallop on his ear. Stanley cried out. He staggered backwards clutching his ear. 'You knobber!' Mervyn wandered off rubbing his knuckles.

'What a knobber,' Stanley muttered, still holding his ear.

Ewan considered himself sufficiently involved to offer an opinion. 'You got off lightly there, Stan. If he'd taken you on proper, he'd have half killed you.'

Worried he was making matters worse, I tried to take the sting out of it. 'Because, you're not at full strength, are you?' Stanley's failing health was increasingly evident. He'd lost some of his bulk, and he sweated a lot these days.

'It's not that,' Ewan said. 'He's a dirty beggar. He's known for it. He'd have slotted you while you were pulling your shirt over your head. You'd have bloody killed him in a fair fight.' The ripple of a smile played at the corners of Stanley's mouth, so Ewan pushed his luck: 'He was slagging you off yesterday, saying you've stopped handling the youngsters. He must think you're getting soft.'

'Cheeky knobber,' Stanley muttered, wandering over to a seventeen-hand chestnut filly, and into Ewan's snare. 'I'm not having Mervyn calling me soft.'

Ewan winked at me, then spoke *sotto voce* as he tucked himself under a sweet-natured bay. 'Good; cos I'm not having my leg broken in the last six months of my apprenticeship.'

The belligerent chestnut was a leaner. It doesn't look dramatic, but when six hundred kilograms of horse drops its entire weight into the leg you're holding up, it's painful. When you've thirty centimetres of red hot-iron in your other hand, it's dangerous.

Stanley was gasping and groaning. Every now and then he straightened and grasped his belly. I offered to hold another leg up – horses can't kick when they're on two feet – but Stanley insisted he could manage. He straightened again, stretched and drew breath through clenched teeth, then he bent and resumed his grunting. Ewan had finished his work so he was swinging mock kicks at Stanley's backside as therapy for every short pay packet, but Stanley was oblivious.

During one particularly energetic tussle, Stanley let rip a fart. He had been prone to what he described as 'gas' for a few weeks, and out of respect for his infirmity we'd sometimes paid him the compliment of ignoring it. This one, however, smelt like chicken sheds. Ewan clutched his throat and I wafted at the fetid daylight. Even the horse stopped struggling. Stanley used the opportunity to keep working, but the stink just didn't go away.

After ten more minutes of breathing in his knock-out gas, Ewan spoke: 'You've shat yourself, haven't you?'

'Oh, shut up, Dolloper.'

'You have though, haven't you?'

'It's not shit. It's horse stunner.' (The filly was looking very dazed.) 'I'm going to patent it.' He clipped a nail off and stood up straight. 'Anyway, I don't know why you're laughing, Dolloper. We've only fetched the one van.'

The thought of being trapped in the Old Van with Stanley whilst he sat in his own horse stunner was horrifying. 'Why don't you borrow a clean pair of underpants from Mervyn?'

'Are you simple, Posh Lad? It's not two minutes since I jumped on him in the lavvy. He'll think I'm a deviant.'

'Horse shower,' Ewan said.

'It's bastard January!'

Ewan dangled the Old Van's keys in his face. 'It's the only way you're coming home with us!' Stanley groaned and set off, straddle-legged, towards the horse shower. 'This is what I call karma!' Ewan grinned, rubbing his hands.

STRATFORD COLLEGE OF AGRICULTURE:

FACULTY OF BLACKSMITHING AND FARRIERY

Apprenticeship Journal for the month of: February.

Comments: I have played an active part in the remodelling of the forge in preparation for the installation of a new chimney. My ATF commented on the speed and efficiency of my work.

Mr Dirk Koetzee, whose training and early practice was undertaken in South Africa, is now supervising the running of the business during the hospitalisation of Mr Lampitt.

Learning Outcomes:

I can assess, file and respond to business correspondence.

I am able to prepare a forge roof for the installation of a chimney.

I understand some of the handling procedures used by South African farriers.

Signed: William Harker. Feb 29th 2016   (Apprentice)

Signed: SL Feb 29th 2016   (Master)

Chapter 18

I was sorting through Stanley's correspondence – which, despite Sandra's return, had remained my morning task – when four hearty knocks shook the front door. Stanley was in the shower, so I answered it. A door-shaped wedge of South African was blocking the daylight and a shovel of flesh thrust out of the murk. 'Dirk Koetzee – pleased to meet you.' As he followed me to the kitchen, Koetzee's eyes were everywhere. 'Nice house, man!' He whistled, then he perched himself on a bar stool and looked me straight in the eye. 'You must be the apprentice?'

'One of them; I'm Will.'

'Is he a baast-ed then, ja?' I was unused to his accent and unprepared for his directness, so I asked him to repeat his question but before I could answer it Stanley had appeared, still buttoning his checked shirt.

Their greeting was like the meeting of two silverbacks, and from where I was, Dirk looked like the alpha male. He had an open friendly face, a pelt of close-cropped fair hair, a ruddy complexion and piercing blue eyes. His white T-shirt was taut across his biceps and on a thong of leather round his neck there rested the incisor of a predator. His faded jeans were stretched across his oak-tree thighs and tucked into heeled cowboy boots. A Yorkshireman would have looked like a transvestite in them, but not Dirk Koetzee.

'Pleased to meet you,' Stanley said, and before he could grill him, Dirk set about the questioning. He seemed delighted that a room in Bling Manor came with the job and Stanley was thrilled that Dirk's Spanish wife was a nurse.

Stanley took Dirk on his morning round whilst Ewan and I practised our shoemaking skills. It hadn't occurred to me that they'd taken Lucky until they clambered laughing from the van at noon with Dirk holding Lucky by the scruff and calling her a 'little shut'. Her stump of a tail was wagging with joy, though she hadn't managed so much as a nibble of South African. 'Lusten, man, a mouthy little terrier is no problem to me,' he said, holding up his predator-tooth pendant. 'I killed this crocodile with one shot!'

Stanley was chuckling for the first time in days. 'Pub then, I think. Then you can go out with the lads this afternoon.'

Over a pie and a pint Stanley regaled us with Dirk's answer to Molly Wainwright's rearing carriage horse. 'So he says to her, "Go and get me an igg please, lady", and she looks at him, all blank like.'

'I had to say it four times, man ...'

'Anyway, she comes back with this egg, and next time it rears up Dirk here smashes the egg between its ears.' Dirk was nodding his affirmation. 'He says, "It won't do it again, lady" – and the bastard doesn't!' It wasn't the solution I'd have favoured. 'How many times has her horse waved its feet over our heads – eh? It stood like a clothes horse after that.'

'Always works, man! Thinks it's smashed its head on the fucking moon, ja.'

'I tell you,' Stanley laughed, 'when she fetched her Shetland out, I thought he was going to upend it!' Dirk laughed warmly and downed his pint, and Stanley threw Ewan the keys. 'You're at Williamson's this afternoon. Two full sets and one trim. Oh, and, Ewan, look out for that fourth leg. It can be a bitch to find.'

Dirk asked, so on the way to Williamson's I told him the tale. I should have known that I'd pay for a tale against Ewan.

*

Dirk confided in us that he had nearly murdered the Jack Russell. 'It tried to take my fucking arm off, man, so I grabbed its mouth, but it still fought like an anaconda!'

'If he shuts you in the van with Lucky, he likes you,' Ewan reassured him. He changed gear. 'You do know he's gay, don't you?'

Dirk had answered before Ewan had released the clutch pedal. 'Is he bollocks, man!' The contrast with Finley made us laugh out loud.

Williamson's was a friendly family yard. Only the hens pecking about unsettled me and I was careful not to hesitate when one pecked nearby; the last thing I needed was Dirk Silverback Koetzee spotting my weakness.

When we'd finished shoeing, Ewan suggested Mrs Williamson book in our next visit. 'Just grab me a pen off the dashboard, would you, Will?' I opened the van door, and a bantam cockerel exploded from the cab. It blinded me with feathers. I dropped the pen and ran. It gave chase, leaping at me with mantled wings. The whole yard was shrieking with laughter. I ran into the barn and slammed the door.

What had amused them had damn near given me a heart attack. I sat on the bales, heart banging, throat dragging at the air. I could hear them chuckling cheerfully and herding the hen. I was furious. Bastards.

When my pulse was nearly back to normal, I opened the door a crack. My hesitancy set them all roaring again. 'It's gone. You can come out!' I opened the door another inch and looked round for more fowl. 'Come on, we need to get going,' Ewan urged.

'Open the van,' I commanded.

'You what?'

'How do I know you've not got another one in there?' Ewan sighed, walked to the van and threw wide the door. 'The others!' I said. He shook his head and trudged round the van opening the doors. I waited through thirty seconds of taunting to be certain no pensive chicken was going to strut slowly out of the van, thrusting its throat and wobbling its wattle, then I sprinted across the yard, leapt in and slammed the door.

'You're supposed to pack up!' Ewan reminded me.

'Get lost!' I shouted.

They packed up, but they interspersed it with a screaming, mincing, arm-waving mimicry of me. By the time they'd jumped in the van – and even though I knew Ewan was showing off for Dirk – I was laughing despite myself.

That evening, I decided to put in another hour with Precipitant. She whickered a greeting as I crossed the yard towards her stable and I was touched; she was the sort of horse who'd have been happier on a small yard with a single handler. I rubbed her forehead, threw a rope round her neck and walked past Pippa who was filling a hay net in the open barn.

'How's she getting on?'

'Great,' I answered, and I would have elucidated, but Pippa had already returned to her task.

In the school, I slid the rope off her neck and sent Precipitant away. I praised her quick response and signalled for her to circle me. Her ear flicked and locked on me, and I was about to turn her round when the door rumbled. I kept my gaze on the circling horse but my heart was floating in my chest. Here was Pippa, about to be jaw-dropped in wonder at my moment of greatest success.

'Sorry!' That didn't sound like Pippa. I turned. I was looking at a small red-haired girl in the livery of Eckersley Equine Vets. 'Have you seen Mr Jennings?' I turned back.

'Try the house.'

'I've tried.'

'Office?'

'Thanks.' The door rumbled, then stopped. 'Is that horse-whispering?' My mother hated that term, so I bristled on her behalf.

'Natural horsemanship,' I said. I felt the girl's eyes on me as I sent Precipitant back out onto her circle. Only when the horse had moved up into canter did the door rumble closed.

Chapter 19

Jennings' set-up was spotless. The drive was tarmacked, the stables on small interlinked yards were purpose-built, and a post-and-railed gallop poured over a velvet hill like a band of ribbon in the land of Oz. All the equipment on Jennings' yard was spanking new. Jennings' staff wore green and purple livery and the horses never left the yard without their purple exercise sheets. Richard Jennings bought from the best bloodlines. He had, however, been in the winner's enclosure only six times that year. Mervyn had been in it thirty-five times.

Mervyn's yard was smack on top of Scorthwaite Moor. When Jay had dared to suggest the place needed a lick of paint, Mervyn had asked if he thought 'the 'osses give a bugger?'

Despite the flaking paint, the mismatched exercise sheets and the jockeys in jeans, Mervyn's horses were winners. He'd won the Betfair Chase, the Champion Hurdle and the Albert Bartlett in the previous season and owners clamoured to put their horses in his converted shippons and sheds.

A hundred thousand guineas' worth of horse flesh could often be seen rolling in the mud like a hippo in a drystone-walled wilderness of twenty or thirty acres. Neither did Mervyn believe in paying for a bloodline. 'It's not its mam and dad as has to run, is it?'

For two whole seasons Jennings regaled owners with a tale of standing beside Mervyn at the Doncaster sales whilst he bid a thousand guineas for a one-eyed yearling. 'I said to him: "You do know it only has one eye?" And do you know what he said?

He said, "It has four legs, hasn't it?"' Richard stopped telling that tale after Diddy C had stood in the winners' enclosure at Haydock.

Mervyn's equipment was tied together with baling twine, his horse-walkers were housed in old silo towers and twice a week every horse went for a hack into Scorthwaite like a riding school dobbin. He insisted that they met traffic, stood at junctions and stepped over manhole covers, so they'd 'dick about less at t' races'. It also meant that Mervyn's horses had a life after racing.

The first time I rode for Mervyn I was on the first lot at seven a.m., so I could work with Precipitant and, hopefully, gaze on Pippa Jennings for the rest of the morning. Jay had me mounted on Bernard's Dream, a sensible eight-year-old handicapper who knew his job. To reach Mervyn's gallops we had to walk down a long dirt drive then cross the moor road. It was a sharp morning and sixteen of us were mounted on fresh thoroughbreds, keen for the thrill of speed.

I was at the front of the string, upsides Jay, and Bernard's Dream was snorting, head-tossing and skittering sideways. Jay's mount was bucking and blowing dragon breaths when a mechanical roar shook the hushed morning. Sixteen racehorses whipped round and squirted to all points of the compass. As I fought for control, Mervyn's laughter wafted over the ruckus. He had fired up his digger.

'Idiot,' Jay seethed.

Once we'd coaxed the fizzing horses back into formation we continued down the drive, but the digger was following us now. I felt the back and shoulders of my mount lift as it drew level. Jay turned to the cab. 'You're a bloody pillock!' he shouted – in response to which Mervyn dropped the digger's bucket. The almighty smash was more than the strung-out beasts could bear. I flicked my feet from the stirrups and sat straight. Suddenly, it was Agincourt. Panicked horses were running amok among prone bodies strewn in the dirt. *Don't grab the reins*, I told myself. Mervyn was hanging out of the cab, lapping it up.

'You're still on then?' he shouted over the din.

Jay answered for me: 'No thanks to you! You berk!'

'Just checking he can ride,' he laughed, then trundled off, unconcerned by the peril and carnage he had created.

Jay's horsemanship had saved him and my horse had saved me but the less fortunate were now resurrecting their bodies and catching their mounts. Within a few minutes a one and a half mile breeze up the gallops had blown away their disgruntlement.

'You can ride for me if you want,' Mervyn grinned when I dismounted on the yard. 'You're more use than some of these gormless beggars!'

Heading down Jennings' drive an hour later I smiled at the contrast between the two trainers. On either side of me Jennings' horses were turned out in individual paddocks to spare them from kick injuries. They were rugged, booted and neck-wrapped in his green and purple livery and their leather head collars bore their names on brass plates.

Richard Jennings had asked to watch me work that morning so he sat himself on a hay bale in the indoor school, and I began insinuating Precipitant through increasingly narrow gaps. 'Mum thinks it's either claustrophobia or sensitive flanks – or both,' I explained when she was walking calmly between a wheelbarrow and the wall. At each pass I slowed the mare down until I finally stopped her between me and the wall. She was twitchy. Her head was up and she flinched at my touch so I sent her on and repeated the exercise. At length, she stood there more happily. 'She needs to associate narrow gaps with refuge,' I explained, and by the time we broke for lunch, the mare was at ease between a jump wing and the wall.

Jennings dragged open the rumbling door and suggested I try her in a trailer after lunch. Right in our path was a beaming

stable hand. I'd noticed him before. I'd seen the way he followed the horses with his eyes and I'd listened to his formation
of naive questions in broken English. Jennings walked on
without acknowledging him but the stable hand jogged after
him. 'Ruudi ride?'

'We've been through this, Ruudi. Get this mare sponged
down.'

'Is why I come!'

'You came to muck out.' Ruudi took Precipitant's rope
from my hands as Jennings disappeared into the tack room.

'Can you ride, Ruudi?'

'No, but I like,' he said, stroking her neck.

'You can't learn on one of these, though.'

'Is why I come.'

'Every blessed day,' Jennings grumbled when I walked into
the tack room with Precipitant's bridle. 'Heaven knows what
they told him in Poland – or wherever he's from.' I glanced to
where Ruudi was wiping down Precipitant and I felt sorry for
him. Horses are a Class A drug that Jennings had never been
deprived of.

By the end of the afternoon we had Precipitant walking
happily into an open trailer and standing between the narrow
partitions. Jennings was delighted. 'Come to dinner on Sunday,
Will.'

'She's not in the stalls yet!' I laughed.

'We should be doing more of this here,' he went on. 'I'd like
you to talk to Pippa.'

I was thrilled, but Ewan put a different spin on it.

'What would your mother have charged him?'

'Ewan! He's as good as set me up with his daughter!'

'And what does Pippa Jennings want with a bastard
Thunderbird puppet?' Stanley scoffed. Predictably, Ewan
doubled over his anvil.

Chapter 20

I was sick of reading the fire like a mediaeval yokel. 'You should be proud,' Stanley insisted. 'How many young farriers can still do that – eh?'

Ewan backed me up. 'They can't light a fire with flints either, Stanley. I failed my exam because of that pile of outdated crap.'

'You failed your exam because you were too bloody lazy to learn the temperature of a pale yellow shoe.' Ewan rolled his eyes and turned away. Stanley put the bellows down. 'I'm tryin' to teach you a craft here, you pair of ungrateful wasters!'

We were convinced it was a cover-up for his spectacular tightness, so when he announced that he'd picked up a second-hand forge we were elated. 'About time!' Ewan grinned.

'It'll need a new hole in the roof though.' I looked at Ewan. Ewan looked back at me. He was thinking what I was thinking.

'A coke forge?'

'Of course a coke forge!'

'Stanley,' Ewan sighed, 'nobody uses them any more.' But Stanley had picked up a sledgehammer.

'Shut your whining, Dolloper, and get on the roof.'

Ewan folded his arms. 'I aren't going up.'

'If you do it now we'll still have time for a breakfast sandwich.'

'It's daft, Stanley. We'll have less room, and another forge nobody wants.'

'Get on that roof before I boot you up!'

The scuffles between Stanley and Ewan were becoming

more frequent and less funny, so I offered to go onto the roof instead. Stanley conceded, like he was doing me a favour.

He propped the ladders on the outside wall and handed me the sledgehammer. Its weight unbalanced me for a second, but I adjusted my gait, climbed a few steps and shoved it onto the roof ahead of me. I climbed the rest, hauled myself onto asphalt and unfolded gingerly. To my left the roof of Stanley's Porsche shone like sheet snow and to my right, the slow prowl of the Hathersage Road traffic growled to a halt at the lights.'Opposite corner, Posh Lad.' I lifted the sledgehammer and cautiously crossed to where plastic sacks were covering cracks in the asphalt. 'Just put a hole in where we repaired it. We can make it pretty later.'

I took a deep breath, raised the sledgehammer to chest height and let it drop. It was an experimental blow, but it unbalanced me. 'What the bloody hell was that supposed to be?' I ignored him, took a step back and spread my legs wide. Feeling safer, I swung again, but harder, and this time the whole roof bounced. 'Give it some bastard welly!'

'It feels like the whole roof will cave in, Stanley!'

'Will it buggery! It's all rotten in that corner. It'll be like butter if you aim it right.'

I repositioned my feet and raised the sledgehammer over my head. I lined it up, took a breath and brought it down with as much force as I could. It blasted straight through the roof. Tools clattered and hammers bounced. There were *Jesus Christs* and *what the fucks*. Tins tumbled, coals scattered, nails sprayed. The clanging racket culminated in the plaintive spin of a paint-tin lid – then there was silence.

I moved to the edge of the three-foot hole. Beneath me, a sledgehammer was lying amidst devastation. Stanley was under his workbench. Ewan was crouched in a corner covering his head. Black paint was everywhere; on the floor, on the walls, on the workbench and on Stanley. Eventually, Stanley's bewildered face emerged between the splintered trusses. He stared up through startled eyes. 'Why the fuck did I send you up there?'

I was convinced all hope of a breakfast sandwich had crashed, but Stanley changed out of his paint-spattered clothes and ordered us into the Old Van. An imminent operation, a devastated forge and a hole in the workplace roof could all be soothed by a breakfast sandwich. On our way to Peggy's Café, I apologised again. Stanley nodded a grudging acceptance. 'If Dolloper hadn't been so bastard belligerent, you wouldn't have been up there to piss the job up, would you!' Ewan stared out of the window. It was just another wave of injustice, breaking over his head.

The breakfast sandwiches arrived. They had become the highlight of our week. They were served between seven and ten at Peggy's Café, and for £2.50 you got two rashers of bacon, one slice of black pudding, two sausages, six fried mushrooms, a fried tomato, a fried egg and a spoonful of baked beans, all on an oven-bottom muffin. 'Wait while our South African gets his laughing gear round one o'these, eh. It'll put hairs on his chest.' I suspected that Dirk Koetzee already had hairs on his chest. Stanley wiped a stripe of egg yolk off his chin. 'Seeing as how you two can't knock a hole in a bastard roof without triggering a tsunami, t'South African'll have to build t'new coke oven.'

Dirk Koetzee would arrive to find a paint-spattered shambles with a metre-wide hole in the roof and the job he'd been employed for impossible to do. He'd have to repair a roof, put up shelves, organise stock, build a forge and install a chimney before he could touch a horse.

'That's a big ask …' I remarked.

Stanley pushed his plate aside. 'We'll fill him full o' Yorkshire ale and steak pie – then we'll ask him.'

'When?'

'Sunday.'

'I've been invited to Jennings'.'

Stanley leant across the table. 'I do not care if you have been invited to bastard Balmoral. You will be at the Fleece on Sunday night – comprendo?' I nodded.

On the way out, Peggy stopped us. 'Was your sandwich all right, Stan?'

'It's me guts, Peggy,' he explained with one hand on his belt.

For my sake the Jennings had deferred their meal until eight thirty, so at six thirty on Sunday evening we met Dirk and Maria Koetzee in the Fleece before they'd had time to unpack, let alone glimpse the forge. Stanley kept the drinks coming and in no time at all I had four pints lined up.

'Get 'em down you,' Ewan said as I trod from foot to foot. 'They'll settle your nerves!' In less than two hours' time I would be sitting at the same table as Pippa Jennings. 'Go on,' he went on, proffering an untouched pint. 'I'll drive you.' The closer it crept, the more it looked like an ordeal. I wanted to impress Pippa – and her mother. I'd never even met her mother. I gulped at my pint. Would they serve something tricky, like lobster? I downed another draught and Ewan patted my shoulder.

'Use your cutlery from the outside in.' I gave him a withering look and he laughed. 'They know their own sort, don't they?'

'What are you talking about, Ewan?'

'I'll bet Richard Jennings doesn't even know my name.'

'I helped him with his horse!'

'And you talk like a newsreader and drink Earl Grey.'

'I drive a Vauxhall Astra!'

Stanley's voice sliced through our different perceptions. 'Oi, Posh Lad. Tell him what you did with that bastard sledge-hammer!' The room swam a little as I turned, but I propped an elbow on the bar and described my ineptitude. 'So you see,' Stanley finished off, 'we're in a bit of a mess.'

'I enjoy a bit of bricklaying.' Dirk grinned, and he raised his pint to salute the coming project.

It was ten past eight when Ewan dropped me at the corner of Briar Lane. I hoped the short walk might clear my head, but everything started to go wrong when I noticed a policeman darting in and out of pools of yellow light behind a pig. I don't really know why I didn't walk on (four and a half pints of lager probably had something to do with it), but very soon I was running, waving and slithering on the shit of three pigs. The pigs darted one way, I darted the other way, the policeman feinted, the pigs galloped past. One barrelled in the direction of the gate then dead-legged the officer so he finished up on his backside. More than once I sent the pig towards the gate only for it to squirt off down the road. After a near-miss with a Fiat Multipla, the officer decided to call for back-up. 'I'm going to look a right charlie,' he said, cracking his radio to life.

'I know!' I said, before he'd had the chance to speak. 'Fetch us a kebab.' He laughed out loud.

'I'm on duty!'

'Not for us! To tempt the pigs in.' He let go of his radio.

'Do you reckon?'

'They love food.'

He hesitated. 'It'll look bad, a uniformed officer, queuing in the kebab shop.'

'It'll look worse calling for back-up.'

'Fair enough.' He shrugged, and climbed into his patrol car.

I guarded the blind bend until the officer came back. 'There's one with yoghurt, one with chilli and a plain one,' he said, handing them over. I broke the end off the chilli kebab and flung it in a pig's path. It scoffed it and trotted up for more. I dropped another chunk. The two remaining pigs approached with enthusiasm, and I made a kebab trail. Within seconds all the three pigs were in the field and the gate was shut. I shook greasy hands with the policeman and finally headed for the Jennings'. It was only as I crunched down the gravelled path, breathless, sweaty and spattered in chilli sauce, that I remembered I must be very late.

Richard Jennings opened the imposing black door and welcomed me in as if all were normal. He ushered me across chessboard tiles, past a mahogany chiffonier and into an opulent dining room generously swagged with tasselled yellow curtains. Pippa and her mother were at an oval table, bejewelled with silverware, glassware and bone china. Neither of them appeared to have any lips. Richard poured a large whisky. 'We were expecting you at eight thirty, Will.' My eyes drifted to the spangled chandelier.

'Sorry.'

'We were also expecting you to have taken a shower,' Pippa added.

'Sorry,' I repeated. I listened to the ticking of the antique clock, less concerned than I should have been that the room had fallen grave-side silent. 'I've been chasing pigs.' It hadn't helped. Richard swilled the whisky round his glass.

'Are you drunk?' Mrs Jennings demanded.

'Not any more!' I laughed – but nobody joined in.

'Why were you chasing pigs at nine at night?'

'I wasn't—'

'You just said …'

'I *started* chasing pigs at ten past eight.'

'Why?' Richard asked, after a beat of stillness.

'They were loose. Here, on Briar Lane.'

'Oh, I see!' he exclaimed. 'That could have been dangerous…'

'He should have called the police!' Mrs Jennings shouted.

'The police were there,' I explained, and she threw her hands wide.

'So what had it to do with you?' The room fell silent again. Richard Jennings almost whispered his next question.

'Did you catch them?'

I nodded. 'With a kebab.' At that, Mrs Jennings rose to her feet.

'You were eating a kebab on the way to dinner?'

'No! No, we bought them for the pigs!' But she was walking away, and Pippa was following her. The heavy door slammed shut. I looked across at Richard by the mantelpiece. His grimace over the rim of a whisky glass was fighting to form itself into a smile. 'They'll have been Lawrence Simpson's,' he said, indicating that I should sit. 'I'd have given you a hand if you'd knocked.' I dragged out my chair and Richard uncovered a terrine of pâté. 'I'm afraid it's pork.'

STRATFORD COLLEGE OF AGRICULTURE:

FACULTY OF BLACKSMITHING AND FARRIERY

Apprenticeship Journal for the month of: March.

Comments: Damage to a vehicle parked close to a horse could, I believe, have been lessened if the handler's response had been based on Natural Horsemanship techniques. However, my position as junior apprentice currently restricts my influence on the practice's methods. I hope to change this over time.

Learning Outcomes:

I understand (and have assisted in) the building, painting and fitting of a new coke forge.

I understand the shoeing style necessitated by the requirement for additional traction in the hind feet of a driving horse.

Signed: William Harker. March 31st 2016   (Apprentice)

Signed: Dirk Koetzee AWCF   March 31st '16   (Master)

(pp Stanley Lampitt DipWCF)

Chapter 21

Soundtracked by Dirk's toothy whistle, I saw afresh the random spatters of black paint, the collapsed shelves, the buried sink, and the heap of bricks that had once been a second-hand forge.

'Was the sledgehammer tied to a fucking petrol bomb?' I managed to force a weak smile through my embarrassment, and Stanley pointed to where he thought a box of size five shoes should be buried under the rubble.

'We're doing four sets at Mervyn's.'

Dirk appraised him. 'You look like *shut*, man.'

Stanley tried to stand more upright. 'I'll be reyt.'

'Man, you shouldn't be working.'

'I've to show you t'ropes this week.'

'I can show him.' Ewan grinned.

Stanley let the workbench take his weight. 'That's what I didn't want.'

'Get back inside,' Dirk ordered – and for once in his life, Stanley did as he was told.

Dirk was concentrating on unfamiliar roads, Ewan was humming 'What a Wonderful World', and newly arrived curlews were soaring over the peat moor. I was telling Dirk how their rising whirr always lifts my sprits when he brought the van to a halt before a row of traffic cones. The moor road was closed. Ewan leant out of the window and addressed a policeman. 'We only want to go down that drive!'

'Ah,' the officer answered, all theatrical, 'but how do I know you're not going to drive straight past it, eh?'

Dirk raised his eyes to the skies. 'Because you'll bloody well see us turn in there, ja!' The policeman turned away. 'It's fifty yards away! What's the bloody hazard?'

'The road's closed from this point, sir.'

Dirk was having none of it. He flung open the van door and jumped out. The policeman turned back, but Dirk had already walked to a traffic cone and picked it up.

'What are you doing with that?'

'I'm moving it out of the bloody way!'

'Stop that immediately!' the officer shouted, but Dirk had flung the cone. It hit the drystone wall and landed on its side on the verge. Ewan was grinning from ear to ear; this sort of showdown passed as entertainment on Cribbs Estate, but I was getting twitchy. I'd already had a semi-automatic at my head. The policeman was marching back to us, but Dirk had picked up another cone. 'Don't you dare throw that!' But Dirk threw it, and lifted another. The policeman started rifling in his belt and when Dirk turned to fling the third cone he faced an outstretched arm with a can at the end of it.

'What have you got there, man? Mustard gas?' He flung the cone and as he bent to pick up a fourth the nozzle followed him.

'I'll do it! I will! I will!'

Ewan laughed, so the policeman aimed the nozzle though the passenger window. 'I'm warning you! It's mace!' but Ewan was lapping it up. He jumped down from the van and threw a sixth traffic cone aside. The officer swung his aim back at Dirk who was carrying on regardless. He held his arm outstretched as cones ten and eleven hit the verge, then he lowered his arm. 'Oh, what the heck! Go where you want! See if I care!' Dirk laughed and with the road ahead clear, he and Ewan leapt in the van on either side of me.

We trundled past the sullen policeman on the forbidden

tarmac and as Ewan waved at him Dirk asked what Stanley would have done. 'Same,' Ewan said, but I disagreed. Stanley would have cursed and sworn, then driven round the long way. Working with Dirk was going to be altogether different.

Dirk was delighted to be working for Mervyn Slack. 'My dad says your goal against Uruguay in 1977 was one of the best he's ever seen.'

Mervyn chuckled his thanks. 'Do you follow football?'

'It's a religion in South Africa! Do you?'

'When I can. I'm busy wi' t'racing job most Sat'days.' Then, pointedly, for Ewan's benefit, 'When they have their bloody shoes on.' Ewan shook his head and continued unloading the van.

'Is there a problem keeping their shoes on, Mr Slack?'

'There is, aye. All it needs is another nail in every front foot, but he's set in his ways, is Stanley.'

'I can do that for you, Mr Slack.'

Mervyn grinned broadly and patted him on the back. 'You want to take notice of this young fella, lads! It's a tonic having a farrier who's open to new ideas.'

When Dirk walked to the back of the van for a paring knife, I put him in the picture.

'Stanley says it'll smash their feet up.'

'It will.'

'These are top racehorses. They can't have smashed feet.'

Dirk put his hands on his hips. 'So what do we do, eh? Argue the toss every time we see the trainer, or let him find out he's wrong?' (Outside Yorkshire, that might have been sound reasoning, but he was dealing with men who were never wrong.)

'They'll blame us.'

'They'll blame *me* – and I'm only temporary.' I couldn't dissuade him and Mervyn had wandered over with a sleek bay gelding.

'It's short-coupled, you see, so it overreaches.' Dirk was nodding. 'An extra nail will make all the difference.'

'Whatever you say, boss.' Mervyn grinned at Dirk's deference and disappeared into the house rubbing his hands.

'Watch yourself with that,' Ewan advised, before following Jay to where we'd been assigned the removal of two sets. 'It's a bit quick behind.'

Ours was a simple job and we'd done it in no time, but Dirk wasn't onto us yet, so rather than risk being given another, we sat on a low wall and Ewan asked how I'd got on at the Jennings'. I put my head in my hands, rested my elbows on my knees and recount my pig-chasing interlude, culminating in my turning up late, pissed and covered in pig-shit, to a meal they'd rearranged for my convenience.

After a stunned silence in which he stared at me for longer than was comfortable, Ewan shook his head. 'You utter pillock.'

'I know. And I've blown any chance I had with Pippa Jennings.'

'Stanley will kill you with his bare hands if we lose that yard.'

'Why would we lose the yard?'

'Caroline Jennings,' he said, standing up and heading back towards Dirk. I would have asked him to explain but Ewan's roar of distress wiped out all other thoughts. I dashed round the corner.

Striking Distance (son of Ikdam out of Constant Companion, winnings to date £162,000) was trussed up like a Christmas turkey. A rope ran from its near hind fetlock, under its belly and emerged on the right side of its wither. From here it passed over the left of its neck and was tied to a ring in the wall. The horse's head was in the air, its eyes were rolling, and it was erupting in sweat on its flanks and quarters. I ran to untie it, scanning the yard for signs of Mervyn.

'What the hell are you doing?' Ewan begged.

Dirk was nonplussed. 'Stopping it from kicking me – ja?'

Ewan's free hand was in his hair. 'You can't do that, Dirk!'

'What, here on this yard?'

'Here on this planet!'

'How the fuck else do I stop it kicking?'

'Ask Will!'

'And what's he? A fucking wizard?' Ewan set about untying its foot. 'It'll fucking kill you, man.'

'You've frightened it.'

'It's fucking frightened me.' A hind hoof whistled past Ewan's right ear. 'I can't believe what you guys put up with.' Ewan picked up the hammer and resumed where Dirk had left off, intermittently displaying the footwork of Amir Khan. When he had driven in the last nail, Dirk congratulated him. 'You can hang them up by their fucking hind legs in South Africa!'

On the Friday of Dirk's first week, Stanley declared himself well enough to work, so at eight o'clock we set off for our Friday treat. The long front seat of the Old Van would only accommodate two silverbacks, so Ewan and I were flung in the back with the propane gas, the rasps and the hammers. It was both lethal and illegal.

The café was already full of lorry drivers when we piled out, bruised, but Peggy had saved our corner table and ran a grey dishcloth over the formica for us. 'Breakfast sandwiches?'

'Aye, three, and a big mug of tea.'

She put her hands on her hips. 'Are you not so good again, love?'

'I'll be reyt,' Stanley conceded. 'They're sortin' me out next week.'

'You can have a breakfast sandwich on me, when you're right,' she said.

Stanley grinned. 'Give me six weeks, Peggy.' She swept up the dishcloth and disappeared behind the counter where she fried bacon, eggs and black pudding in full view. The smell alone must have been torture for Stanley. After she'd slathered three muffins in butter she waddled over with three breakfast sandwiches and a mug of tea. I'd stuffed half a sausage in my mouth and Ewan had doused his egg in HP sauce when we realised that Dirk was staring down at his plate.

'What's up?' I asked him, through sausage.

Dirk looked up. He placed the palms of his hands on the table top. He leant forward. He took in our gazes and when he spoke it was in a hushed tone. 'Jesus Christ, man. You're all gonna be dead by the time you're forty.'

We stared back, jaws stilled, bacon rind dangling. It was incredible, unbelievable to us that a grown man could eschew Peggy's breakfast sandwich. Even more distressing to us was our inability to find room for it.

Stanley bemoaned the waste of that sandwich all the way to Lofthouse Riding School. 'You wouldn't even let me take it for the bastard dog!'

'And I don't even *like* that bastard dog, man.' It was unfathomable.

'Is it because your wife's a nurse?'

'It's because I don't want to die, man.'

'Well,' Stanley pulled on the handbrake, 'I hope you're not going to be depriving these lads of their Friday breakfast sandwich. Because I would consider that a breach of their human rights.'

'Feeding them that much cholesterol is a breach of their human rights, man.'

Stanley turned to us. 'Listen, lads, I'm paying your breakfast sandwiches on at Peggy's for the next four weeks. I don't want you wasting away on his bastard granola or whatever guinea-pig-shit his wife feeds him. She's filled my bastard cupboards with all sorts of crap.'

'What crap?'

'Sun-dried tomatoes – what the fuck's that about?'

'What's your problem with sun-dried tomatoes?'

'God made tomatoes wet! And olive oil!'

'It's for cooking in!'

'It's for marrying bastard Popeye! Lard's for cooking in.'

Chapter 22

The fallout from my pig-chasing escapade was almost as bad as Ewan had predicted.

Stanley indicated his phone. 'Caroline Jennings doesn't want you on her yard again.' I'd dreaded the embarrassment of going back there, but this was worse. 'Have you been snogging her daughter?'

'In his dreams!' Ewan quipped.

'Well he's done summat to upset her!'

'It's not her daughter!' Stanley stared at me, unsure.

'You keep your dirty hands off my clients, Posh Lad – comprendo?' and before I could prevent it, he'd snatched my phone and was scrolling through my contacts. 'Who's these?' I made a lunge for the phone, but Stan was twisting away from me. 'Alex Bentley! Have you snogged her?'

'No!' I made another grab.

'*No*, or *no, not yet?*'

'No!' He thrust my phone behind his back.

'If you snog Alex Bentley you stick with her – do you hear?'

'Can I have my phone back?'

'You break Alex Bentley's heart and I'll break your todger.' He resumed scrolling through the pictures. 'Paula Bridge!'

'So?'

'I've seen more meat on a butcher's apron.'

Just at that moment, and for the amusement of the gods, who should ring my phone but Alex Bentley. The undisguised delight on Stanley's face had identified her before I'd seen her face flash up. He turned his body so I couldn't reach the phone. 'Hiya, Alex … No, he's just nipped round the back with one of the stable lasses.' He raised his voice. 'Will! Alex is on the phone!' I snatched for it, but he swung away, and pretended to address me again. 'Oh, come on, Will! She can do her own buttons up!' I thought Ewan would wet himself. Stanley returned to the mouthpiece. 'He won't be a minute, love.' Then he stared at the phone. 'She's hung up.' I glared at him hard before I snatched the phone back. Stanley strolled off, chuckling at his own wit.

Riding work for Mervyn was what his Irish jockeys called a craic. They trotted off the gallops laughing, and the horses had their ears pricked. This morning I was nervous though; Mervyn had asked me to ride a piece of work upsides Jay. I'd have to follow precise instructions.

As I walked between the looseboxes, stomach somersaulting, Jay was leading Enville Lad towards the mounting block and grumbling. 'Why've you put me on this moose, Mervyn?' Enville Lad's head was so big the lads called it Anvil Head.

'I'm trying to fathom if it's a chaser or not.'

'I'm trying to fathom if it's a horse or not,' he chunnered, swinging onto its back.

'What's to do with it?'

'It can't jump, Mervyn! It has more letters after its name than the Lord Chief Justice.'

'That's not because it can't jump!'

'Conor Doherty's still in hospital!'

'That's because it can't *land*!' I chuckled at his logic, but I was relieved to see Silent Shannon led out for me. She'd put a few of the jockeys on the deck, but I'd worked her out. I mounted softly and let her follow Anvil Head to the gallops, like it was all her idea.

There was no sign of Mervyn so we decided to make a start. I tucked in beside Jay and we cantered for a steady mile. 'I'll bet his knackered old quad won't start,' Jay muttered as we pulled up and scanned the blank horizon. After circling for a few more minutes, Jay ran out of patience. 'Come on,' he said, picking up canter again. 'Push Shannon on a stride at the next marker.' When the moment came, Shannon pulled away as if I'd changed gear. Jay caught me up and pushed Anvil Head on, so we alternated our lead up the gallops. We were on the second circuit when Mervyn's quad roared into view. He clattered upsides, causing Shannon to bang into Anvil Head who dived right. Shannon followed him, putting thirty feet of Yorkshire wind between me and Mervyn's bronze-age quad. He hollered something into the air

'What?'

Yorkshire growls struggled against the thundering of hooves and the clattering of engine.

'Can you tell what the fuck he's saying?' Jay shouted. I shook my head. There was more yelling and a few wild arm gestures then Mervyn roared off. We cantered on, clueless.

'Do you think he told us to jump?'

'Fuck knows!' We alternated canter with gallop whilst Mervyn dismounted the quad and climbed on a mound of earth for a better view.

We came off the bend and I lined Shannon up for the first chase fence, but I saw Jay had taken the outside track. It was too late to change my mind. Through spattered goggles I could see Mervyn jumping up and down on the little hillock. The fence was approaching. Shannon soared it. Mervyn was waving and hollering, but it could have been at either one of us. In for a penny, I thought and took the second. We were a long time in the air. Whether I was right or not, I was enjoying the ride. Anvil Head kept pace, stretching, digging deep and glad to be earthbound. By the time I'd taken six more chase fences Mervyn was gesticulating like John Terry after a red card.

As we neared the end of the gallops he cupped his hands at his mouth but still his every word flapped off in the breeze.

We slowed to a trot and Mervyn ran down his mound of earth and headed for us. I was convinced I was for it, but he grabbed Jay's jacket.

'I've a good mind to pull you off it, you bloody chicken!'

'I couldn't hear you over the quad, Mervyn.' Jay turned Anvil Head away, but Mervyn was so furious he hung on.

'The fucking farrier could hear me!' His face was brick red.

'Well let the fucking farrier take it round Aintree then!'

'Don't tempt me!' He released Jay's jacket and roared off on his quad.

'Sorry,' I said as we turned for home. 'Are you riding at Aintree?'

'Only schooling round.'

'What Becher's Brook and the Chair and that?' He nodded. 'I'm surprised they let you.'

'Mervyn knows the right folk.' I whistled in admiration.

Back on the yard I was surprised to find two missed calls and a voicemail message from Richard Jennings: *'Hi, Will, just wondering where you are. I thought we were trying Precipitant in the stalls this morning. Give me a ring.'* I listened again. Did he and his wife not communicate? I rang him. 'We must have got crossed wires,' I said. 'I'll come now.'

I climbed out of my car to be welcomed by Richard who chatted about the miserable weather and the state of his gallops and showed me to a stall where Ruudi was bridling up Precipitant.

At his first glimpse of the trainer, Ruudi spoke. 'Ruudi ride?' I took the reins from him.

'Have you ever been on a horse, Ruudi?'

'No, but I like.'

I turned to Jennings. 'Is there nothing quiet he could have a go on?'

'No one has time to teach him.'

'I will,' I said. 'If there's something quiet enough.' Then I turned my attention to Precipitant. It was the day of reckoning.

In the paddock I released her, circled her, sent her through the gaps she was comfortable with, then – as part of the flow – as if it was no big deal, I sent her towards the starting stalls. She trotted through them without hesitation. Jennings exclaimed his surprise, but I didn't stop there. I sent her between the jump wings, then between the fence and a wheelbarrow and then I stopped her. I praised her stillness, sent her to the stalls, stopped her there, then sent her on again. Within five minutes she was standing comfortably in the stalls with the gates closed and her ears pricked, just like she'd have to at the races.

Richard Jennings was thrilled – and so was I. I was also knackered. I'd ridden four horses and schooled another, but waiting on the yard, holding a fat piebald pony by the reins, was Ruudi. I would have deferred the lesson but Ruudi's unrestrained joy at the realisation that he was to sit on a horse was irresistible.

'Is quiet, yes?' Jennings laughed out loud then he patted me on the shoulder.

'Your next project, I think!'

Some people have the spirit of the centaur. Their bodies meld with the horses'. Ruudi mounted Pongo so effortlessly I had to double-check his story. 'You've never been on a horse before?'

'No. Take photo! Take photo of me on horse!' I took out my mobile phone and snapped, then Ruudi demanded to have his stirrups up higher: 'Like jockey.' I wouldn't have put it past him to head straight for the gallops.

Over the next half-hour Ruudi fell off four times, but he always landed laughing and was always clambering back on before I'd crossed the school. There were moments that looked like courage and others that looked like recklessness. He would have gone on all afternoon, but after thirty-five minutes Pongo's willingness diminished and to be fair on the old pony, I called time.

'Tomorrow?' Ruudi pleaded.

'Next week,' I said, envisaging one horse-free day in the week.

'Is Sunday tomorrow. Is good day!'

The radiance of Ruudi's enthusiasm was like sunshine. Even knackered old Pongo lifted his head up.

'Let me think about it.'

He took the reins of the sweaty pony. 'I telephone you? Yes?' I was already regretting sending him that photograph.

The following day Ruudi was waiting for me in an ill-fitting riding kit – and beside him was Pippa! I felt the fizz of possibility rising in my throat. 'I don't want Pongo overdoing it,' she said, 'so I thought I'd supervise.'

When Ruudi was safely mounted, Pippa allowed the lunge line out so the pony could walk on a large circle around her. Heart hammering, I focused my attention on Ruudi. 'Heels, hips and shoulders in alignment, Ruudi.' Pippa stopped the pony.

'He wants to ride racehorses, Will!' She walked to the centre of the circle and racked up Ruudi's stirrups by five holes. 'Just balance there, over your knees, Ruudi.'

Ruudi dropped his heels and crouched with a back as level as Barry Geraghty's. 'Like on gallops!' he grinned. My own racing position wasn't as good.

Professional shit-shovelling had afforded him good core strength, so aside from an initial wobble he barely budged. Within five minutes the pony had picked up trot and Ruudi was still crouched over his knees. I complimented him on his strength. Many races don't last that long. 'I practise on a chair!' he grinned. Pippa was allowing him a brief rest before attempting a canter when Richard Jennings stuck his head round the door.

'Will, could I have a word, when you've done in here?'

'Ruudi ride!' he shouted, but the barn door rumbled closed.

Despite my preoccupation with Richard's mysterious order and the distraction of Pippa in jodhpurs, Ruudi was soon maintaining his racing position in canter.

'Tomorrow?' he asked as he slid off the biddable old pony.

'Sorry, Ruudi, I'm working.'

'After?'

I would be knackered after a day of bending double under horses, but the possibility of seeing Pippa again was impossible to resist. I looked at her. 'Six o'clock.'

She nodded.

'I ride on gallops, yes?'

'No!'

'We'll see,' Pippa conceded. Grinning with his victory, Ruudi led Pongo back to the paddock.

Richard Jennings was feeling down the right foreleg of a skittish grey when I finally approached him. I half feared he'd tell me to stay away from his daughter but he greeted me warmly and told me to let Stanley know I was welcome as a farrier as well as a guest. I fought down a smile. My prospects at Jennings' yard were in the ascendant.

Chapter 23

We'd agreed that Dirk and Maria would take Stanley to hospital in Leeds whilst Ewan and I sealed the newly installed chimney and repainted the forge. By lunchtime though, Dirk and his TVR had not returned, Bling Manor was still locked and Lucky was yapping in the kitchen. 'Do you think he's done a runner?' Ewan asked. It had crossed my mind. We climbed the back steps and peered in at the windows. Ewan pressed his finger against the glass. 'Maria's handbag's on the table. She wouldn't leave that.'

I blew on my frozen fingertips. 'Double bluff?'

'If he's not back by one, we'll have to go to Tracy Prichard's on our own.' I didn't relish it. Tracy Prichard was a pinched little woman who bought other people's throw-outs. The last time we'd been at her yard she'd watched Ewan shoe all four feet of her gypsy vanner, then refused to pay, insisting her horse had been used as practice for Stanley's monkey.

We agreed that we'd get the money upfront today. I was warming my hands on my mug and considering abandoning my sandwiches in favour of a tray of chips when we heard an engine. We locked glances and walked to the door. Dirk was emerging from a taxi. The broad grin on his face was at odds with his black eye and the long cut running from his cheekbone to the corner of his mouth.

'I've just had the best adrenalin rush of my entire fucking life!' he yelled. 'Gatepost to tree! Tree to gatepost! Gatepost to wall! Five seconds of pure fucking, magic, man!' He punched the thin March air in triumph. 'Shame it's cost me a TVR.'

'You've hurt your face,' I observed.

'Oh, that's just where Maria whacked me with the passenger wing.'

Despite destroying his car and jeopardising his marriage in the same morning, Dirk insisted on driving us to Tracy Prichard's: 'I need to get the hang of this ice, man!'

I objected loudly, but Ewan reasoned that Dirk needed to learn the techniques if he planned to drive the Yorkshire moors in bad weather. He instructed him patiently all the way: 'No ... no! Foot off the gas!' I'd stopped breathing. '*Off* the gas, Dirk!' Dirk whooped in delight. 'Into it! Steer into it, remember!'

We passed fields framed white, where drystone walls had shaded the frost. The crisped skeletons of last year's cow parsley bristled by the roadside. Sugared holly bushes dotted red against a cobalt sky – but I enjoyed none of it. By the time we arrived on Tracy's yard, I was peeping through slits between my fingers.

I struggled to settle my nerves whilst Ewan wrangled the advance cash out of her. Dirk set about explaining the nuances of shoeing her driving horse to me, but I wasn't paying attention. Was he planning to drive us back? Would the roads be as bad in an hour? Had enough sunlight dribbled between the bulging clouds to melt some ice? Pippa's name flashed up on my phone. My chest bubbled. I touched the message icon.

Ruudi on gallops. No need for lesson.

The bubble burst. Surely old Pongo wasn't up to the gallops? But neither was Ruudi. What was she thinking?

I was relieved when Ewan sat behind the wheel of the van at the end of the job; even his nerves, tempered in the forge of Cribbs Estate, could take no more of Dirk's driving for today.

*

Richard Jennings met us with his easy geniality and whilst he issued our instructions I scoured the yard. No Pippa. I was dragging my attention back to Richard's concerns for a grey filly's tendon injury when his wife began crossing the yard. I looked away, but she stopped in her tracks and stared at me like I was a soiled bed sheet. 'You!'

'Caroline, darling ...' Richard cut in, 'this young man has an absolute gift with horses—'

'I'll speak to you later!' she spat, snatched up her car keys and stomped through the puddling slush.

Meanwhile, the grey filly had been tied to the wall in front of the Old Van and Dirk was running his hand down her tendon. 'We'd need to take her toe back a bit, and roll the shoe ...'

Jennings was still nodding when his wife's Range Rover hissed past, lifting an arc of meltwater. It soared skyward, then spilt, spattering the filly's flanks. The horse swung away and hit the anvil. The anvil toppled, smashing the van's tail lights. The filly reared, snapping her halter. Ewan lunged for her, but she shot backwards. She hit the van and kicked out. The exhaust pipe clattered onto the concrete. Her next kick detached the bumper. It was like watching a pile-up. Each impact was predictable but unstoppable. Ewan grabbed her rope but the filly swung through three quarters of a circle, touching the van again and crashing her hind hooves on metal. Dirk walloped her flanks. She leapt clear. She swung round to survey her adversary, then stood, head high, ears pricked, flanks heaving like she'd crossed a finish line.

Rivulets of blood were rolling down her white legs. Her leather headcollar was dangling uselessly about her neck. 'Whoa ... ooa. Whoa ... ooa,' Jennings was crooning. We stood like fence posts for fear of spooking her again. 'Easy, Lily, goo ... od girl.' Her ears flicked as she acknowledged her surroundings. Jennings took a step towards her. 'Whoa there, Lily.' He put a hand on her shoulder, and we breathed. She stretched her nose towards her trainer who, slowly but deliberately, took the lead rope from Ewan. 'Not a clever place to put the anvil,' he said to Dirk as he turned her towards an empty stable.

She'd lifted a flap of skin above her fetlock so when she was safely inside, Jennings dialled the vet's number.

I was heating the last shoe of the morning when Ruudi's shape formed out of a cloud of burning-on smoke. His left side, from ankle to earhole, was mud-caked. He was grinning as usual and his two front teeth were missing. 'Fell off two times!' He pointed at the empty space behind his lips. 'Like A.P. McCoy!' I shook my head in wonder at him. 'I go again now. You watch?' I turned to Dirk, who nodded his permission.

The first person I saw on the colts' yard was Pippa. She was mounted on a skittering bay with its tail towards me. I pulled my attention to Ruudi who was climbing onto a feisty sixteen-hand black. As he made contact with the saddle the horse leapt into a little rear, then plunged its head between its forelegs. 'Just drop your feet and relax,' Pippa instructed. 'Take your right-hand wide and he'll circle.' I wouldn't have wanted to ride it.

'Are you sure he's ready for this?' I asked her.

'We'll see, won't we!' she laughed, and headed for the gallops. I noticed Pippa was rising to the trot whilst Ruudi was standing above it, but when they reached the gallops he crouched like a cheetah. His horse curled then unfolded under him and Ruudi's wild laughter travelled on the wind as he disappeared over the brow of the hill. When they emerged into view again I was relieved to see Ruudi still mounted.

I waited for his mount to fall into step beside me. 'You've got some bottle, Ruudi!'

'Bottle?'

I might have bothered to explain had I not seen Pippa's eyes following the vet's car up the drive. I pre-empted her question: 'Lily's cut her leg.'

She was off. Ruudi's mount made to follow, and the un-expected jolt unbalanced him. I grabbed his reins. He wasn't ready for thoroughbreds who flick from sleep to terror in a demi-second. 'Is fine!' Ruudi said, pushing my hand away.

Pippa was already on the yard when the vet climbed out of her car. I recognised her as the girl who'd interrupted my schooling of Precipitant. She reached an anoraked arm towards Dirk. 'Millie Routledge; pleased to meet you.' Dirk shook her hand then she turned to me. 'We've met, haven't we?' but before I could answer she had been distracted. 'Heck,' she said, 'that looks a mess.' My heart took on the weight of a sandbag. If Jennings sued for the mare, it could finish Stanley's business.

'How much do you think it'll cost?' I asked.

She answered me without looking up. 'Hard to say. There could be more going on underneath.' She looked at Dirk. 'What do you think?'

'You're the bloody vet!' Dirk thundered.

Millie looked startled. 'I know.'

'Well have a bloody look, then!'

She raised her cool cat-like eyes to his. 'At your van?' He crumpled into relief-edged laughter, and Millie walked to the horse. She was neat, slim and her movements were composed. 'How did this happen?' she asked, crouching at the horse's feet.

'Ewan spooked her,' I answered mischievously.

Ewan's neck ratcheted round. 'Are you for real?'

'You did grab at her,' I reminded him.

'She'd been hit by a freaking tsunami!' Millie's conspira-torial twinkle showed me whom she believed.

'Tidy lass,' Ewan conceded as her estate car slid off the yard twenty minutes later.

'Shame she's not a motor mechanic though.' His gaze had returned to the Old Van. Dirk sighed and pushed his hand across his scalp.

'We'll have to shoe out of the New Van, for now.'
'We won't all fit in it.'
'You'll have to follow in your Astra.'

Chapter 24

'That tree branch is a bit close.' I followed Dirk's gaze to where the bough of a birch tree was waving inches from the new metal chimney.

'There's a saw in the shed,' I said, and went to put the kettle on.

Dirk was crossing the lawn with the saw when Ewan arrived. 'Will's going to saw that branch off.'

I walked out of the forge. 'I'm not!'

'You're the smallest!'

'Look what happened when Stanley sent me on the roof!'

'You'll be up that tree like a little monkey!'

I looked to where its lacework branches were outlined against a leaden sky. 'It'll be wet.'

'You're the one that's bloody wet, man.'

I grudgingly donned a pair of gardening gloves and assessed the task. The offending branch emerged about six metres up. Dirk planned to tie a rope to the handle of the saw and throw it over the branch so I could hoist it up when I was in the tree.

After three attempts the saw was in position and Ewan and Dirk were offering legs up and lift holds. I didn't trust them. Instead I shimmied up the trunk with bark scraping my cheeks and neck, until I could grab the first branch. Once there, I hoisted myself up it and sat astride it to get a breather.

'What did I tell you, man? Easy!'

With the trunk to steady me, I uncurled to a standing position, gripped the branch above, cautiously raised a knee and hefted myself onto it. The whole tree was swaying. I paused, breathing my way to stillness.

'Go on!' Ewan yelled. I leant over the branch above, and the ground seemed to rush towards me. Every movement I made seemed to create a counter lurch. I straightened again. 'Get on with it!'

With a surge, I hoisted myself onto the branch nearest to the forge roof and straddled it. I took hold of Dirk's rope, hoisted up the saw, then edged along the branch. The further out I shuffled, the wobblier the tree became. I decided I'd rather saw for a long time where the bough was thick than for a short time where it was thin. I raised my saw.

'Not there, man. It'll take you all morning! Move along!'

'It's too wobbly!'

'It'll wobble anywhere!'

'It's not wobbly here!'

'It is! See!' Dirk flung his massive bulk against the tree and shook it. Several whippy twigs from surrounding boughs hit me in the face. Gales of laughter travelled up the tree trunk. I grabbed for the branch.

'Move a bit further on!'

'All right! All right!' I edged out another two feet.

'See, it's not as bad there, is it!' Pretending to prove his point, Dirk shook the tree again, but this time Ewan joined in and my branch whipped and sprang like a bungee. I grabbed it with both hands and the saw clattered to the ground, whipping its rope tail with it. It only narrowly missed Ewan, but it didn't stop him shaking the tree. My body was snaking and twisting as if on a rodeo horse. Suddenly, I was fired from the branch. I grasped it as I fell, catching it momentarily to slow my descent. I did the same on the next bough before my weight lashed the branch from my fingers. Miraculously, I landed on my feet. The pair of them were close to wetting themselves.

'You wankers!' I screamed. 'You could have killed me!' Ewan was sitting on the wet grass nursing his guts, and Dirk was leaning against the tree trunk wiping his eyes between volcanic blasts of laughter. 'I dunno what's so funny about attempted murder!' Dirk's volcano blew again and he slid down the tree trunk. Ewan rolled onto his side, oblivious to the sodden grass. 'I could have broken my legs, you dickheads.' I stormed to the forge and was nursing a solitary cup of tea when Dirk tried to persuade me to go back up. I just laughed at him.

After several failed bribes and threats, Dirk turned to Ewan. '*You'll* have to do it, man.'

Ewan suddenly recovered his wits. 'No way! Not with him murderous for revenge!' It was my turn to laugh. Dirk pressed him with promises and rolled out assurances, but Ewan wouldn't shift.

'Well, I can't go up, can I?' Dirk insisted. 'I'll bring the whole fucking tree down!'

The bough was still tapping the chimney when Ewan and Dirk set off for their next job. I'd offered to go to the wholesalers instead. I knew they'd be quoting my utterances like kids re-enacting a favourite episode of *The Simpsons*. '"I could have broken my legs",' would be followed by the flapping of limp-wristed hands as they joyously relived my near-death experience. I had deluded myself I was fitting in, but Ewan's new allegiance to Dirk left me exposed. How had Dirk slid in from South Africa to Hathersage so seamlessly? He was easy in the company of Bob Entwistle and I knew he'd be comfortable with Flashman Freddie.

It was a blustery spring afternoon and the newly arrived lapwings were performing their plunging acrobatics against a boiling grey sky, so I stopped the car on Scorthwaite Moor to think. Beneath me, the whole of Eckersdale was spread out like a tablecloth. Now and then the distant River Ecker sparked, unpredictable as a firework. I wanted to scoop up a handful of houses, or scrub a miniature car on its back wheels and let it go down Throstle Lane. The springy grass was damp, so I perched on the barrier which separates cars from the Yorkshire sky and remembered fishing from Whitby pier with the sea buckling all around me. I felt at sea now; a tide was dragging at my legs. A lapwing swooped, spiralled like a skater then soared skyward. Cold spits of rain stabbed the side of my face. If I was clinging to the pier, Ewan was bobbing on the brine, dipping and rising, grasping the chances that floated past. There had been no malice in Ewan's stealing Stanley's boot or pocketing Joan Mitchell's twenty quid any more than in a lapwing's gulping down of a worm. It was survival. Daggers of slanting rain were stabbing my ears now and the lapwings had fallen silent. I shifted my weight on the cold barrier. I couldn't blame Ewan for enjoying a respite from Stanley. Besides, I reasoned, Dirk wouldn't always be in Hathersage. I stood up and hunched inside my jacket. I'd collect the horseshoe nails then I'd eat my lunch at Mervyn's on the way back; I always felt at home there.

Mervyn's yard was deserted when I pulled up, so I walked towards a barn lined down both sides with stables. Only the occasional snort broke the whispering rhythm of chomping. I wanted to sit on a bale of wood shavings, breathe the sweet drug of horse dung, and think. I slid back the barn door to see a Labrador-sized creature trotting towards me – but it wasn't moving like a Labrador. It was moving like a sheep – but it wasn't shaped like a sheep. I stood my ground until it emerged from its backlighting, trotted straight past me, and out onto the middle yard. It was a pig.

I was still trying to make sense of what I'd seen when Jay stuck his head out of the feed room. 'Was that a pig?'

'It was.'

'Did you fetch it?'

'Why would I be driving about with a pig on the passenger seat?'

'Well, where the hell has it come from?'

We retraced my steps to find a mottled black pig snuffling

round the stable doors for the scraps the horses had dropped. It looked up with what appeared to be a smiling mouth, allowed Jay to scratch its bristled head, then returned to its snack. 'It must be Mervyn's,' he concluded, though I couldn't see why Mervyn would want a pig. We watched as Bernard's Dream lowered his vast neck to investigate and the pig lifted its smiling face in answer. They stood there together, pig and racehorse, nose to nose. 'What are you doing here anyway?' Jay asked, handing me a finger of KitKat.

I shrugged. 'At a loose end.'

I put up my hood against the drizzle and the pig waddled towards me like a portly grandma, then sat up on its haunches and begged for the KitKat. Jay laughed out loud and I was sharing the chocolate finger with it when Mervyn walked onto the yard and stopped dead.

'Is that a pig?'

'No, Mervyn, it's a racehorse,' Jay answered. Mervyn ignored him and the pig grinned up at Mervyn who couldn't help scratching its bristly head.

'Did you fetch it?'

'No!'

'I'll have a ring round; see if anybody's lost a pig.'

'What if they haven't?'

'Bacon butties!' he said, rubbing his hands.

'You wouldn't!'

'No! I'd enter it in't' Topham Chase.'

Jay laughed. Mervyn told him it would be about as useful as he is and sent him to change Sovereign's bandages.

'Do you fancy 'avin' a jump round Aintree?' he asked when Jay was out of earshot

'Me?'

'Silent Shannon could do with seeing the fences and you're about the only one who gets on with her.'

I stared at him. 'Are you serious?'

'I'll have to put somebody on its back.'

'What about Jay?'

'He can bugger off.'

'Fintan?'

'He'll be schooling Rubicon round.' I bit my lower lip.

'Have a think about it.' He stalked off, then he turned back. 'Are you coming, Pig?' Pig stood and trotted behind him like she'd known him all her life.

A hazy rainbow was melting into the hilltop, painting the clouds above Eckersley in stripes of soft colour. A pair of sleepy gulls crossed it, unaware of its stain on their wings. I watched until it bled back into the sky and only when the faintest pink glow ghosted its place did I realise I was smiling.

STRATFORD COLLEGE OF AGRICULTURE:

FACULTY OF BLACKSMITHING AND FARRIERY

Apprenticeship Journal for the month of: April.

Comments: Our vehicles have needed unexpected repairs requiring us to be flexible and inventive. Unforeseen events during a foot preparation reinforced the necessity for strict adherence to health and safety measures. Thankfully, no horse or farrier was hurt.

My A.T.F. has listed our health and safety procedures, described their functions and advised us in detail of when it is appropriate to use them.

Learning Outcomes:

I have prepared feet for the application of glue-on shoes.

I understand the flammable nature of the materials used in nail-less shoeing.

I have helped implement bio-security measures for strangles.

Signed: William Harker. April 30th 2016   (Apprentice)

Signed: Dirk Koetzee AWCF   April 30 th '16   (Master)
(pp Stanley Lampitt DipWCF)

Chapter 25

The following morning I parked my car on Hathersage Road, locked it, and turned the corner of Bling Manor. A shocking expanse of Yorkshire sky fronted me like an act of defiance. The silver birch lay felled and Dirk had a foot on it, like a great white hunter with the corpse of a slaughtered elephant. My mouth fell open.

Maria was gesticulating furiously, hands on hips. 'He here one week and he smash up van of Stanley and tree of Stanley!'

'The branch isn't too near the fucking chimney now though, is it?'

'No!' Maria yelled. 'Is too near the fucking ground,' and she slammed back inside.

Dirk gestured with his coffee cup. 'She's always bad-tempered when she's on nights.'

I took a deep breath. 'Stanley won't be pleased.'

'It's a fucking tree, man! What is it with you eco-warriors?'

Ewan turned the corner and stopped. A gulf of silence opened before he whispered one word: 'Jesus.'

'It was a fucking tree, man!'

'It was a fifteen metre silver birch.'

Dirk drained his cup. 'Jeez! I'm working with fucking Greenpeace!'

Following them to the first job, I could see Ewan ranting at Dirk. There was tension in his shoulders and every now and then his hand rose in a finger splayed gesture of incredulity. It shouldn't have, but satisfaction rustled in me like a pocketed sweet wrapper. We were to shoe at Lord Hathersage's yard but Dirk was remonstrating too much to take in the grandeur of his surroundings. 'If you had gone up there like I asked and sawn the bloody branch off, I wouldn't have had to take such drastic action!' he protested, slamming the van door.

'Don't try to blame me!' Ewan shot.

'It's a fucking *tree*, man!'

'It might as well be a newborn baby when Stanley gets to hear about it!'

Dirk held up his hands. 'OK, OK – but the van was a bloody accident.'

'You parked it too near the stables!' I was enjoying their altercation.

'Stanley says there are no accidents. Only fuckwittery,' I put in.

'Well, it wasn't my fuckwittery!'

'You'll be sunning yourself on the Western Cape while we're paying for that van and that tree!' Ewan raged.

The morning didn't improve. Lord Hathersage's groom had failed to tell us that there was a strangles outbreak on the yard, so in next to no time we were all packing up. 'The chinless parasite could have got his lackey to give us a ring,' Ewan grumbled, picking up the diary. He flicked a page. 'There's a couple of cast shoes at Mervyn's and a trim at Throstleden we've been struggling to fit in.'

'Then what?' I asked.

'Then,' Ewan sighed, 'you and me should get some forge practice in, I suppose.'

'Or ...' Dirk smiled, keen to curry Ewan's favour, 'we could do a spot of car hunting.' They high-fived triumphantly and by eleven o'clock I was driving my Astra towards the Leeds city car dealerships. Our smoked-horse smell and farrier's attire earned us some scathing glances in the Mercedes showroom and the Lamborghini salesman wouldn't let us anywhere near his cars. Land Rover were more understanding, but by ten to four Dirk had bought a new Toyota Hilux. We were piling back into my Astra, when Ewan pointed out how close the hospital was.

'Let's surprise him!' Dirk grinned.

The swinging doors of the ward had barely swung shut when a prim nurse with tight grey curls approached us. I was about to ask her where Stanley was but she pointed her stiff little arm at the doors and spoke one word: 'Out.'

Dirk took an affronted step back. 'I thought visiting was till five?' She let her eyes travel from the tip of his hard-toed boots to the top of his sweaty scalp, noting every horse hair, grease smear, scorch mark and mud crust then curled her lip.

'It is *never* visiting time for *dirt.*' Her pointing finger had not wavered. Ewan, meanwhile, had located Stanley who was waving enthusiastically at us from his bed.

'Five minutes?' Ewan appealed.

'Not even five seconds.' She bustled his shoulder to turn him and as she did so Dirk caught sight of Stanley. He gave him the thumbs up and Stanley responded in kind. 'Go home, get washed, get changed, and come again.'

'Visiting will be over by the time we've done that,' Dirk complained; his blue eyes were bright against the dirt of his face.

'I cannot let you on my ward in that state.'

'Look! He's seen us now,' Ewan begged. She hesitated. It was the encouragement he needed. One glance at her name badge burst him into song.'*Come on, Eileen! Oh I swear well he means'*– the twinkle of a tiny smile sparkled at the corner of Eileen's lips – '*at this moment, you mean everything!*' She held up her palms.

'Right; this is what I'll do. Through those doors is a shower room. You scrub up in there whilst I bag your clothes and fetch you clean hospital gowns. That – and only that – is the one circumstance under which you will enter my ward.'

'Eileen, you're a princess amongst women!' Dirk stated, blowing her a kiss, and Ewan picked up where he'd left off:

'With you in that dress, my thoughts, I confess, verge on dirty. Ah, come on, Eileen!'

We *toora-loora-rye-ay*ed our way to the showers over Eileen's lecture on MRSA and antibiotic resistance, then scrubbed, rinsed and poked our heads head round the shower curtains where we each found a blue hospital gown and a pair of disposable towelling slippers. I was draping my gown on my damp skin when I heard Dirk's voice over Ewan's *'Poor old Johnny Ray ...'*

'Does yours shut, man?'

Ewan broke off.

'Nobody's does. We'll have to brave it.' Bubbles of girly giggling bounced into the shower cubicles.

'It shows my crown jewels, man!'

The bubbles burst into guffaws, but Eileen's voice rang out clearly: 'Turn it around!'

'It'll show my arse!'

'Your choice!' Her footsteps receded.

Dirk's shower curtain scraped back, so I stepped out too. Dirk was wearing his gown like a coat clutched shut at the front. It was all the more absurd for ending above his knees. 'We can't go out like this,' he hissed. Then Ewan's curtain swished back and he posed beside it like a drag queen at the Bradford Alhambra; hip cocked, arms outstretched.

'If we've got to look prats,' he announced, 'let's make a proper job of it!' He relaxed his posture. 'Do you know "Hot Stuff", off *The Full Monty*?' He began the guitar intro: *'Dooby dooby dooby, dooby dooby dooby, dooby dooby dooby, doo-oo-dum.'* Dirk joined in the finger clicking.

'We can't!' I protested over the rhythm.

'It's the only way to save face, man!' and as Ewan hit the lyrics in a surprising American falsetto, Dirk added the *dooby doobys*. They began filing into the ward. *'Sittin' here, eating my heart out waitin', waitin' for some lover to call …'* Dirk in front, crouching, finger-clicking and *dooby do*-ing, Ewan clapping over his head, shoulders swinging, bare arse beaming, and me, at the back. *'Dialled about a thousand numbers lately, almost rang the phone off the wall. Lookin' for some hot stuff, baby, this evening …'* If they could brave it, so could I. I put my hands on my hips and struck up a strut. *'I need some hot stuff, baby, tonight, I want some hot stuff, baby, this evening, Gotta have some hot stuff, Gotta have some love tonight.'*

It took three renditions to get down ward B2. I couldn't look round, but stitch-splitting laughter accompanied us, and when we arrived at Stanley's bed the whole ward burst into applause. Ewan took a bow that thrust his bare cheeks ceilingwards.

Settled on cold plastic chairs, we enquired after Stanley's health but he dismissed the topic and reached towards his bedside cabinet. 'See here,' he said, handing me a pink Get Well card depicting a bandaged kitten.

I flicked it open. 'It's from Katie.'

'I know it's from Katie!' He raised his eyes as if I were the one with limited literacy skills. 'That's why I'm showing it you!'

'Did you get one from Jonathan?' Ewan asked. Stanley snatched it back.

'You've always to piss on the party, haven't you, Dolloper? Can't you just be suited I got one from Katie?' That shut us up. 'How's Lucky?'

'Still psychopathic,' I said.

'Aunty Dorothy?'

'Grand,' Ewan answered.

'Is she laying?'

'Not yet.'

'Is the chimney up?'

'Ja.'

Then Stanley lumbered into the territory I most feared. 'You might have to lop a branch off that tree, you know, Dirk.'

Dirk was utterly at ease. 'Have you thought that maybe that tree is a bit too big for the garden?'

Stanley was defensive. 'It's a grand tree, is that.'

'But the roots, man. Have you thought about the damage those roots might be doing to the house?' It was like watching a dodgy insurance salesman. 'Or worse, to your neighbours' house. I mean, yours'll be insured, but if the roots undermine next door, you could be liable.'

Stanley rubbed his chin. 'D'you reckon?'

'Ja! You could be liable for thousands.' Stanley was silent, and for a moment Dirk could see the finish line, then Stanley flapped a dismissive hand.

'Nah, it's miles off next door's house.'

'Jesus, man, they're like fucking icebergs those trees! Two thirds of them are underground.' I wondered if it was ethical, to worry a sick man like this. 'I'll tell you what; I'll have it checked out. It could be sorted before you came home if need be.'

Ewan must have been gazing into the same gulf of honesty as I was, because he soothed Stanley's discomfort with an appeal to his greed. 'Imagine how many bags of firewood there are in that tree, Stan! At three pound fifty a bag, you'll be minted.'

Stanley grinned. 'Aye, get it checked. I can payt' solicitor off wi' logs if need be.'

After half an hour Stanley was tiring, so with our wax jackets over hospital gowns, we headed for the car park. Ewan snatched back the double doors. '*Go on now, go, walk out the door, Just turn around now, cos you're not welcome any more ...*'

Dirk joined in: '*Weren't you the one who tried to hurt me with goodbye? Did you think I'd crumble, Did you think I'd lay down and die?*'

And then me: '*Oh no not I, I will survive, Oh, as long as I know how to love, I know I will stay alive ...*'

Chapter 26

Dirk was pacing the space where the New Van – the Only Van – should have parked half an hour before. If Ewan was late, it usually presaged disaster.

'Have you rung him?' I'd been ringing him every three minutes for the last twenty. Dirk looked at his watch. 'We should be at Lower Beck by now!'

Dirk slammed back into the house and I tried Ewan again. This time, he picked up. 'Where the hell are you?'

'I've had a bump.'

'Another!' A voiceless crackle on the line worried me. 'Are you all right?'

'Yeah, I'm fine.'

'How bad is it?'

The line crackled again before Ewan spoke. 'It's a bit battered ...'

'Where are you?'

'Cribbs Road, just past the Esso station.'

'I'll see you in about fifteen ...'

'Don't fetch Dirk!' It was music to my ears. I glanced to where Dirk's outline was a fragmented shape behind Stanley's Italian blinds and jumped, grinning, into my car. Within seconds my rear-view mirror framed Dirk waving and yelling at the top of the drive.

For a moment, I couldn't make sense of the picture I saw just past the Esso garage. I told myself it must be the angle – but the nearer I drew, the clearer it became that the New Van was embedded in a bus. Steam was curling from under its bonnet, its engine was on the tarmac and a policeman was crunching on a carpet of glass as he controlled the traffic flow around it. Another was measuring two black lines where the New Van had unwound a ribbon of rubber on to the road.

A small group of pedestrians (formerly bus passengers) was milling on the pavement and the uniformed driver was on his mobile phone. Ewan was leaning on the wall of the Busy Bubbles Launderette with his toolbox at his side and his hands in his pockets.

'A bump?' I said.

Ewan pulled back his lips in what was more of a grimace than a smile. 'They can look worse than they are – can't they?'

'That's head wounds,' I told him.

We waited in sick silence until a pick-up truck arrived. After a brief word with a policeman, its driver hitched chains to the New Van's rear axle. The New Van groaned its way out of the bus, dropping nuts, bolts and door handles like a drunken aunty spilling her handbag in the street. We watched, dumbstruck by the unfolding horror. Ewan shook his head in disbelieving wonder, then sunk it in his hands.

'The forge!' Ewan raised his head. 'The gas forge, Ewan!' We exchanged panicked glances then dashed across to the pick-up driver. He must have felt sorry for us, because he rootled in his cab for a spanner and when the disintegrating vehicle had been chained to his truck he let us climb aboard to salvage Stanley's gas forge. He even helped us stagger it to the Astra before Ewan signed his clipboard, and the New Van was trundled down Cribbs Road to its final resting place. I thought of Ginger on the knacker's truck, but I didn't say so. I didn't want Ewan knowing that I'd watched *Black Beauty*.

I handed him my phone. 'You'd better tell Dirk.' Seventeen missed calls were registered on my screen, and the sight of them did nothing to settle Ewan's nerves. 'Go on. He was your biggest mate yesterday.'

Sitting on the passenger seat of my Astra, Ewan flicked it to speaker phone. Dirk picked up immediately.

'Where the fuck are you?'

'We're on our way back.'

'That doesn't answer my fucking question.'

'I've been in an accident.' (Good move, Ewan.)

'Oh. Are you all right?'

'A bit shaken up, that's all.'

'Is the van all right?'

'Not really.' (Not *really*?)

'Shit. How bad?'

I heard Ewan take a breath. 'It's had it ...'

'*What?*'

'The van. It's a write-off.'

'You are *fucking joking* me, man!' There was despair in his voice. 'Are you telling me we have no fucking van?'

I heard Ewan swallow. 'I suppose so.'

'He only had two fucking vans, and now he has no fucking van!'

'He only had one silver birch tree, and now he has no fucking silver birch tree.' (He gave me the thumbs up when he said it.)

'What the fuck did you hit?'

'A bus.'

'A bus! How could you miss a fucking bus?'

'I didn't miss it. I hit it.' (I burst out laughing now. So did Ewan.)

'Get your hides back here – ja? We need to make a plan.'

Ewan hung up. 'Arsehole.' It was business as usual again, so I happily settled back into my role as mediator.

'Ewan, you've just written off our only functioning vehicle.'

'Our Lee'll have the Old Van ready by Tuesday.'

'Stanley comes home on Tuesday!'

'He might not notice.'

'They've removed his bowel, not his eyeballs.'

Ewan suddenly swivelled his head to me. 'What if he makes me pay for the New Van?'

I pulled on the handbrake. 'I wouldn't worry,' I said. 'It can't have cost as much as the fire extinguisher.'

Chapter 27

Peggy did a double-take when we arrived a day early for our breakfast sandwich. 'What's this? When the cat's away?' None of us wanted to admit that we'd wrecked both of Stanley's vehicles in the space of a week, so we laughed it off. Our usual table was taken, so we settled Dirk at the only free one and walked to the counter. 'Three, is it?' Peggy asked.

'Just two.'

She flicked her head towards Dirk. 'What's to do wi' 'im?'

'He's foreign,' Ewan explained. (He said that about people born west of the Pennines.) Peggy grunted and set about buttering up, and we returned to our table where Dirk was perusing the menu.

'Do you think she does soya milk?' Ewan's answer was unequivocal.

'No.'

'Muesli?'

'No!'

'Skinny latte?'

I tried to explain. 'Dirk, it's Peggy's Café' – pronounced *caff* – 'not Starbucks.' I'd spoken too loudly. Peggy popped up from behind the counter.

'What's he after?'

'Latte,' Ewan answered.

'You what?' (I raised my eyebrows at Dirk in a told-you-so expression.)

'Foreign coffee,' Ewan explained.

'Tell him I have Nescafé.' Pronounced *Nescaff.*

'She has—'

'I bloody well heard her!' Dirk snapped.

When Peggy arrived with our oozing breakfast sandwiches, Dirk had still not placed an order. She plonked our plates down, took a notebook from her pocket and addressed him. 'Right. What can I get you, love?'

He hesitated. 'I don't suppose you have Greek yoghurt.'

'You suppose right.'

'Granola?'

Her pencil poised over her pad, she turned to Ewan. 'What's he after?'

'Rabbit food,' Ewan answered through a mouthful of bacon.

'Does it look like a bloody pet shop?' She pocketed her notepad and picked up the menu. 'I've toast, I've toasted teacakes, I've creamy porridge, I've curd pie, I've fruitcake …'

'Just fetch me a glass of water please, lady.'

'I've hot chocolate!'

'Water's fine.'

Peggy shook her head and bustled off. When she returned she slapped the glass down with such emphasis that lumps of water leapt out and splashed the formica table top. 'I don't know how you reckon to shoe horses all day off a glass of corporation pop!'

The truth was we weren't going to be shoeing horses all day. We were limited to Mervyn's yard, where he had his own forge. Fortified by a breakfast sandwich though, Ewan started to think logically: 'We've ten of Mervyn's to do before Monday, so let's try to get them done today and I'll ring up Lower Beck Showjumpers and offer them a discount if they'll fetch their horses to us tomorrow.' Ewan was pleased with his solution and Dirk was nodding appreciatively, but that still left us with a dozen horses to shoe, on four different yards.

Dirk was silent for a minute, then he turned to Ewan. 'We'll just have to get the Old Van back.'

'It won't be ready.'

'Ring your brother and tell him we have to have it.'

Ewan rubbed his chin. 'I could give it a try.'

Both Mervyn and his pig were grinning. 'Well, well, well, you've got yourselves in a reyt pickle, haven't you?' We grunted our agreements as we unloaded farriery tools from the boot of my Vauxhall. 'How long's he been in hospital? Ten days and you've written both his vans off?' He folded his arms over his belly.

'We've written *one* off,' Ewan argued. 'The other's nearly fixed.'

'*You've* written one off!' Dirk corrected him.

Ewan slammed down the tripod. 'So have you! You wrecked a TVR!'

'That was my own bloody car!'

'That bloody tree wasn't yours though, was it?' He turned to Mervyn. 'He's cut his silver birch down.' Mervyn burst into delighted laughter. 'A fifteen metre silver birch,' Ewan swept a palm parallel to the ground for emphasis, 'flattened.'

Mervyn rubbed his hands. 'I wouldn't like to be in your boots, lads!' Then he addressed his stable jockey who had ambled round the corner. 'You've seen Stanley's temper, haven't you, Fintan?'

But Fintan turned to me. 'Have you thought any more about Aintree?'

I had. I'd even rung Matty; a conditional jockey now who'd ridden in the Grand National the year before. A part of me had wanted him to say I was a lunatic; to tell me I'd be risking life, limb and livelihood – but he hadn't. 'You lucky sod, Will,' is what he'd said.

I was scared stiff, but I knew I would despise myself if I turned the chance down. 'Fintan'll be upsides you,' Mervyn urged, 'and he's ridden in the Grand National twice!'

'When is it?'

'Next Wednesday.' I breathed a sigh of relief. Dirk couldn't spare me so soon, but before I could say so, he'd had spread his hands in a gesture of magnanimity.

'Go on. We'll manage without you.'

'Hang on!' Ewan protested. 'How come he gets time off?'

'He doesn't,' Dirk reasoned. 'He'll be working for Mervyn.'

We worked on wordlessly. I was nursing fear, and Ewan was sulking. Only when the light began to fade did he break his self-imposed silence and suggest we pack up the Astra. I dropped Dirk off at Bling Manor and continued with a sullen Ewan towards the Cribbs Estate. The breath left my chest in a gush of relief when he climbed out of the car.

Ten minutes later I was driving down Jennings' drive to my agreed tuition of Ruudi. I parked in the post-and-railed car park and stared through my windscreen. Cloud towered on the distant strip of moor like whipped cream. Closer to me, a nut-brown wren was flickering on the fence, dipping, bobbing and busy. I sighed, put my elbows on the steering wheel and let my head drop into my hands. I was considering cancelling the lesson when Ruudi's diminutive figure walked out of a stable, waved, dashed to the railings, and began climbing them. I wasn't in the mood for his obstinate cheeriness, but he was banging on the window.

'I ride already!' A gush of relief sank me deeper into my seat.

'I ride Tomahawk today!' Tomahawk? No one wanted to ride Tomahawk. As soon as a jockey's foot was in the stirrup it was rearing, spinning, running backwards, or doing all three at once. Jockeys were often off before their backsides had hit the saddle. I lowered my window.

'On the gallops?'

'Yes. You watch tomorrow?'

'Ruudi, I don't think you should be riding Tomahawk.'

'He say only Tomahawk.'

'Who says?'

'Mr Jennings. He say Ruudi stablehand, not jockey.' I was about to be outraged when Pippa Jennings appeared in my rear-view mirror; lit red by my tail lights and spangled diagonally with drizzle, she was running towards my car.

'Sorry! I meant to text you!'

'No worries,' I said, relieved to be going home.

'Ruudi's really coming on.'

'He'll need to if your dad's putting him on Tomahawk!'

'Ah – he said, then?' I nodded and fired the engine.

'The lads wanted Ruudi back on stable duties, so he *offered* to ride Tomahawk.' I didn't want to argue with her but a solution to Ruudi's problem was taking shape in my mind.

Chapter 28

One of the Lower Beck showjumpers needed glue-on shoes. Glue-on shoes require a spotlessly clean hoof or the resin won't stick. This means that the horse can't be allowed to put its foot down from the moment you start cleaning the hoof with alcohol until the shoe is on – and even then it has to be immobile until the glue is set. That degree of restraint takes at least two people and several failed attempts per hoof are common.

Dirk trimmed the horse's feet and told me to clean the hooves whilst he shaped the shoes. Ewan found Stanley's spray-on hoof cleaner, passed me the can and, to deter the horse from struggling, lifted a back foot whilst I worked on a front. I was working as quickly as I could but within minutes the huge animal was rocking, swaying and leaning on me. A deserved dig in the ribs would have caused it to jump, snatch its foot away and slam it down, so I had no choice but to work fast. I was making steady progress when a Rhode Island Red caught me in its gimlet eye. It was a daily hazard since the tree had destroyed Stanley's chicken-run fence in its descent. 'If you let go of that foot, I will take my bloody hammer to you,' Ewan said through gritted teeth. But it was advancing, its livid wattle wobbling as it raised then lowered alternate scaly claws. 'Just squirt it,' he shouted, keen to speed up my labour. Of course! I was armed. Relief rushed in like floodwater. I waited until the fowl was near enough, then I turned the nozzle on it, and squirted. The bird was only mildly ruffled. It jumped, flapped, settled its feathers and stalked towards the forge. I breathed again. I had been gripping the horse's foot like a human vice.

When the foot was surgically clean, Dirk applied the resin, aligned the edges and carefully fitted the shoe. The patient was at last allowed to straighten its knee and place its foot on the ground. One down, three to go, I thought. Ewan walked to the front of the horse and, familiar with the pitfalls, he leaned his weight on its knee to dissuade it from lifting the newly shod foot before the glue was set.

We were enjoying the five minutes of ease that comes between the wrestling of each foot when a shout followed a slosh and a dripping wet hen shot underneath our horse. The horse reared. Ewan staggered backwards. Dirk streaked past us and I groaned. There on the concrete was a white plastic shoe. I picked it up and flung it on the workbench. Whilst Ewan and I were shaking our heads in despair, Dirk had caught the hen and was walking back across the lawn with it under his arm. 'I swear to God we're jinxed, man!'

'Why the fuck did you chuck water all over it?' Ewan asked.

'What was I supposed to do? Use the fire extinguisher?' Dirk turned the bird round and Ewan guffawed so suddenly that the horse jumped again. A few roasted quills sprouted from the hen's bald and blackened rump. 'It went up like a Roman candle!' Ewan laughed louder. 'Its whole fucking tail was ablaze! It was spontaneous fucking combustion, man!'

I'd read about spontaneous combustion when I was eight and for years I'd been afraid of ending up as cinders in my own slippers. I'd since dismissed it as nonsense, but chill trickles of realisation were troubling me. 'Did it get too near the forge?'

'Don't be bloody dumb – ja! If flesh were combustible, we wouldn't last a fucking morning!' He was towelling off the remaining feathers when I sheepishly held out the can of spray cleaner. Dirk looked from the can to my eyes. 'Tell me you didn't.' I bit my lip and he let his head roll back so that his

Adam's apple pointed at the clouds. 'Jesus Christ! I should flay your fucking hide, man!'

Dirk was still drying Aunty Dorothy – it would have to be Aunty Dorothy – when Lee pulled up in the Old Van. It was a glimmer of hope, a change in the empire-wrecking juju guiding us to the destruction of Stanley's former life. We filed down the drive, full of expectation. We lined the kerb, inspecting Lee's work, and by degrees our relief warped into disappointment. Our luck hadn't changed at all. Bare metal was visible on the uneven door panel and one yellow door was fastened to one white door with a hasp and padlock. He followed our eyes. 'I mean, I'm not saying Stan won't notice ...'

'You could have bought new shittin' doors, Lee!'

'You can't get that shade of yellow any more!' Banana yellow brush strokes fringed the reattached bumper. The horse in its tweeds with its cheery thumbs-up was gone. 'It's not as tidy as I'd have liked, but you said you were desperate for it—'

'How much?' Dirk interrupted.

'—and I couldn't have painted that horse back on anyway. You need a sign writer for that ...'

'How much?'

'And I've only taken fifty for my labour ...'

'HOW MUCH, LEE?'

His answer was almost a whisper. 'A hundred and fifty.' Dirk told Ewan to take it from the cash box and walked away with the half-cooked hen. Lee watched the bird's disappearing rump, then turned back to Ewan. 'Do you fancy a Kentucky for your tea?'

It took us hours to finish the showjumpers; so long, in fact, that the Fleece had opened by the time they were back in the horsebox. We decided that the struggle with the glue-on shoes and the double shock of Aunty Dorothy and the Old Van deserved a pint.

'Stanley not with you?' the landlord asked as Dirk approached the bar. Dirk shook his head.

'Shame. Birdie's in.'

Dirk scanned the pub. Reclaiming Stanley's overdue two-hundred would redress the balance of our offences. 'Where?'

The landlord looked up from the pump and furrowed his brow. 'Oh ... he was here ten minutes since.'

Chapter 29

'OK, let's get this straight: we had the tree looked at, and it was undermining the foundations – ja?' I nodded. We were surrounded by the tree, in its new incarnation as firewood. Logs were stacked in every conceivable cranny, and outside under tarpaulin.

Ewan was sitting on the floor staring fixedly ahead. 'I'll have to admit to the New Van.'

'We'll always park the Old Van with its good side to the house, ja?'

Ewan leaned on the wall of the forge and closed his eyes. 'I'm going to have to admit to the New Van.'

'And *don't* open the chicken coop until I've mended the run.'

Ewan leaned forward. 'I'll have to admit to the New Van, won't I?'

'Ewan, man, we'll have to admit to it all, but a bit at a time, ja?'

'So, does Ewan go straight in with the New Van, or do I start with the hen and build up to the New Van?'

Ewan sat bolt upright. 'I am not *starting* with the New Van! Jeez – he'll rip my fucking liver out.'

But before we could discuss it further, the sound of a diesel engine announced Maria's arrival with Stanley. We filed from the forge, a sheepish welcoming party, and he emerged slowly through the passenger door. Maria guided him down the Old Van's nearside, where it bore no scars, and Ewan greeted him: 'A'reyt, Stanley?'

'Dazzled wi't' daylight.' He grinned. 'Hasn't it made a difference, wi't' tree gone?' Maria had obviously delivered her script.

'Ja!' Dirk responded. 'You'll get a suntan now.'

'It's bastard Yorkshire,' Stanley grunted, then he looked round. 'Where's the New Van?' Ewan mouthed like a codfish for two seconds, and Maria's eyes darted like a trapped bird's.

Dirk attempted a rescue: 'We've been shoeing from my new Hilux.'

'Why?'

'I've fitted a forge in it!'

Stanley whistled. 'How much did that cost you?'

He hesitated. 'Nine.'

'Nine hundred? That must be a good 'un. What make?'

'Erm ...'

'Pro Forge!' I said.

'Pro Forge? Really? They're normally half that price ...'

'No. Not Pro Forge. I forget.'

'Let's have a look at it, then ...'

Dirk ran a finger under his collar. Maria tried to help: 'Come, Stanley; is no good for you, stand in cold.'

'I'd like to see this new gas forge.' Dirk made no attempt to move.

I tried a diversion. 'You've not seen the new coke forge yet ...'

'I'd rather see a nine hundred pound gas forge. What's it do? Fit the bastard shoes an' all?' Dirk made a lame pretence of patting himself all over for his car keys – then the truth exploded out of Ewan.

'There is no new gas forge!'

Stanley turned theatrically. 'Dirk just said he'd spent ...'

'It's out of the New Van!' He was like an erupting boil. 'I smashed the New Van into the side of a bus. It's utterly fucked. Banjaxed. Bollocksed.'

For long, gaping seconds Stanley stared at him, whilst Ewan

squirmed like a slug in beer.

'So I believe,' Stanley said, folding his arms.

'You what?'

'Mary Westwell rocked up, white as a sheet. Her bus had just been rammed by a van. Turns out, t'van driver were t'same fox as lobbed my boot in her garden a few weeks since.' Ewan swallowed. 'If your mate Nurse Eileen hadn't taken me phone off me, I'd have blasted you from here to Barnsley!'

'Stress bad for recovery,' Maria said, and made another attempt to guide Stanley towards the back door of Bling Manor. He was nearly there when he turned. 'And tell your brother I want the Old Van *one* colour. I don't care what it is, but I don't want it two-tone.'

For some seconds after the back door had closed our eyes remained on the frosted glass.

'They should be scrambling the fucking air ambulance by now,' Ewan whispered.

'He's the one who dabbles in the fucking juju,' Dirk sighed.

Before we'd walked to the forge, Maria opened the door. 'He say only Posh Lad to drive.' She would have closed it again, if Dirk hadn't challenged her.

'You told him I crashed the TVR, didn't you?'

Her hands dropped to her hips. 'He want to know why we have new car!'

'So you told him I'd wrapped the old one round a tree?'

'Is true! *Por qué inventar?*' Dirk turned his back and headed for the forge but she followed, ranting in Spanish. Her tirade picked up speed and volume and in no time at all her remembered near-death experience had her stabbing the air and stamping her feet. Soon Dirk was holding up his palms like a man surrendering but Maria was raging and frothing and poking him in the chest. She stormed some more then stomped towards the door, then she remembered another offence and erupted again. She swiped a horseshoe from the work bench and though Dirk was appealing and apologising she let it fly with impressive force. It sliced through the air and pinged off the metal chimney an inch above his head before clattering to the concrete. Its rolling diminuendo finally dropped the room into silence.

I unfolded from my crouched position. 'What the hell was all that about?'

'Fuck knows,' Dirk answered.

'Shouldn't you go after her?'

'No,' he said, pulling a hammer from the toolbox. 'She'll have forgotten by lunchtime.'

Chapter 30

Scorthwaite Manor is nestled in a little valley backdropped by ancient woodland. That morning, daffodils were stiffening themselves against an easterly wind and lilac was struggling into bloom before the manor's mullioned windows. Dirk declared it the epitome of an English country house. Ewan grinned. He hadn't prepared me for Scorthwaite Manor either and it was only now, in the build-up to Dirk's first encounter, that I realised it had been a deliberate omission. Ewan had wanted to see my reaction, and I wanted to see Dirk's.

Ewan showed his familiarity with the estate by guiding Dirk past the fountain to the equine showers, solarium and the purpose-built shoeing bay. Beyond the stables is a row of spacious centrally heated kennels where four sleek Labradors were waving their tails in greeting, just as they had six months earlier. Beside the kennel block is a neat drystone wall which, just as before, was enclosing four well-rugged chestnut Arabs. Dirk was taking it all in with saucer eyes, and Ewan was especially gratified by Dirk's response when we rounded the next corner.

'Lekker!'

'It's a Harris hawk,' Ewan announced, then pointed at the next two aviaries. 'A buzzard; a lanner falcon.'

Dirk was poring over the raptors in wonder when their owner emerged from behind the aviary. 'A'reyt, Ewan?' He was dressed from head to toe in tweeds: tweed cap, tweed jacket, tweed plus fours, leather boots and shooting socks.

'A'reyt, Saeed. You know Will?'

'A'reyt, Will.'

'And this is Dirk Koetzee.'

'Koetzee. Dat's not a name you 'ear in Yorkshire, innit?'

Dirk's expectations were wrestling with the reality in front of him. 'I'm South African, sir. Mr Saeed,' he stammered, and I could see from his grin that Ewan was enjoying Dirk's discomfort.

'Pleased to meet you, mate. I'll get Parvarti and Laveesa fetched in.' He put two fingers in his mouth and whistled. The first time I'd witnessed this I'd been groping for a handhold on reality and had half expected the Arabs to gallop in like mustangs in a movie, but then, as now, his whistle set the dogs off barking and brought out a little woman in a pale blue salwar kameez. Saeed addressed her in Gujarati then led us to the shoeing bay. Minutes later a pasty-looking lad was leading in two of the Arabs. Without a word he tied them up and took off their rugs.

'What d'ya reckon?' Saeed asked.

'They look well,' Ewan assured him.

'Dey vintered a'reyt, to be honest. I'm just doin' a couple of qualifiers wid'em next month. I fancy t'Royal International dis year.'

'Not the Horse of the Year Show?' Ewan asked, as he began removing Parvarti's front shoes.

'Or dat. Yeah.' With my eye on Dirk's expression, I fired up the forge.

'What do you use your birds for, Mr Saeed?' Dirk asked.

'Huntin' job, innit.'

'Tell him about your eagle,' Ewan prompted.

'Oh, aye. Th'eagle! Bloody 'ell!'

'Go on, then!'

'After t'huntin' ban, reyt, I paid free fousand nicker for a bald eagle for t'hunt.'

'Proper hunt,' Ewan put in. 'He rode with the Hathersage Harriers, didn't you?'

195

'Aye, I war t'whipper-in for two seasons. Any road; I bought dis bald eagle, cos I thought, law dun't say nuffin about huntin' wiv birds, only wiv dogs. One over on Tony Blair, innit?'

'Tell him what happened though.'

'First meet, reyt. October time – and it's brilliant. Not too cold; no vind. Lovely orange colours in t'trees, like. Ground's good and th'eagle goes up, riding de fermals.' He was demonstrating with a hand against the rafters. 'Proper majestic, innit. Horses all followin' and t'bird swoops! It's got one! We 'ave it cracked! Sorted. Take dat, Mr Blair!'

'But tell him what happened, Saeed.'

'Master of de 'unt sends t'hounds to finish t'job – cos it's t'chase dat's illegal, not t'kill, innit – an'dat's when it all goes to shit!' Ewan's already chuckling. 'Cos de hounds fink dey've been sent for th'eagle, innit!'

'Oh! Man!' Dirk was feeling it with him.

'I know! Free fousand nicker!'

The woman in traditional dress had put an anorak over her pale blue silk, but the tail of her head wrap was floating behind her. She laid a silver tray and china teacups on a little table, nodded and walked away. Saeed reached for a biscuit. 'You wanna try one of deez, mate; magic.'

Anticipation of the following day's ride round Aintree had robbed me of appetite, but Saeed insisted that I take one. It tasted spicy and buttery. ('Caraway seeds, innit.') As we sipped tea and nibbled on what Saeed told us were khari biscuits, Dirk resumed his fascinated questioning: 'So don't you hunt now?'

'Nah. Sickened me off, dat did. I shoot, like, in de vinter.' An idea brightened Saeed's eyes. 'I have a freezer full of pheasants. Do you want some?'

'Really?'

'I can't eat 'em canna? Not halal, mate. You can all 'ave some – and some for Stanley; get well gift, innit!' He whistled again. The silk-clad woman came to the door, and he yelled at her in Gujarati.

'You fly-fish an' all, don't you?' Ewan prompted Saeed.

'Oh, aye, I do a bit o' fly fishin', and I hunt wiv me raptors.'

'He's the proper country gent!' Ewan added.

Saeed beamed. 'I do me best, innit.' The woman deposited four Waitrose carrier bags at Saeed's feet. 'How is Stanley?' He lowered his voice. 'My vife says they've sewn up his bumhole.' (I couldn't imagine that dainty Pakistani lady saying bumhole.)

'They have,' Ewan affirmed.

'Shit!' Then he recognised the irony of his words and laughed until he had to wipe his eyes. 'It's not funny though, innit.'

At length we waved Saeed goodbye, wished him well in his qualifiers and crunched up the immaculate golden gravel drive. Dirk was silent, but I knew he was encrypting a search engine of politically incorrect questions. Working for Stanley exploded stereotypes and replaced them with unaskable questions – like *Is Saeed a drug dealer?* and *If Bob Entwistle worked for sixty years, why has he no money?*, and *Why do Ewan's family listen to Radio 4, when the rest of the Cribbs Estate is watching* Jeremy Kyle?

'The Maharaja of Scorthwaite Manor, they call him,' Ewan offered. 'He started off selling jeans on Fowlden market.' Dirk let out a low whistle.

'How come you know him so well?'

'His brothers were at school with me.' Dirk fell silent and I thought of the gap Saeed had travelled from Eckersley Comp, where Ewan said the only competitive sport was spitting over the mezzanines, to Scorthwaite Manor and a string of Arab horses.

'You'll feel better when you've met Lord Hathersage,' I said.

'Why's that then?' Ewan snapped.

I shrugged. 'Closer to expectations, I suppose.'

'Expectations of what? Unfairness in British society? At least

Saeed sold jeans to get that place!' I couldn't see how flogging jeans gifted Saeed any more worthiness than an inheritance did, but I didn't want a political discussion. 'Come the revolution,' Ewan snarled, and tightened his grip on Lucky's quarters.

Chapter 31

It was five in the morning when I climbed into the cab of Mervyn's horsebox, my guts lurching. I'd watched Richard Dunwoody's *Grand National Course Walk* six times before bed, but now I wanted to avoid all thought of the coming challenge. I took control of the conversation: 'Are you still looking for work riders, Mervyn?'

'I might be. Who're you thinking of?' Mervyn asked as he checked the traffic.

'It's one of Jennings' stable lads.'

He pulled the wagon onto the silent moor road. 'Is he any good?'

I hesitated. 'He doesn't jump yet, but he has loads of bottle on the flat.'

'Yet?'

'He's not been riding long.' A barn owl ghosted the wagon's passenger window. We watched it disappear towards a copse before Mervyn coaxed the rattling engine into third gear. 'Will it piss Jennings off?'

'Probably.'

'Aye, go on then!' Fintan, in the middle seat, laughed out loud.

I wasn't faintly interested in the progress of Leeds United through the football league, or the injuries besetting the current England team, but I listened attentively and made Mervyn explain the finer points, so that when he clattered the wagon into Aintree's car park I'd almost forgotten why I was there.

The sight of the course stretching away to my right quickly reminded me though, and my guts swilled cold.

Mervyn dropped from the cab, walked round the wagon and lowered the ramp. I'd competed enough to know the drill. You check the horses, offer them water, settle them with hay and walk the course. I was wondering if I'd have time to stop at Red Rum's grave, when I saw Fintan walk straight into the wagon and untie Rubicon. I paused in the zipping of my jacket. 'Aren't we walking the course?'

'No, we're just feckin' riding it.'

'I'll just have a walk down to the first, then,' I said, finishing my zipping up.

'You'll see it from the horse!'

'I know … but …'

Fintan's hands stopped their work on the lead rope. 'Trust me, Will, you don't want to be standing next to those fences.' My body felt suddenly light and insubstantial.

Mervyn led Shannon from the wagon and I concentrated on tacking her up, checking and double-checking every buckle and strap. She was dancing in anticipation and my palms were wet and shaky. 'Don't send them,' Mervyn was saying. 'We're not after speed. Just let 'em enjoy it.' His instructions seemed to be arriving over a great distance, even though he was right beside me. 'You're drip white, lad!'

'I'm remembering that seven foot drop at Becher's,' I said. My mouth was dry too.

'Six foot ten!' he countered, like two inches made a difference.

'Ach! You'll be grand over Becher's,' Fintan added. 'It's nothing like the drop it used to be.' I was unconvinced, but I nodded out of courtesy.

'Aye,' Mervyn agreed. 'It's the Canal Turn you've to worry about.' I caught Fintan's scowl at him as he double-checked my girth and tucked a bridle strap into its keeper. Satisfied I was safely tacked up, Fintan put his hands on my shoulders.

'Stick upsides me, and you'll be fine. I've ridden in two Grand Nationals already.' I managed a grateful smile before Mervyn legged me up. 'Now breathe,' Fintan advised.

Once in the saddle, some of my tension trickled away. Shannon had relaxed and though the whole Grand National course was stretched out before me, every televised Grand National since I was four made it look like a computer mock-up.

'We'll trot in,' Fintan announced. I needed more time.

'Aren't we showing them the first fence?'

'No. We're just feckin' jumping it.' We picked up the trot. 'OK?' My stomach was churning, but I nodded.

We picked up canter, and the first fence started gaining on us. I knew it was four foot six, the smallest on the course, but it looked massive. Fintan glanced sideways. 'All right?' I couldn't answer. I was locked onto the huge hedge that was pulsing ever closer. He counted us in: 'One, two, three – fly!' Hoof beats silenced. For ethereal seconds we were free from the drag of earth; airborne! Then the sound resumed. Shannon had landed in her stride, and her hooves were beating the rhythm again. A smile tightened my face.

'Fantastic!' Fintan yelled.

Don't relax yet, I told myself. *Becher's is the sixth.*

The second was approaching; another plain hedge; four foot seven. It sucked my concentration like a vortex. Fintan counted us in. We flew it together and landed, barely interrupting Shannon's canter. I grinned at Fintan.

'Brilliant!' Fintan shouted. 'I've now got further than I've ever got before!' I glanced across. He wasn't joking. If I'd known that two minutes earlier, I wouldn't have started.

Next was an open ditch in front of a big hedge. I reminded myself that the natural take-off point is well before the ditch. 'Don't look down,' Fintan yelled. After a long time in the air, we landed in a stride. 'Jaysus; you need a feckin' pilot's licence for that one!'

201

The wind in my face and the heartbeat rhythm of pounding hoofs transformed the towering hedges of fences four and five into the familiar.

'Becher's!' Fintan stated as we landed after the fifth.

The approach to the most famous fence in National Hunt history renders it no more intimidating than the others, but perhaps a surge of nerves had transmitted to Shannon, or a flash of hesitation had stopped me from riding straight, for as Fintan counted us in I knew I was too close to him. 'Sit back!' he shouted. I slipped my reins for a backward seat and felt my stirrup clip Fintan's. My leg shot forward. I drew a sharp breath. I wobbled. Shannon stretched for the turf and – God bless that horse – she landed and galloped away, folding and stretching underneath me with the grace of a leopard. Rubicon had pecked on landing, but behind me, Fintan gathered up the reins, rebalanced the horse and was galloping again. It was my turn to ask if he was OK. 'I could do with a bit more feckin' room!'

I was enjoying it now. The feared fence was behind me and the Foinavon in front. Shannon's ears were pricked and my knuckles were rubbing her mane which was rising and falling with every thrust of her quarters. Exhilaration had wiped out my caution. I was in a stride and heading for the Canal Turn. I met the fence straight, intending to hang a left on landing, but two strides behind me, Fintan was riding it like a jockey should – on the diagonal! Rubicon slammed into Shannon's shoulder. I gasped. She staggered, mid-air. I was flung sideways. I grabbed for neck – then, somehow, Shannon was under me again, and stretching for the earth. She buckled on landing, but found a leg, heaved herself up, and was away. 'I said take the diagonal!' Fintan yelled. It was too late now, we were belting towards Valentine's. Shannon's head was pumping the rhythm of her pounding hooves and the sweet smell of horse was in my nostrils.

Valentine's was bigger than I'd expected. 'You've got it,

now!' Fintan grinned as we landed together. We sailed the plain hedge and the open ditch at ten and eleven, with matching strides. Fence twelve has a ditch on the landing side but if you're on a good stride the horse doesn't know it, so I let Fintan count us in and enjoyed the silence of the long airborne moment. Shannon stretched her front legs, found her rhythm and picked up the pulsing beat of her gallop. The next two were plain hedges, then the Chair; the height of my mother with a six foot ditch in front of it and a landing side higher than the take-off.

'We're going for a long one!' Fintan shouted. It was the only way to take it. The earth rushed up to meet Shannon's hooves. 'Stay on a long one!' he yelled as the water jump loomed. I enjoyed the shallow soaring, but as we cantered away, I took a pull. The six-minute adrenalin rush of a lifetime was over. Shannon had the power to go round again, but she steadied to a rocking horse canter, then a trot. I let myself find the saddle, reached down and swept my hand over her silken, sweating neck.

A small group of racecourse staff was applauding from the rails and in my elation it was the roar of the winners' enclosure. By the time Shannon was in walk, I had populated Aintree's famous mound with a roaring crowd and Liverpool ladies wearing peacock colours were waving their race cards in the Queen Mother Stand. I almost waved back at them.

Mervyn was approaching with a sweat rug. 'She looked after you at the Canal Turn, my lad!' I didn't answer him. Still smiling, I slid off the mare, loosened her girth and patted her neck.

'That was absolute magic!' Fintan grinned, dismounting from Rubicon. I agreed, but ecstasy, exhilaration, pride and gratitude had coagulated as a lump in my throat and a glimpse of Red Rum's grave over Shannon's back tore a sudden tear through my smile.

I let Mervyn lead Shannon away and walked to where Red Rum is forever paused, by the paddock; bronze head up, ears pricked, gazing towards the course. I reached out and ran a hand down his raised right fore. I hadn't wanted to arrive at Aintree, and now I didn't want to leave. I took one last look at the distant deserted course from the Lord Sefton Stand, and returned to the wagon.

On the journey home I talked Mervyn through every stride, then I rang my mother and relived the experience for her. I rode it all over again for Matty in Lambourn and I'd have ridden it again for Fintan, but he reminded me that he'd been there.

My face was still stiff with smiling when the wagon pulled into Mervyn's yard. I was in no mood for work, but I collected my car and drove to the forge as promised. Dirk was sharpening his paring knife when I walked in.

'Hey! You've got four functioning limbs, man!'

Ewan looked up from sorting through shoes. 'Did you do it?'

'Course I did it!'

He addressed Dirk: 'Has Lord Hathersage's groom re-booked their yard?'

' ... best adrenalin rush of my entire life!'

'Not to my knowledge,' Dirk answered him.

' ... I needn't have been afraid of Becher's. It rides a heck of a lot better than it looks ...'

'You've got the business phone,' Ewan replied.

' ... It was an absolute blast!'

'No, then,' Dirk confirmed for Ewan.

' ... Valentine's rode bigger than I thought it would ...'

'We need to ring him,' Ewan stated.

' ... and I was nearly off at the Canal Turn; we collided in mid-air!'

Ewan finally turned to me. 'Are you going to shoe some horses this afternoon, or are you going to ride that Grand National course for the next three hours?' My mind clattered back into the forge.

'Sorry. Yeah. I'll get changed.' I turned away, wishing they were more impressed. I understood why Ewan was sulking, but I'd hoped Dirk might be interested beyond my mere survival.

I was at the boot of my car when Dirk called after me. 'Forget it, man!' I turned round. 'You're no bloody use in this mood. Go talk racehorses to someone who gives a shit – but come back ready to work tomorrow!' I could hear Ewan's protestations as I walked, grinning, to my car.

The road out of Hathersage crosses a narrow stone bridge before an elbow bend spreads the swell of the moor in the windscreen. Spring had spattered the verges with primroses, lambs were bleating in the low pastures and my heart bubbled. Exhilaration seemed to lift me out of the valley and onto the sparse moor which billowed about me like a floating sheet before falling steeply into Briardale. I was driving back to Mervyn's for one more rush of reliving and one more look at Silent Shannon.

I was surprised to find Ruudi there. My plans for him were taking shape faster than I'd expected. At five o'clock that morning Mervyn hadn't known of his existence. He was wearing his cobbled-together riding livery and leading a tacked-up horse into Mervyn's barn. When I shouted his name he turned, grinned, and showed the black rectangle where his front teeth had once been. 'I have trial with Mervyn!'

'Already?'

'He call my number this morning!'

It was then that I recognised Enville Lad. 'You've not ridden that, have you?'

Before he could answer, Mervyn had walked out of the barn. 'He's got some bloody bottle, your lad, hasn't he?'

I was jaw-dropped. 'He's only been riding two minutes, Mervyn!'

'Fair play to him.'

'Fair play? You'll kill him!' But like every jump jockey I'd ever known, Mervyn believed in immortality.

'Will I 'eck as like! I've told him he can go over t'jumps on his twenty-first.'

'Key of the door!' Ruudi grinned.

'*Never been twenty-one before ...*' Mervyn sang, strolling towards the house. I helped Ruudi untack Enville Lad then followed Mervyn through the front door with its brass knocker of two clashing heads, left open to give Pig permanent ingress and egress. I walked past the photo gallery of framed newspaper cuttings, the England team photographs and the racing trophies and straight to the kitchen. Mervyn looked up. 'Do you fancy a sausage?' He was placing a frying pan on the Aga.

'Mervyn, you can't put Ruudi on Anvil Head!'

He dropped a dollop of lard in the pan. 'He's a grand lad, that, isn't he? They're making Estonians like they used to make Yorkshiremen!' Was Ruudi an Estonian? I'd never asked. Mervyn pointed his spatula at me. 'Do you know what I'd do, if I were Jennings? I'd get that useless lass of his mucking out, and I'd get yon Estonian lad riding.'

I was doubly indignant. 'Pippa's a good jockey!'

'Get away!' Mervyn yelled and flung a raw pork sausage in my direction. I caught it, let it go, caught it again, let it slither down my jacket then trapped it on the table. 'She couldn't ride one side of a Bridlington donkey. You want to listen to your brain and not your pants. Anyway, I've told Jay to get the lad jumping, and I'll take him on. If Jennings can't spot a talent, I can.' He slithered the remaining sausages into the pan. 'Do you know what Jennings is doing? He's making that lad's mother stop in a caravan.'

The whole monologue had moved too quickly for me. 'Whose mother?'

'Your Estonian's. It's his twenty-first birthday. His mother's coming, and he's making her stop in a caravan.'

'He *lives* in a caravan.'

'Aye. Wi' three others! Anyway, I've told him, she can stop here.'

'Who can?'

'Dagmar.' My brow must have furrowed. 'His bloody mother. Keep up!' Just as I handed over my sausage, Ruudi walked into the kitchen. Another sausage flew his way and he caught it in one lizard-like flick. 'Reflexes, you see!' Mervyn crowed. 'I'll bet he wouldn't have been out of the plate at the Canal Turn.' I knew who'd be schooling round the Grand National course next year.

'You come to pup crawl, no?' Perhaps it was tiredness, but the evening's dialogue seemed as slippery as the sausages.

'Oh, aye!' Mervyn cut in. 'Me and the lads are taking Ruudi round Fowlden on Friday night for his twenty-first.' How had Ruudi secured a new friendship group, a new job, a guest room for his mother and a twenty-first birthday party in the space of an hour? He was a walking wonder.

'It's Good Friday,' I said. 'I'll have to check there's no family stuff on.'

'He's only twenty-one once, you miserable streak of drippin'!'

'You best English friend!'

'I know, but we always go to my granddad's ...'

'You teach me ride!'

'I know, but if I can't I'll take you to the Fleece next week.'

'Is not birthday next week!' He held me with his imploring eyes. 'Come after Granddad's, yes?' I considered it. 'We'll be out while closin',' he insisted, in his newly evolving Yorktonian.

I was beaten. 'Go on, then,' I said.

I arrived at the forge the following day to find Ewan on the telephone. 'Sorry, no can do, love.' He raised his eyes at us. 'I know, I know we always come on a Friday, but it's a bank holiday this week.' We could hear her tinny indignation at his ear. 'But we never nail on on a Good Friday. It's company policy.' The client couldn't see the thumbs up grin that he was giving us. 'Because it would be in very poor taste!' There was a hiatus. 'No, no, not at all. I'm not offended. Have a nice Easter.' He slung the phone on the draining board just as Stanley walked in carrying Aunty Dorothy. We'd come to dread Stan's arrival. He wasn't yet well enough to work, but he was bored enough to interfere. He squared up to Ewan and I expected a challenge about why he was turning down business, but his concern was different.

'Right then, Dolloper, what the hell's happened to my hen?'

Ewan turned away. 'It's nowt to do wi' me!'

'No wonder it isn't bastard laying!' Ewan ignored him and set about checking his tools. 'Come on, Dolloper! Why is my hen halfway to a Sunday dinner?'

Ewan flicked his head in my direction. 'Ask him!'

'It just got a bit too close to the forge,' I said, like it was no big deal. Stanley looked at the height of the forge, then at the hen in his hands.

'And how did it do that then? Was it on bastard stilts?' I glanced at Ewan, but he was deliberately preoccupied.

'We lit the gas forge in here.'

'In here?' It was the wrong answer. 'We have two perfectly functioning coke forges and you lit the gas forge in here?' I said nothing and Stanley's nose lifted a slow arc. 'Un-be-bastard-lieveable! We have two – *two* – coke forges in this building and you light a gas forge on the floor!' He turned to Dirk. 'You're supposed to be in charge! Have you never heard of health and safety?' Dirk opened his mouth to speak, but Stanley didn't wait: 'When I think of the effort and the expense I go to for the safety of you feckless fuckwits, I could cry!' He paused for effect. 'There's steel toecapped boots, there's quick release ties, there's fire extinguishers, there's safety guards, there's ear protection, there's first aid kits, there's regularly serviced vehicles ...' Ewan slithered me a sideways look of incredulity. 'There's safety goggles, there's back supports ...' He could bear no more of Stanley's fantasy.

'You called me a lazy bastard when I wore a back support!'

'You are a lazy bastard! It should be in the stomach muscles at your age!'

'You don't let us use the ear protection either!'

'You won't be able to hear what's going on! Safety again, you see!' I could feel a smirk curling at the corner of my mouth, but Stanley had folded his arms and resumed his lesson. 'You were lucky to finish your apprenticeship without major disfigurement in my day, but a splinter off the bastard firewood and you lot are on to some "No Win No Fee" chancer!' A fizz of laughter frothed behind my nose. 'I've had more nails in me than Jesus of bastard Nazareth ...' A snort of laughter blasted out. 'It's not funny, Posh Lad!' but Ewan was doubtless remembering his Good Friday conversation and had given in to it too.

'The pair of you want to bloody well grow up!' he bellowed, then stormed out, slamming the door behind him.

I accepted a bottle of Kopparberg from Granddad and felt a smile snake my lips. Stanley wasn't even in the room, and I could hear him: *What you drinking that for, you big lass? It's a lasses' drink, is that!* I refused a glass and scanned the room full of tweedy ladies and men dressed as Jeremy Clarkson; this was my family. Even the hum had a timbre I'd come close to forgetting; it was the drone of insects, shattered randomly by the chink of china or the rattle of cutlery. It wasn't the echo and heave of the Fleece. Piers was approaching me; after a gap year in India, he was wearing a kurta and sandals. Imaginary Stanley shook his head: *It's eight bastard degrees outside!* Piers' long hair was worn in a top knot and bracelets were bejangling his wrists.

'Hi, Will, how's it going?'

'Fine,' I answered. 'You?'

'Amazing,' he said. 'It's been such a privilege to experience another culture, you know? I mean, there are people in India who have nothing. I mean, nothing – but they're happy, you know?' I nodded. 'I mean, really happy. They have a different outlook. I mean, totally.' I nodded again. 'Different things matter over there. Totally different values.' I sipped from my bottle neck. 'You stayed in Yorkshire, didn't you?'

'I did, yeah.'

'Really, Will, you should travel; broaden your horizons.'

He wants to get a ribbon in that bloody hairdo. Big jessie. 'So, what are your plans now you're back?'

'Oxford. They've held my place.'

Granddad pushed a plate of canapés under my nose just as Piers was accosted by an eavesdropping second cousin of my mother's. 'Which college?' I didn't hear Piers' answer, but when I looked up, Granddad was shaking his head at his other grandson's retreating back.

'Absurd,' he snarled. 'Nine months in India and he thinks he's Pandit Nehru.' I laughed.

'Do you mind if I duck out early, Granddad?'

He patted me on the back. 'Off with you, young man, you're only young the once!'

I crossed to my mother, who was looking like an impostor in a slinky black dress, and told her I'd be staying at Mervyn's. 'But you've no night things with you!'

'I'll be fine.'

'What'll he think?'

'Mumma, he keeps a pig in the house.' She raised her eyes and kissed me on the cheek and I stepped into the chilly night air.

The Station Inn's welcoming lights were in sight when my taxi pulled up in the parking zone. I was about to walk under the viaduct which straddles the town's central roundabout when I heard a shout.

'Hey! Will!'

I turned. Five giggling girls wearing cowboy hats and

skyscraper heels were tottering on the other side of the street. Their concentration seemed to be focused on staying upright and retaining handbags, so it wasn't one of them.

'Will!'

I looked about. The slow hiss of passing traffic had muffled the voice but it had seemed to be male. A man in a dark jacket walked out of the pub and through a pool of lamplight; the timing was wrong for it to have been him.

'WILL!'

It was coming from my left. I stopped and squinted at a vague movement on the roundabout. I took a step towards the kerb. What looked like a massive chrysalis was propped against the roundabout's central decorative lamp-post. It had feet which were planted amongst the primroses of *FOWLDEN IN BLOOM*.

'Ruudi?'

'Is me!'

I crossed to the roundabout. 'Ruudi, how long have you been here?'

'Five minutes.' His voice was ebullient with its usual enthusiasm. 'And five minutes outside the Bull; five minutes outside the Coach and Horses.'

I started to look for the end of the cling film so that I could unwrap him.

'Five minutes outside the Farmer's Glory, five minutes outside the Golden Cross, five minutes—'

I interrupted. 'I need scissors.'

'Is very funny, yes!' Ruudi was grinning his toothless grin. 'They come. Carry me in pup.' Sure enough, Jay and three of the jockeys were crossing the road, joshing and guffawing. All but Jay greeted me, and with the ease that comes from frequent rehearsal, they hefted Ruudi over Jay's shoulder. Marc and Peter supported the length of his body and Michael checked the traffic and opened the pub doors for them.

Ruudi's arrival was greeted with a roar, a cheer, a round of applause, and what must have been the umpteenth rendition of 'Twenty-One Today', because Ruudi knew the words by now. They propped him against the bar – he couldn't have sat – and plonked before him a pint with a straw in it. Ruudi was as efficient as a vacuum hose.

'What if he wants a pee?' I asked.

'I pee in here!' Ruudi grinned. 'Is waterproof!'

His tormentors' eyes sparked with consternation. Ruudi's inability to differentiate between English tenses had panicked them. Without a word, they abandoned pint glasses, hoiked him up and spirited him to the Gents even faster than they'd hefted him off the roundabout.

Meanwhile, Fintan bought me a pint and suggested I join his table. He seemed more on edge than he should have been at a twenty-first birthday party, but I followed him to where a middle-aged woman was silently gazing on Mervyn's crumpled profile. 'Ruudi's mother,' Fintan explained as I sat down opposite her. She didn't shift her gaze. 'They've told her the cling film's an English tradition.' He took a gulp of his soda and lime. 'Now, Will – just so you know – Jay's got wind of your ride round Aintree, and he's not happy. I thought we should tell you.' I'd not hidden my ride from Jay, but nor had I told him. It made sense now that Jay hadn't greeted me on the roundabout. My ride round Aintree had trodden on his toes.

'What has he said?'

Mervyn answered, 'What has he said? Never mind what *he's* said, the cocky little waster, I'll tell you what *I've* said! I've said it's come to a pretty pass when my bloody farrier's a better jockey than my bloody head lad! "Never mind complaining!" I said. "You should be skulking about with your tail between your bloody legs!" He can either raise his game, or else learn to nail shoes on. The cheeky bastard!' He put a hand on my shoulder. 'Don't you worry about him, Will. They're my 'osses and I decide who rides 'em.' He raised his pint to his lips. 'Cheers!'

At that moment a beaming Ruudi emerged from the Gents, free from his cocoon. The jockeys surrounding him were discussing the cling film. 'Surely it'd be yellow?'

'Sniff it.'

'I'm not sniffing it!'

Ruudi winked at me and downed the rest of his pint.

Chapter 32

Dirk and Ewan stopped talking the second I walked in. I stopped in my tracks.

'All right,' I said. 'Where is it?'

'Where's what?'

'The hen.'

'What hen?'

'If you've not hidden a hen, you're plotting to.'

'We're not!'

'So what's the big secret then?' They flashed a shared glance.

'Have you been on Facebook this morning?' Ewan asked.

'No. I have a life.'

'I'll bet that new vet's added you.'

I flung a used horseshoe at the scrap bin. 'That's a bit random, isn't it?'

'Go on! Have a look.'

I took out my smart phone and flicked the screen. There it was; a request from Millie Routledge. I looked up. 'How did you know?'

'She was in Rafferty's last night.'

'And?'

'And she was asking about you.' I pressed Confirm.

'You're in there, man!'

I would have asked more questions but Stanley strode into the forge and declared himself well enough for a breakfast sandwich.

'Let's have a proper look at this motor then,' Stanley said, climbing into the Hilux beside Dirk. Ewan and I sat in the back and as soon as Dirk started the engine Stanley pushed the Hilux's window button and watched the glass sink into its door panel. He waited, and then with another theatrical button stab he raised the window and watched its upward journey. He leant forward and twiddled the knobs for heat-setting and air-direction. Even from the backseat I could feel Dirk's irritation. 'Roomy, in'tit? It's more like a car.'

Dirk bristled. 'More like a car than what?'

'A van!'

'It is not a bloody van!'

Stanley leant forward and pressed another button. He waited. 'That's not working.'

'It's the Bluetooth.'

'The what tooth?'

'To connect to my phone.'

Stanley folded his arms. 'It's bloody noisy.'

'It's four-wheel drive!'

He reached for the gear lever and Dirk smacked his hand like he might a ten-year-old's. Stanley withdrew it.

'My Porsche's not this noisy.' He watched the terraced houses reel past the window. 'Does it have satnav?'

'No.'

'My Porsche has satnav. It has an electronic log book an' all.'

'Ah! But does it have dusk-sensing headlights?' Ewan challenged.

'What's the bastard point in dusk-sensing headlights, when you have dusk-sensing eyeballs?' None of us could answer.

Peggy was delighted by our arrival. She took Stanley's massive paw in both her pudgy ones. 'Hey up, Stanley! How are you?'

'I'm well enough for a breakfast sandwich, Peggy!'

'It's on me, love. It's grand to have a man appreciate me food.' She glared at Dirk as she said it, and then addressed

Ewan, as if Dirk were a dog. 'Is he havin' owt, or is he just going to take a chair up?' Unruffled, Dirk smiled at her and asked for wholemeal toast.

'Toasted brown,' Ewan translated. 'And they've fetched their own teabags.' She took the Earl Grey from me and red bush from Dirk like they were dirty hankies. 'No milk!' Dirk added as she waddled away.

Stanley spent the time it took for Peggy to cook three breakfast sandwiches complaining about the state of the forge. 'It's like there's been a bastard explosion in there!' I could have pointed out that we had less room since he'd installed a coke forge that nobody wanted but I resisted. Stanley was emphasising the iniquity of mixing up the plain and the fullered shoes when Peggy arrived with three breakfast sandwiches, a slice of toasted brown bread, a mug of Earl Grey and a mug of red bush. Stanley reached up for his plate. 'I've dreamed of this, Peggy.'

'Aye,' she said. 'And I've dreamed of the days when customers were satisfied with what I had on my menu.' She slid another contemptuous glance at Dirk then looked at my cup of Earl Grey: 'I don't know how you can stomach that muck. It's like bloody eau de cologne – pardon my French.' I laughed, then tried to explain it, but faced with two blank, bacon-dripping maws, I abandoned the effort.

The breakfast sandwiches shut us up until Stanley was mopping up the last of his egg yolk with his oven-bottom muffin. 'Where are you off to this morning?'

'Mervyn's,' Dirk answered through the last of his wholemeal toast.

'I might as well come with you,' Stanley announced. I glanced at Ewan.

'Are you sure you're up to it?'

'I can sit in t'van if it gets too much.'

Dirk pointed beyond Peggy's net curtains to the silver 4×4 parked against the kerb. 'That,' he stated, 'is not a van.' Stanley laughed, knocked back the dregs of his coffee then stood. He steadied himself on the furniture and made his way to the door where the bell tinkled our exit. 'Ta-ra, love!' Peggy shouted from the counter.

I had barely lowered the Hilux's tailgate when Mervyn dashed over, reached in and swiped a hammer. Without a word he strode purposefully towards Jay and proffered it. 'Fancy a do?' he yelled. 'They have all th'equipment if you fancy a do.' Jay ignored him and Mervyn turned back. 'You'd think he was Ruby Walsh, not an also-ran in two bumpers and half a dozen novice chases!' He watched Stanley stepping carefully from the passenger seat. 'Anyway, how's life, Stan? Can you still have brews?' Before Stanley could answer Jay was returning and Mervyn was holding out a pair of horseshoe nails. 'Here you are, lad – come and have a do at this!' Jay walked on and Stanley looked at Mervyn quizzically.

'Come for a brew,' Mervyn beckoned, 'and I'll tell you t'tale.' I didn't know how Stanley would react to the knowledge that I'd been jumping round Aintree on his time, but when he emerged from the house an hour later, he'd been totally distracted by Dagmar.

'There she is in a little shortie dressing gown – a right big girl.' It was the word 'girl' that threw me at first, then I remembered that any woman under fifty was a girl to Stanley. 'I'll tell you what – her feet are firmly under t'table!'

'No,' I said. 'She's just over for her son's twenty-first. He rides a bit for Mervyn.'

Stanley folded his arms. 'She's here for t'duration, Posh Lad. You mark my words.'

STRATFORD COLLEGE OF AGRICULTURE:

FACULTY OF BLACKSMITHING AND FARRIERY

Apprenticeship Journal for the month of: May.

Comments: I have compared my experiences with those of other apprentices on block release and recognise that ours is an unusually diverse client base. On my return, a group of clients attempted to avoid paying for our services. My ATF left the yard following a diplomatic resolution and having received payment in full.

Learning Outcomes:

I recognise seedy toe and have examined exposed laminae and the periople.

I understand the implications for the administration of biotin.

I have given practical experiences a theoretical context. (Further details on college report.)

Signed: William Harker. May 31st 2016   (Apprentice)

Signed: Dirk Koetzee AWCF   May 31st '16   (Master)
(pp Stanley Lampitt DipWCF)

Chapter 33

I returned to a depleted year group. Neither Lewis nor Andy had found apprenticeships; Stewart had found one too late and dropped back a year; Richard and Ryan had packed in and Sam had converted to blacksmithing. So the remaining half-dozen of us met in the college bar and I listened to their tales of patient masters, state-of-the-art forges, brand new company vehicles, Christmas bonuses and lavish tips. I took a lungful of air and reminded myself of the laughs, the landscapes and the life experiences granted by working for Stanley.

Our tutor surveyed the single line of desks with raised eyebrows. 'When the going gets tough, eh?' and we grinned at one another; a row of survivors. For the first time in my life, I was uninterested in the classroom window. The diagrams on the whiteboard jigsawed satisfyingly with my Hathersage experiences. There it was: a heart-bar shoe to support the pedal bone, just like the one we'd used at Sylvia's. The next slide was a three-quarter bar shoe, protecting a false quarter. We'd used one at Mervyn's. Then there was a rolled toe shoe, like the one we'd used on Jennings' mare. The forging was trickier, though. As Ewan had predicted, I was the only apprentice using a coke forge at home, so the others worked the gas forges with more confidence – but Ewan's mumbled temperature mantra had stuck, and I fumbled through.

David Hodgkinson, Fellow of the Worshipful Company of Farriers, pulled at his beard. 'Stanley Lampitt,' he said as

I sat down for my assessment interview. 'Haven't we another apprentice with him?'

'Ewan Grimshaw.'

'Ah.' I said nothing whilst he turned the pages of a thick file in his lap. 'Ewan's not always been happy there, has he?' I pretended ignorance whilst Mr Hodgkinson chewed his tongue. 'You get on with Mr Lampitt, do you?' (No one could get on with Stanley.)

'Yes,' I nodded. 'Fine.'

'There've been no ...' I didn't help him, 'bullying issues?'

'No.' (Aside from being savaged by his dog, attacked by his hens and tricked into picking up white-hot shoes.) He turned over another page.

'He pays you when he should?'

'Yes.' (Unless that's you plural; when it's no.)

'No health and safety concerns?'

'None.' (Apart from the out-of-bounds fire extinguisher, forbidden goggles, forbidden ear protection and unused back braces.)

'And you feel you're receiving good tuition, do you?'

'Yes.' (From Ewan and Dirk.) He closed his file.

'Would you say you're happy there, William?' And to this question, I didn't have to lie.

'Yes. Yes, I am.' My ready answer had shocked me. I smiled and Mr Hodgkinson smiled back.

'Good. Some of our students haven't stayed the course with Stanley Lampitt.' I thought about Fetch-It and Fuckwit. He stood up.

'Well, we're happy with your progress, William. Just speed up your forge work a bit, and we'll see you later in the year.'

I thought Stanley had put some weight on when I got back home; he was certainly cheerful.

'Is that knob Hodgkinson still there?'

Ewan defended him. 'He's a Fellow of the Worshipful Company.'

'He's a knob. "You should have a fire extinguisher, Mr Lampitt." "Why are the goggles locked away, Mr Lampitt?" "Show me your first aid kit, Mr Lampitt."' I flicked Ewan a glance but he changed the subject.

'That vet's missed you.'

'Get lost, Ewan.'

'She has! Her face proper dropped when we said you were at college.'

'Same rule applies!' Stanley yelled from the van.

'Who can I snog, Stanley? Do you want to give me a list?'

'Dolloper here has no bother sticking to the rule, have you, Dolloper?'

'Piss off!' Ewan shouted, and Stanley's self-satisfied laughter tumbled into the forge.

We set off for Rodrigo's with a redundant Stanley in the passenger seat, and after a morning of shoeing polo ponies Dirk threw his toolbag in the footwell and asked where we could change the gas cylinder.

'Cribbs industrial estate,' Ewan said. 'Behind our house.'

'Is there nowhere else?'

'There is, but you'll lose your deposit.'

He still hadn't started the engine. 'How much is the deposit?'

Stanley smirked. 'You're worried about your van, aren't you?'

'It's *not a van*.'

'It's not like we're parking it up and leaving it.' Ewan laughed.

Dirk started the engine. 'We've got some bad vehicle karma round us, man.' Against his better judgement, he drove his brand new, four-wheel-drive, silver Toyota Hilux Invincible to the car park of Cribbs industrial estate.

'Here,' Stanley said as the vehicle glided to a halt, 'I'll pay for this,' but as he fumbled through his wallet he dropped his cash into the footwell.

I had been answering a text so my realisation that something was wrong occurred only when Ewan hissed at Stanley to stay down. I looked up and saw a teenager's pimply face in each front window. Ewan and I were hidden by tinted windows and Stanley was groping for his money, so the thugs must have thought that Dirk was alone.

The face at Dirk's window was long, lean and framed by a grey hoodie. The other was more menacing and had a skull and crossbones bandana tied low across the forehead. The Hoodie's muffled voice penetrated the glass: 'Open the fucking door.'

With a mighty roar Stanley smashed the door open and knocked the unsuspecting Bandana Boy to the floor. He was on top of him before the lad had gathered the wits to stand. The Hoodie ran for it, but Dirk had grabbed a rasp and was after him. Ewan grabbed another, threw me a hammer and we were off.

By the time we'd caught Dirk up he had the Hoodie by the throat and was waving a rasp over his head. I've never heard such terror as that croaking from under Dirk's grasp.

'Don't hit me!' the Hoodie was bleating. 'Please don't hit me with that!' but the sight of two more armed men about to pile in gave the Hoodie a surge of strength. He kicked, squirmed, slithered and was off. I swung a flying tackle at his ankle but it only slowed his first few steps. I would have followed but Dirk grabbed my sleeve.

'Why d'ya leave Stanley?'

'Shit!' We'd forgotten he was post-operative.

Back at the car, Stanley was still sitting on Bandana Boy. 'Ring 999!' he shouted as we approached. I obeyed, and in the time it took for Dirk to sit on Bandana Boy in Stanley's stead a police car was pulling up.

'Help me!' Bandana Boy started bawling at the policeman.

'He's hurting me!' Shouldn't we have been the ones appealing for help? I glanced at Ewan, but he was turned away. 'This is common assault!' Bandana Boy was whining. A solidly built police constable with a shaven head was calmly putting on his cap. 'I want to press charges, officer!'

The officer didn't even look in Bandana Boy's direction; instead he turned to Ewan who had dropped his rasp and was opening the door of the Hilux. 'All right there, Ewan?'

'Why shouldn't I be?' Ewan's voice was unexpectedly sullen.

'Your Lee being a good lad, is he?'

'I dunno. Ask our Lee.' This must have been the default survival mode for Cribbs Estate. I'd never seen it before.

The officer's eyes remained on Ewan. 'Oh, I will. I will indeed.'

Bandana Boy was shouting 'traitor' and 'Judas' at Ewan and I was becoming increasingly confused. The police officer took out a pair of handcuffs, and over cries of 'I've been assaulted,' and 'It's these you should be cuffing,' he calmly cuffed him. He lifted him to his feet and with Dirk's help, pushed Bandana Boy into the back of the police car, then he turned to us.

'Look, lads – if you don't put those tools away, I might start wondering who the criminal is round here.' I looked at the hammer still in my hand and lowered it to the floor. Dirk followed suit. The policeman turned and addressed Bandana Boy: 'What's your name?'

'Justin Bieber.'

He sighed and turned to Stanley. 'Perhaps you'd like to explain what happened, sir?' So Stanley set about the tale.

The officer cracked his radio to life; he gave a description of Hoodie and I added a detail: 'He'll be limping.'

The policeman flicked off his radio. 'Why's that then?' Ewan was making cut-throat gestures at me from the other side of the Hilux, but I was impressed by my vigilante blow and bowled on.

'I kicked him.' Ewan squeezed his eyes tight shut. The officer looked down at my steel toecaps and closed his notebook.

'Well, you can't help it if he twists his ankle jumping a fence, can you?'

'But he didn't,' I persisted, then I caught sight of Ewan, who'd buried his head in his hands. Realisation sprinkled me like a cold shower. 'Could I get into trouble for kicking him?'

But the policeman had given up on me. He was addressing Bandana Boy again. 'What's your name?'

'Jeremy Kyle.'

World-weary, he closed the car door and turned back to me. 'Listen,' he said, 'he caught his leg on that fence. He fell, and he twisted his ankle.' I chewed the inside of my cheek. 'Now, do you think you're ready to make a statement?' I nodded.

When all our statements were signed, the police officer slid the clipboard onto the driver's seat and said something else I wasn't expecting. 'Next time, just drive off, eh? Jeremy Kyle and his mate are just a pair of low-life chancers, but they could have had guns.' (Could they? Here? In Hathersage?)

He addressed his captive again: 'Have you decided to be sensible?' There was no answer. 'What's your name?'

'Osama Bin Laden.'

He sighed again. 'Right then, Osama! I'm charging you with offences against the Terrorism Act of 2006.'

'You can't do that!' The voice had come from Ewan. We all turned to him, but it was the policeman who spoke. '*I* don't know why he was stealing a car. Do you, Ewan? This way, young Osama here gets slammed in a cell for forty-eight hours and I start questioning him after forty-seven.'

Ewan looked at his shoes. Dirk shuffled uneasily and Stanley spoke.

'Bloody hell,' he said, 'it's hardly Dixon of Dock Green, is it?'

'Amir Asif,' Ewan said, flatly, and a volley of abuse erupted from the back of the police car. 'I'm trying to help you, you daft sod!' Ewan shouted back.

'Thank you, Ewan.' The officer smiled, but there was an edge of sarcasm in his tone.

'The other's Kabir Hussain,' Ewan went on. 'His mam and dad have the Bengal Star on Cribbs Road.'

The officer made a note, put his paperwork away, smiled and opened the driver's door, releasing another tirade of abuse from Amir Asif. He slid into the driver's seat and lowered the car window. 'Evenin' all,' he said, tapped his imaginary helmet, and drove off.

Chapter 34

Sitting on a carjacker had lifted Stanley's spirits. He'd seen a glimpse of the man he had once been and it had bolstered him. By the time the tale had done a circuit of the Fleece, Stanley had, single-handedly, disarmed three gunmen and pistol-whipped two of them. Pints he wasn't allowed to drink were lined up on the bar and before long he was talking about coming back to work.

'No! No! No!' Maria insisted in her very Latin way. 'In eight weeks is reberse procedure. Then maybe.'

'What am I supposed to do for eight weeks?'

She put her hands on her hips. 'How you bend double all day?' Stanley was silent. 'Rebersal, June; bend over, August.'

Stanley swung round. 'August!'

'If you sensible. If you careful.'

He threw himself onto a kitchen stool, and behind his petulance I noticed the shadow of a wince betraying his bravado. 'What if I just do half days? No bending. I'll just do the anvil work.'

Maria sat on the stool beside him. 'Estanley,' she said, in the tone of a kindly school teacher, 'is possible farrier work become too hard— Not now' – she was reacting to a change in his expression – 'but later.' His silence proved that this had already occurred to him. 'Is big operation.'

Despite Dirk's residence and Sandra's daily presence, the mail still fell to me, and over the next few weeks it included brochures for HGV courses. I read out the deals and prices,

228

terms and conditions and Stanley nodded vaguely though he must have been taking it in because before long he was taking instruction and our weeks had fallen into a new pattern. In the mornings Stanley joined us, and bragged about what a piece of cake driving a forty-ton articulated lorry is, and in the afternoons he headed off for more (unnecessary) instruction. Lucky's weeks were different too. Four of us wouldn't fit in the Old Van and Dirk refused to let 'the little shut' in the Hilux, so she spent her days with Maria when hospital shifts allowed it. The scars on our hands began to fade.

It must have been late May when we received a call from Flashman Freddie. His farm cum scrapyard was the gathering point for some of the thousands of travellers who every year make their way to Appleby horse fair. It would be a full week's work for all four of us, but Stanley couldn't resist it.

'We'll take both vans,' he said, 'because we'll need plenty of stock.' Dirk was mouthing *It isn't a van*, but Stanley was still talking. 'There'll be everything turning up; heavy horses, gypsy vanners, trotters, Shetlands – you name it, we'll have to shoe it!' He was gabbling like a four-year-old on his way to a birthday party. 'You've never been to Flashman Freddie's, have you, Dirk? You won't have seen the like of it. He's one on his own, is Freddie!'

'Except when he's in Strangeways,' Ewan put in. 'Then he's one in three thousand.'

'Your mates aren't so squeaky clean, Dolloper!'

'They weren't my mates.'

Dirk's eyes had widened. 'This Freddie's been to prison?'

'He's all right, is Freddie! In my job, I have to pay tax. In his job, he has to do a stretch now and then. It's how it is.'

Dirk pushed a palm through his pelt of blond bristle. I could see he was struggling with this as much as I had.

The steep road out of Fowlden is wooded on its lower slopes, and the sharp sunlight on its canopy dappled my eyelids so I felt I was blinking. White-saucer blossoms of elder splashed the dark verges as the tall trees thinned. The narrowing carriageway foamed with hawthorn blossom until the only survivors were the scraggy rowans, sloping against a remembered moorland wind. At length even they petered out and our last companions were the drystone walls, tramlining us between the waving grasses of Yorkshire's rooftop.

Flashman Freddie's stony lane was barely recognisable as the winter wilderness I had visited. A candelabra foxglove stood proud in frothy meadowsweet, so that the coloured cobs and flighty trotters tethered in groups along the approaching verges looked to be hock-deep in soapsuds. The previously deserted gravel was lined with Range Rovers, camper vans, modern caravans, traditional caravans, wagons and horse-trailers so that we struggled to park side by side.

Stanley had devised a slick system whereby he would heat and shape the shoes, Ewan and Dirk would nail them on whilst I dressed and finished feet, and collected payment.

There was a party atmosphere amongst the travellers. Many hadn't met for a year and, though it was only nine in the morning, they were sitting outside caravans drinking lager from cans. I'd clenched up a 15.2 skewbald vanner and Freddie pointed me in the direction of its owner. A bulldog of a man was bulging out of his checked shirt on the steps of a shiny silver caravan which was corrugated like those in American films. He was surrounded by a group of men, all in high spirits. I wore my most genial expression and led the well-mannered mare towards her owner. 'Here she is,' I smiled, 'all done.' I handed him the lead rope, and realised that he wasn't going to ask me the price, so I braced myself, and said it. Unlike earlier customers, he didn't baulk. He just reached into his back pocket and drew out a roll of notes. (Stanley once told me that each roll is two thousand five hundred pounds – which put several million in cash on Flashman Freddie's farm that morning.) He peeled off three twenties, I thanked him and pushed them into my jeans' pocket – but something of their grain didn't feel right. I looked up to see two dozen gypsy eyes on me in varying shades of menace and I decided not to mention it. Instead, I walked to the anvil where Stanley was tapping at a tiny Shetland driving shoe. With my back to the silver caravan, I handed him the cash. 'Feel,' I whispered. He flashed me a glance, took them between his finger and thumb and rubbed them gently.

'Cheeky bastard,' he said, lifted the little shoe from the anvil, placed it in the forge and took a step towards the silver caravan.

'Are you mad?' I hissed. He looked at me. 'That's twelve lawless travellers versus you and your colostomy bag. Because I'm not fighting.'

It was too late though. The travellers had seen our exchange and a dozen of them were already swaggering across the car park. I could feel my heart in my throat. Stanley retained his bellicose stance as they fanned around the van. They had formed a semicircle and were beginning to close in. The bull-dog was in the centre. His shoulders were back, his arms were dangling and even the tilt of his head was pugnacious. 'Is there a problem?'

'Aye,' Stanley said, as coolly as if it were a conversation at a shop counter. 'One of you clowns has tried to pay me with bastard Monopoly money.' He let his eyes travel slowly round the semicircle.

The bulldog took a step in. 'And what are you going to do about it?' He pushed him in the chest and Stanley staggered backwards. A rustle of laughter shuffled the crowd and I was backing towards the van when, like the cavalry in a Western, Dirk barged through the travellers. He grabbed the bulldog by the scruff, spun him round and slammed him against the side of the Hilux. 'Give the man legal tender!' A good foot taller, he was speaking to the crown of his victim's head.

'Or else?'

'Or else we take the shoes off your horse and stick them

up your bloody arse – ja?' A few of the travellers murmured amusement, but I couldn't see this ending well.

I was groping behind me for a rasp to sneak to Stanley, when Flashman Freddie's voice rang out: 'I'll have that, Posh Lad!' A dozen pairs of eyes locked onto me. Sick and tremulous, I handed Flashman Freddie the rasp. He held it aloft and strode to where Dirk had loosened his grip on the bulldog. I had no idea which one of them would get the rasp. My mouth was dry, my palms were wet and I waited. When he was sure he had the stage, Flashman Freddie shoved the rasp in the traveller's barrel chest and held his other hand out, palm up. Breathing heavily, the bulldog reached into his pocket and passed a roll of notes to Flashman Freddie who tossed them to Stanley. Whilst Freddie eyeballed his guest, Stanley removed the elastic band from the roll and fingered the notes.

'All dodgy,' he announced.

'Fire them,' Freddie commanded without taking his eyes off the bulldog. Stanley pushed the counterfeit money into the white-hot gas forge. The assembly gasped. The notes flared. Within seconds they were burnt and a murmur ululated the crowd. 'Expensive set of shoes, Dukey!' The bulldog was silent. 'Now take your horse, take your trailer and piss off my land.' His tone was pure menace; closer to a hiss than a voice. Dukey's friends started to disperse, but Dukey found a late flash of mettle. 'Come on, Freddie. It's not like the blacksmith's one of us!'

'DON'T,' Freddie roared, 'take the piss out of my muckers!' The rasp fell to the floor with a clatter and Freddie landed Dukey a blow on the jaw which buckled him. Dukey groaned. He nursed his face, then without another word he uncurled and headed for his caravan. 'Oi!' Freddie called. Dukey turned, his hand still on his jaw. 'I want sixty notes off you at Appleby!' He then peeled sixty pounds from his own roll of readies and handed them to Stanley.

'Thanks, Freddie, I appreciate that,' Stanley muttered.

Flashman Freddie clapped Stanley on the back. 'Ach, I don't see why you should be out of pocket just because your man there's an eejit. Do you want a cup o' tea?'

Six months earlier I'd have turned a brew down, but I sat on a straw bale, nursed a mug of Yorkshire tea in shaking hands and laughed as our fear was rewoven as a tale to be told in the Fleece.

Chapter 35

It was the morning of Stanley's HGV test and he was plotting his future. 'I can see it now: *S.Lampitt: Horse Transporter.*' Stanley's hand wiped the air in the arc of his imagined sign.

'*Get thy 'oss shifted 'ere,*' Ewan added, mimicking his action.

Stanley elbowed him in the side and grinned. 'I like your thinking, Dolloper! We could have all t'vehicles painted the same. Corporate, they call it! You could run t'farriery, and I could run t'transport!' There was such excitement in Stanley's voice, that even though Ewan was carrying a full box of horse-shoes, he stopped.

'Seriously, Stanley?'

'Aye. If you pass this summer!'

'If *you* pass this morning,' Ewan countered.

'It's in the bastard bag!' Stanley shouted, tossing his car keys in the air. He caught them in a swipe and headed for his Porsche.

The mention of exams put Ewan in a dither. Even though he'd now passed the one he'd failed a year ago, he still felt disadvantaged by Stanley's coke forge. 'I'll have a word with Moneybags Morrison,' Stanley offered. 'He has a big gas forge.'

Dirk spent our journeys randomly barking colours at Ewan. 'Yellow!'

'Twenty thousand and ten.'

'White!'

'Twenty-one thousand and ninety.'

'Red!'

'Which red?'

'What do you mean, which red?'

We arrived at Mervyn's to find Ruudi sweeping the yard. 'Jockey school soon!' He grinned. I congratulated him and Dirk reversed his grilling of Ewan.

'Twelve hundred!'

'Blood red.'

'Fourteen hundred.'

'Cherry red.'

'You'll walk it, man!'

Just then, Mervyn sauntered from the house followed by Ruudi's mother and the pig. Dagmar teetered towards us on scarlet stilettos, her thighs in their tight jeans threatening to froth uncontrollably into the daylight. Her bright red sequinned shirt plunged to a plump cleavage and her doughy features looked like a squeeze would remould them. I was still trying to decide where best to look when Mervyn introduced me: 'Have you met Ruudi's mother? Dagmar, this is Will.'

I held out my hand. 'Hello, Dagmar. I saw you at Ruudi's twenty-first, but we've not been introduced.'

Before I'd finished speaking she had clutched me to the pillows of her flesh. 'You are Will! Thank you! Thank you, Will! You make hippy!' Then she burst into Estonian.

'You – are – gift – from – God,' Ruudi translated, deadpan. 'You – are – sent – from – angels – to – solve – problems – of – poor – woman.' I tried to explain over the ebb and flow of her Estonian tide that Ruudi's meeting with me had been luck, but she squeezed me once more into her doughiness. Perhaps Ruudi's translation hadn't been up to it. He went on, unmoved: 'You – have – brought – career – of – dreams – to – boy, – and – man – of – dreams – to – mother …'

I waved my hands clear of his mother and told Ruudi that it was a chain of events, like everything else in life, but Dagmar's gushing gratitude didn't abate. She pressed herself into my chest again, displaying an inch of grey parting in her straw-like hair.

Mervyn tried to defend me. 'You're embarrassing the lad, Dagmar!' Dirk and Ewan were visibly amused as a tentacle Mervyn had already removed suckered onto me again. 'Come on, love. You've the bathroom floor to finish yet.' It seemed an age before Mervyn was holding both Dagmar's wrists aloft and facing her shoulders in the direction of the farmhouse. He finally sent her on her way with a playful spank to her rear. She giggled, threw me a baleful look and I remembered Stanley's prophecy with a smirk.

'How do you do it?' Ewan asked, shaking his head.

'What?'

'Look at you; you're five foot five on tiptoe with muscles like cockles – and women are all over you!'

'Not Pippa Jennings,' I remarked, but Dirk was shaking his head.

'It must take every gram of her will power! Now go and get the fronts off that chestnut, will you?'

'It won't take him so bloody long,' Mervyn cut in. 'Its feet are in bits.' Sure enough, the brittle horn had crumbled and was no longer holding the nails. 'I never had any bother with their feet when Stanley was shoeing them.' Dirk continued silently removing a hind shoe. 'I don't know what you got taught in your South African farriers' school, but it has a brittle hoof, has the thoroughbred.'

'Is that right?' I could hear the irony in Dirk's voice.

'Did you learn on bloody zebras or summat?' Dirk tossed a used shoe across the yard so it hit the metal toolbox with a clatter. 'It stands to reason; banging all them nails in is going to smash their feet up.' (Stanley would have smashed Mervyn up by now.) 'Stanley knows how to shoe a racehorse, I'll grant him that.'

Dirk was a South African; he was impassive from his crocodile tooth pendant to the strips of biltong in his glove compartment. 'Dark orange!' he shot at Ewan.

'Sixteen hundred and fifty.'

Dirk paused. 'Are you certain their dials are in Fahrenheit?'

Ewan groaned. 'I need a pint.'

We were ready for our promised afternoon of celebration. At five past twelve we heard Stanley's Porsche pull into the drive. Ewan downed his tools, Dirk put on his jacket, and I started tidying the workbench. It would be drinks all round in the Fleece now that Stanley had his HGV licence – but Stanley didn't appear. Instead, the door of Bling Manor slammed shut. We looked at one another.

'He must need the bathroom,' Dirk said. Five minutes ticked to ten, and Dirk decided to check on him.

'He can't have failed,' I reassured Ewan – and myself.

'He's failed,' Ewan stated, opening up his Tupperware dish. 'An abdominal haemorrhage wouldn't have stopped him from gloating.'

Dirk was gone a long time. I was washing our mugs out in the sink when he walked back into the forge with a hangdog Stanley behind him. He managed a subtle finger on lips gesture before speaking with theatrical kindness. 'Stanley's morning's not gone quite according to plan ...'

'Oh no!' Ewan exclaimed, like an am-dram actor. 'And you were so confident.' Stanley's eyes narrowed to murderous slits.

'I told him, pass or fail, a beer's the answer, so we're off to the Fleece anyway. You coming?' I started to say that we'd eaten, but Ewan was on his feet.

'We're coming.' He wasn't going to miss this one for all the rhubarb in Rothwell.

Fifteen silent, shifting minutes later with pies and pints in front of us, Ewan dared to ask what we were all dying to know. He asked it casually, with a forkful of meat and potato pie on its way to his mouth. 'So, how come you failed then, Stanley?'

Stanley halted his fork on its mouthward journey. 'Because

the instructor was a berk,' he said, then stuffed the lump of pie in.

'How do you mean?' Ewan persisted, courageously.

I let my pie command all my attention as I waited for Stanley's answer.

Stanley put down his fork. 'We're cruising along the top road over Scorthwaite, right – not a vehicle in sight – and he says to me: "Mr Lampitt," he says, "in a few seconds I'll slam my clipboard on the dash, and when I do, you are to react as if a child has just run out in front of your vehicle." So I keeps bowling on, and he slams his clipboard on the dash, and I'm on them brakes like a tramp on chips! That rig's at a standstill in a bastard nanosecond; no snaking, no juddering, t'rig stops dead. I was that bastard fast, his seatbelt locked. Then – as a joke – I lower my window and stick my head out and I shout at the kid.'

'You shout at a kid that isn't there?' Ewan asks.

'Aye, I thought it'd be funny!'

'What did you say?'

'I said: "Oi, you little twerp! Do you want to get yourself killed? Look where you're bastard going in future. Now piss off home and get your mam to buy you some bastard glasses!" I turned back to him, smiling like, because I thought it were funny – but he looked like he'd been suckin' a wasp!'

Ewan was sucking his teeth.

'I mean you'd think he could have had a laugh, wouldn't you?'

Ewan's head was almost shaking.

'Everything had been bob on; coupling, parking, reversing, emergency stop – but he turns to me and he says,"Mr Lampitt, I'm afraid I am going to have to fail you."' Dirk and I made appeasing gestures of disbelief and outrage. 'Two words, he says. Two bastard words: "Undue aggression."'

Ewan stretched out his legs. 'The thing is, Stanley, if a child did run out in front of you, that's exactly what you'd do.'

Stanley sat back. 'Course I would! Stupid little bastard!'

'Well then?'

'"Well then"! What do you mean, "Well then"?'

'I mean, he had a point.'

Stanley reached out and snatched the beer mat Ewan had been playing with. 'Are you trying to say he should have failed me?'

Ewan looked up; his finger and thumb still poised as if the beer mat were between them. 'No, I'm saying that what you did could be seen as aggressive.'

'Aggressive?'

I took a slug of my pint to disguise my grin but my teeth hit the glass in a giveaway clatter.

'I'm saying that to somebody who doesn't know you ...'

Stanley suddenly stood, knocking his chair backwards. 'Are you saying I'm aggressive?'

Dirk touched Stanley's arm. 'I think he's just saying—'

Stanley shook Dirk off, balled his fist, and leaned across the table to Ewan. 'I hope you're not saying I'm aggressive, you little dolloper, because I swear, lad, that ...'

Ewan looked up at Stanley's reddened face. 'You'll what? Hit me?'

There were only two others in the Fleece, but both of them were staring at our table. Stanley let his arm drop and straightened. He flung the beer mat back on the table, turned and walked out.

It was Bob Entwistle who eventually broke the silence. 'I'll have that pie, if he's not coming back.'

STRATFORD COLLEGE OF AGRICULTURE:

FACULTY OF BLACKSMITHING AND FARRIERY

Apprenticeship Journal for the month of: June.

Comments: I am currently finding the lack of a large gas forge limiting. (Waiting for the coke forge to heat then continually feeding it slows my work rate.) However, my revision has been helped in other ways.

Learning Outcomes:

Improved precision in forging technique (as advised by Mr D. Hodgkinson FWCF).

Increased confidence in gauging temperature based on the colour of metal.

Signed: William Harker. June 30th 2016   (Apprentice)

Signed: Dirk Koetzee AWCF June 30th '16   (Master)

(pp Stanley Lampitt DipWCF)

Chapter 36

'Listen here,' Stanley said as he stood on the kerb with his overnight bag in his hand. 'No arguin'; no settin' fire to my hens; no lumberjackin'; and no crashin' me bastard van.' He turned to Dirk. 'And ring t'council to see how much they'll charge to shift that wasps' nest.' Dirk nodded. The residents of the nest which had formed in the corner of the forge had been annoying us for two weeks now. Maria opened the car door but before stepping in, Stanley turned to Ewan and grasped his shoulder in a rare show of affection. 'Do us proud this week, lad. You're a good farrier, and you work hard.' Then he stepped in the car, and wafted away our good wishes as Maria started the engine.

Ewan seemed to have taken root. 'Did that just happen?'

'Get in the van,' Dirk advised. Ewan threw his bag in the back, followed me into the van then called for Lucky who took up her favoured position with her front paws on the dashboard and her hind legs on his knees.

Two sessions on Moneybags Morrison's vast gas forge had built Ewan's confidence. Moneybags had been a patient teacher and Ewan was working lengths of steel into horseshoes like modern man – but he didn't so much as hum on our drive to the station.

'This time tomorrow I'll be halfway through my first exam,' he said as the van trundled towards the forecourt cobbles.

'You'll walk it,' Dirk said, but Ewan still climbed out looking like a man condemned. I released my grip on Lucky's jaw, wished him well and watched silently until he disappeared under the grey stone arch. Dirk crunched into first gear and the Old Van rattled across the cobbles. It was going to be odd, just me and Dirk.

We had almost crested the rise of the moor when the ping of Facebook Messenger pierced the growl of the Old Van's engine. Blue sky filled the window and a spray of goldfinches sparked from an elder like an unexpected firework. Pippa's face bounced onto my screen gleaming like a Christmas bauble. I tapped it.

Precipitant running in the 2.20 at Ripon.
Spare ticket if you want it.

Even the drystone walls were glistening in the sunshine. 'We've nothing booked in this afternoon, have we?'

'Forge work,' Dirk answered.

'We'll fry!'

'It's not bloody Africa, man!' Then a sigh that could have heaved from a blue whale's blowhole shook his whole frame. I turned to him, surprised. He banged the steering wheel.

'I gotta get home, man.' His emphasis shook Pippa's message out of my head.

'Before Stanley's better?'

'Ewan'll be qualified!' I gazed through the passenger window as the prospect of Ewan as my boss trickled through my thoughts. I felt the van slow down and turned back to see we were pulling into a lay-by.

'What're you doing?'

'Playing at Africa!' he said, ratcheting on the handbrake. Before I could quiz him he jumped from the van and whipped his shirt over his head. By the time my feet were on gravel Dirk was holding his face to the sunshine as if in pagan prayer. 'Aw, man. I miss the heat!' I reached into the glove compartment for the sun block and Dirk started climbing onto the roof. 'The African sun would fry you to this metal!' It felt hot enough to me as I clambered up after him. Dirk stretched out flat on the roof. I sat cross-legged beside him and squinted towards the burnished gold of the far-off moor. Meanwhile, Dirk lost himself in the Drakensberg Mountains. 'Their peaks are like broken teeth, man. There's miles and miles of them, and forests – and rivers and sky! You never see a town, man! I'm going back, for sure, when I get home. There's blesbok and zebra, and eland and cheetahs and leopards.' He raised an arm to shield his eyes from our substandard sunshine. 'See that,' he said, pointing to a buzzard whose creamy underside was bright against the pale summer sky. 'That would be a vulture checking us out.' I watched it wheel a moment.

'When do you think you'll go?'

'Maria's driving the Hilux to Southampton this weekend.' My eyes flicked to him.

'So soon?'

'I have to.' I heard the catch in his voice and left him to squint at the buzzard that was drifting back across the blue.

'You know, we could always do the forge work when the sun's not shining.'

He sat up and stretched. 'You're right.'

'And that horse I've been working on is running at Ripon this afternoon ...' Dirk threw back his head and laughed.

'You crafty snake!' he said. It was good to hear him laugh again.

I arrived at Ripon racecourse just as the 1.50 was finishing, so by the time I'd collected my Owners and Trainers Pass the runners for the 2.20 were amassing in the paddock. The clement weather had made dressing for the occasion uncomfortable but Pippa looked as stunning as ever. She was wearing a pink strappy dress and her honey hair was tumbling over her shoulder. 'Glad you could make it,' she said as she saw me approach.

'I just hope she starts!' I answered, hoping the whole paddock had heard her greet me. I waved at Jay on the other side
of the paddock in the hope that he'd notice my company just
as a floppy-haired young man in a yellow waistcoat arrived at
Pippa's side. She exclaimed in delight and kissed him on the
cheek. My heart seemed to spiral downwards in my chest.

'Toby,' she said, 'this is Will who's been working with
Precipitant.'

'Hi, Will.' He had big teeth.

'Toby's just back from Belgium,' she said. 'He's on the
under twenty-fives UK dressage team.' I managed a weak smile
but my sinking spirits tumbled further as he encircled her with
his arm. I was relieved when Precipitant entered the paddock
and I could feign unconcerned small talk.

'She looks well.'

Toby nodded. 'I'd rather we'd a different jockey on her, but
hey-ho.'

I might have argued Zach's case, but Richard Jennings was
approaching.

'Glad you could make it, Will.'

'Me too. Do you think she has a chance?'

'If she starts!' I laughed at his statement of the obvious,
but for all my work with Precipitant, her starting was far from
certain. The atmosphere of the racecourse, the unfamiliar
surroundings, or the attitude of her handlers could all reignite
her fears.

Jennings had secured permission for Precipitant to enter the
stalls last, and when the runners left the paddock we set off for
the start. By the time we arrived the other runners were shuffling in the starting stalls and a stall handler was taking hold of
our filly's bridle. My heart seemed to be beating in my throat.
Precipitant walked forward. 'Go on, go on,' I whispered – then
her head shot up. The stall handler tugged on the reins and she
planted. Jennings groaned.

'The blindfold,' he muttered, as if the handlers could hear

him. 'Use the blindfold.' Precipitant's ears were pricked; her tail was up. She was taking in her surroundings.

'Just give her a minute, Zach,' I prayed. It was as if he could hear me. I saw him lean down and speak one of the handlers. The handler released the reins. They let her take in her surroundings, then Zach urged another stride. Precipitant took a step. The handler took the reins. She dropped her head and followed him. Five strides and she was in the stall; the gates closed; the handler ducked out; they were under starter's orders; they were off!

Precipitant was the first to show. Jennings gave my shoulder a squeeze, but within six strides his horse had been overtaken, first by a butty little colt, and then by the favourite. They didn't get far ahead though. By the time they were galloping past us, throwing up clods of earth, Precipitant was battling like a bulldog. Half a furlong later and she'd overtaken the favourite, putting her in second place. Pippa started jumping and clapping behind me and Richard Jennings raised his binoculars. On she fought, holding off all contenders. She entered the final furlong with the favourite on her right and a grey on her left. The crowd was roaring, but Precipitant was focused, intent; ears pricked, neck stretched. She could get a place here! On the big screen I saw Zach ask her to quicken – but nothing happened. The favourite was gaining ground now. It drew level. Second place was good, I told myself ... But here was Precipitant, digging in again! That horse wasn't passing her! She pounded and thundered, stretched her neck and flashed past the winning post! Behind me Pippa's scream nearly pierced my eardrums. Richard Jennings' face confirmed what I thought I'd seen. A head! She'd won by a head!

The roar behind me was woven of triumph, surprise, anger, despair and wonder. The tannoy crackled out its confirmation of what we'd hardly dared to believe: *'First: Precipitant; Second: Look A Tuckle; Third: Santa's Uncle.'* Precipitant had never run a race before, and here she was, cantering down to the winner's enclosure. I was bursting with pride for her – and for myself. Jennings was hugging his daughter, his daughter was hugging floppy-haired Toby, and floppy-haired Toby was punching the air. I followed the group as they ran, stumbling and hugging to the railed Astroturf patch reserved for the winner.

Precipitant loped in to the winner's enclosure to polite applause. Zach dismounted and unbuckled her saddle. Toby asked him for a photograph before he weighed in, and it was then I realised that Toby owned Precipitant. He gestured for Pippa to join him, and the beautiful couple and the beautiful racehorse posed for the press photographer. I picked up a bucket and offered water to the horse, but Jennings took it from me and began sponging the filly down whilst answering questions from the racing press. I shook out Precipitant's sweat rug but Pippa swept it from my hands as she received congratulations from a racecourse official.

The winner's enclosure is set up for owners and horses to bask in the glory; for jockeys and trainers to take questions and congratulations; for the horse to be attended to; for the press to take photographs and for the trophy to be awarded. There is no protocol for the bloke who taught the horse to use the starting stalls – but I knew who'd share my triumph. I slipped under the rails, slid my phone from my pocket and swiped her name. I waited. I looked at the screen. I waited some more: *'Lizzie Harker is unable ...'* I sighed and slipped it back in my pocket. Precipitant had her nose in a bucket, so I decided on a drink for myself.

With a slippery pint glass in my hand and the sunshine warming my now tie-less neck, I wondered if Ewan had arrived at college yet.

'... And it's only gone and won!' I shouted when he'd described the torture of a hot train journey. 'At a hundred to one!' He diverted my enthusiasm as successfully as a brick in a culvert.

'And you're in the beer garden with a pint you've bought yourself?'

'They're still in the winner's enclosure.'

'They should be running round it with you on their shoulders!' The line seethed. 'I don't know why you arse yourself with that lot.'

'What lot?'

'Jennings' lot! They're not like us.' Did he just say 'us'? 'Will? Are you still there?'

'Yeah. Sorry.'

'What's up?'

'Nothing.' But he must have heard the smile in my voice.

'How many have you had?'

Chapter 37

I arrived at work at seven o'clock, to find Maria on the drive in her dressing gown, her hair like a comedy wig. The forge's up-and-over door was up, coal was spread across the tarmac, and Dirk was slumped against the wall like a half-deflated lilo. I stepped out of the car.

'Have you called the police?' Dirk wiped a hand across his face then nodded. I walked into the forge. There were no tools on the walls; there were no boxes for us to sit on. Even the kettle had gone.

My mind became a pinball machine. How would we tell Stanley? Why hadn't Dirk heard the intruder? Why hadn't Lucky barked? As one thought demanded attention, another ricocheted across and clamoured for acknowledgement. We couldn't even work! The police wouldn't be interested. Was Stanley insured? Who'd want to steal a load of horseshoes? Then all the bulbs lit up at once: Ewan would know what to do.

When the ring tone stopped there was a clatter then a muffled crackling. 'Whaddya wan'?'

'Ewan?'

'S'middle of the fuckin' night.'

'I thought you had an exam this morning.'

There was a bang, 'Shit!' and a clatter. 'What time is it?'

'Ten past seven.' A long silence followed. 'Ewan?'

'You just scared the shit out of me! I've whacked my head.'

His voice had lost its slur. 'What the fuck do you want at this time?'

'The forge has been broken in to.'

'I'm in fucking Warwickshire!'

'I thought you'd know what to do.' His sigh crackled the line. He was never good in the morning. 'They've taken everything.'

'Tools?'

'Tools, stock, coal, logs. Even the kettle.'

I heard bedsprings creak. 'It'll be some smackhead off Cribbs.' There was a scraping followed by the sound of running water. 'Have they taken the used horseshoes?'

'Every last one.'

'Tell Flashman Freddie.'

'Flashman Freddie?' The rushing water was obscuring his voice.

'They'll try to sell them on as scrap.' Of course! I mouthed *Scrap metal* to Dirk whose eyes brightened with realisation. He snatched the phone from me. 'You are a bloody genius, Ewan!' He blew a noisy kiss into the mouthpiece, and I grabbed it back.

'Good luck this morning, mate.'

'Well, I'll be wide awake for it now, won't I?' It sounded as if there was a toothbrush in his mouth.

Flashman Freddie listened closely. 'So, when I get him, do I have a chat with him?' I was uncomfortable with the notion of Freddie's chat, but the phone was suddenly out of my hands.

'I'm telling you, man, that lowlife scumbag would already be full of buckshot back home!'

'Right y'are. I'll have a chat with him then.'

We cancelled our appointments, repaired the lock and attempted to clean the forlorn forge. Throughout our silent sweeping, the family of resident wasps hovered and darted. Every now and then Lucky snapped at one. Even the cans of

Coke Maria brought out to us were robbed of their pleasure. At eleven o'clock I leant on my broom. 'What now?'

Dirk turned over his palms. 'I was going to suggest visiting Stanley, but Maria thinks we should give it a day or two.' I was happy to defer the explosion. 'Why don't we go for a pint in the Fleece?' It was an appealing idea.

The Fleece was largely empty. Bob Entwistle was nursing a half-pint glass by the window and three others in their forties were sitting under the dartboard. They looked like construction workers. Dirk ordered two pints of lager and the landlord nodded towards Bob. 'He bought that bloody half at five past eleven.' Dirk glanced across at him and Bob raised the dregs of his drink.

'And a half for your friend at the window,' Dirk added.

'Don't be bloody encouraging him,' the landlord grumbled.

'Very decent of you,' came the answer from across the room.

The landlord put a pint glass under the pump and drew the handle towards him. 'Stanley not with you?' I shook my head. 'He'll be gutted. Birdie's in.'

At the sound of his name one of the trio under the dartboard swung his head. I clocked his narrow eyes, pockmarked skin, shiny skull and ape-like crouch, but Birdie was on his feet, knocking back the remains of his beer before the landlord had pulled our second pint. Before we'd chosen a table he'd plonked his empty glass down and made for the Gents.

Dirk carried a half pint of beer to Bob. 'Thank you. You're a gentleman and a scholar.' He smiled, showing his tobacco-stained teeth. Dirk smiled back and made to walk away, but the old man spoke again. 'Slippery as a toad,' he said. 'His father were t'same. He used to come in here and pat his chest all over, reckoning on he'd forgotten his wallet.' Bob put a lip to the froth on his beer and came away with a foamy moustache. He raised his voice again. 'He wants to learn how to pull a decent pint, he does. I only come in 'cause it's local.' The landlord flapped a towel at him. Bob swiped a tweed sleeve across his mouth. Realising that Dirk had decided to stay there, I crossed the pub too and Bob returned to his conspiratorial tone. 'He has cash on him, Birdie. He pulled a proper wad out at t'bar.'

'Ja?' Dirk raised his eyebrows. 'I'll be having a word when he comes back.'

'You'll be lucky! Did you not see him down his pint?'

Dirk glanced over his shoulder. 'He can't stay in the Gents all afternoon.' Birdie's friends were stuffing their phones and keys into their pockets now.

'He'll be out the Gents' window. He's done it before.'

Dirk looked at me. Without a word I strolled to the Gents. I wanted to run, but one of Birdie's mates was the size of a Smeg fridge. The heavy brown door creaked, and whilst I was still wondering if I could muster a pee I didn't need, I found myself standing in an empty room. The breeze was floating a net curtain in and over the sink and the window beyond it was wide, wide open. I dragged the curtain aside. There were two bootprints in the soil under the window. To be absolutely certain I was alone, I pushed on the cubicle door. It swung open.

When I returned to Bob's table, Birdie's friends were at the bar. 'He can't have got far,' I whispered. 'It must have taken him two minutes to struggle through that window.'

Bob's eyes were bright. 'He lives on Tremellen Street.'

Dirk put down his lager. 'Show me where, and your next one's a whisky.' Bob necked his half pint with impressive speed, his Adam's apple glugging rhythmically for a full ten seconds, then he slammed his empty glass on the table. 'Lead on, Macduff!' Birdie's drinking friends said nothing as they watched us walk out on two barely started pints.

'Left at the newsagent's, then right at the corner shop, then Tremellen Street's third on your left,' Bob said. Dirk thanked him and picked up a jog.

'I'll follow on,' Bob said when he saw me dither.

Dirk's jog was my sprint, so I was already breathless when we made a right at the corner shop – but there, strolling happily in the distance, was the relaxed shape of Birdie. Dirk's jog became a lope. Perhaps it was the game-stalking African in him, but Dirk was almost on Birdie when he finally heard footsteps and looked over his shoulder. Birdie took two lurching steps, but Dirk had grabbed his shirt.

By the time I'd caught them, Birdie was slammed against the stone wall of a derelict terraced house. 'Keep your nose out, you foreign bastard,' he was saying. 'It's got nowt to do with you.' It would have sounded tougher if his voice hadn't been strangulated in Dirk's grip.

'Stanley Lampitt is a sick man!' It sounded like 'suck min' but Birdie appeared to understand him.

'So?' His whole body wobbled like a ragged rabbit in Dirk's grip.

'So, I want to give him something to smile about.'

'Tell him Bradford City's being promoted.' He wasn't as concerned as I would have been in the grip of a six-foot-six gorilla.

'You've owed it long enough, Birdie.' This time, Dirk lifted him two inches off the ground.

'I've been away!'

'You've been avoiding us, man!' Birdie was dangling now and gasping a bit as his collar tightened.

The humming of an engine turned my head. A mobility scooter was weaving between the potholes. 'What do you want, you nosy old fucker?' Birdie choked from under Dirk's fist.

'Justice!' Bob announced, pulling his scooter to the side of the road and dismounting.

'Piss off, you silly old sod.'

'Have I to go through his pockets?' Bob asked.

'I've no cash!'

'Yiss you have!' Bob countered, rubbing his hands.

Dirk lifted Birdie another six inches so that his legs were dangling up the wall and Bob went straight for Birdie's back pocket. He pulled out a bulging roll of notes. 'What's he owe you, Derek?'

'Two hundred,' Dirk answered. Birdie was squirming and kicking as Bob counted off the notes.

' ... one hundred and eighty, two hundred.'

'Oi! I owe that to somebody else!'

'Two hundred and ten!' Bob grinned.

'What!'

'Interest,' he said, handing the money to me. (I really didn't want it.) 'And compensation for the trouble Derek here has had to go to.' Only when it was safely in my hand did Dirk drop Birdie.

The impact of landing crumpled him at the knees. 'You're a bell-end,' Birdie grumbled.

'You're lucky we didn't take more interest,' Dirk said as Birdie snatched back his remaining cash, dusted down his clothing and grumbled about Hathersage's lawlessness.

'It used to be nice round here. You used to be able to walk the bloody streets without fearing for your life.'

STRATFORD COLLEGE OF AGRICULTURE:

FACULTY OF BLACKSMITHING AND FARRIERY

Apprenticeship Journal for the month of: July.

Comments: I have enjoyed our collaboration with Millie Routledge MRCVS. I realise that a good relationship with the vet often leads to a positive outcome and look forward to developing it further.

I will enter my second year as Mr Lampitt's sole apprentice, Ewan Grimshaw having now qualified.

Learning Outcomes:

I understand the problem of shoeing a short back and low heels conformation.

I can read and interpret a Wetherby's passport.

I can recognise a foot I have worked on previously.

Signed: William Harker. July 31st 2016   (Apprentice)

Signed: Dirk Koetzee AWCF July 31st '16   (Master)

(pp Stanley Lampitt DipWCF)

Chapter 38

Before I could climb out of my car, Bling Manor's bedroom window had flown open and Maria was hanging out with a toothbrush in her hand and her hair still wild from nightmares. She was gesticulating in fury. 'He pull up Stanley's flowers!'

Dirk looked up from where he was edging the lawn. 'They're bloody weeds, woman!'

'You no' let him touch flowers!' A pile of broad-leaved grasses was heaped on the lawn. I stepped over the herbaceous border and studied one. Last autumn they'd borne bell-shaped orange flowers which had nodded on either side of the path.

Dirk sliced viciously at the soil. 'They grow on the side of the road back home!'

I knew better than to refer to Stanley's likely reaction. Instead I crouched in the flower beds reinstating what plants I could and wondering if Dirk's mother cultivated buttercups. Dirk had told me to stay at home, but it had felt like betrayal. Wordlessly, I pulled up docks, nettles and dandelions.

'They must have backed in, next to the Old Van,' Dirk said, wafting his hand at a wasp. 'There must have been more than one of them.' Not for the first time, I wondered how Dirk had slept through it. He scissored the shears then crossed to the privet hedge and lopped at a straggly branch. 'You go when you've finished weeding, Will.' I was shaking my head when a white transit van began backing into the drive. I could see from the change in Dirk's expression that he wasn't expecting company. Only the Porsche was worth coming back for. The handbrake creaked on. My tongue was thickening. The van door swung open and Flashman Freddie jumped from the cab.

'How's it goin' there, lads?' My relief was like the dropping of a toolbag. He winked, flung open the back doors of the van and gestured to its contents. 'I think you'll find it's all in there.' We crossed the lawn at a sprint.

Our tools and trappings were crammed in the cuboid space. There was the anvil, and behind it Stanley's stock of boxed horseshoes. Each familiar scratch, dent and rust spot declared them to be our friends. I could see a bag of coal, some lengths of steel, the kettle in a bucket and the bin of used horseshoes topped with a pair of nippers. It was unbelievable; incongruous; like bumping into a schoolfriend on a beach in Antigua. 'All present and correct, I think.'

I looked at Freddie with new respect. 'How the heck …?'

He batted my question away like it was a fly. 'Agh! Some little lowlife rolled up trying to sell a ton of used horseshoes – so I had a little chat with him – like I said.'

'Did you call the police?'

Freddie shifted his weight and turned to Dirk. 'This little lot was in a lock-up on Cribbs Estate.'

'What did he look like, this lowlife?'

Freddie laughed. 'Well, let's just say that before our chat he had a brown face and white underpants, and after our chat, the colours were reversed.'

'Is that all you can remember?' Dirk pressed him.

Flashman Freddie rubbed his chin. 'He had on a pirate's bandana.'

'Skull and crossbones?'

'That's the one!'

Flashman Freddie refused a cup of coffee ('Not with all these feckin' wasps!'), told us he was glad to have been of assistance, shook our hands, and waved his good wishes, like Batman leaving Gotham City.

Over the next half-hour we put every nail and coke cob in its rightful place. It gave me unexpected pleasure to see the fire extinguisher back where it belonged. We were still smiling when we walked into the men's surgical ward at Leeds General that same afternoon.

'What are you two to grinning at? Have you burnt my bastard house down?' I laughed at him. 'Is my dog still alive?'

'She's fine.'

'Hens?'

'Yes!'

'Van?'

'Yes! Everything's fine!'

He lowered his eyebrows and nodded at the magazine in Dirk's hand. 'Why are you softening me up with a bastard book then?'

'It's *Practical Performance Car*. It has a load of Porsches in it.'

'We should have fetched him grapes,' I said, as I perched on the edge of the bed.

'Why do I need grapes? I shit myself as soon as I clap eyes on you two grinning your way up the ward.' He took the magazine. 'Come on. There's summat up if you've rocked up with a present.'

Dirk sat on a plastic chair. 'We've got good news, boss.'

'Has my tree grown back?'

'No – but we got your money from Birdie!'

'Birdie!' Stanley tried to sit forward, but he winced in pain. 'How d'you manage that?'

Dirk glowed. 'We roughed him up a bit.'

'Get away! Posh Lad couldn't rough the skin off a rice pudding!'

'Not Posh Lad; me and the old guy in the Fleece.'

'Bob Entwistle?'

'Ja.'

Stanley shook his head in wonder. 'Game old bastard! All of it?'

261

'Every penny, plus ten pounds interest.'

'Well, well, well. It looks like there's less damage all round when Dolloper's away.' I was stung by the unfairness.

'We wouldn't have got your stuff back if it wasn't for Ewan!' Dirk froze.

'Stuff?' Stanley's word was like an icicle. 'What stuff?'

Dirk tried to open a channel in the fast-forming glacier: 'There was a bit of a break-in at the forge, Stan, but—'

'A *bit* of a break-in ...?'

'Ja, but there's no need—'

'When?'

'Monday night.'

'Where the fuck were you?'

'In bed ...' Stanley bashed his *Practical Performance Car* on the counterpane. 'We've got it all back, though, Stanley! Every last cob of coke, man.'

'How?'

'Flashman Freddie!' It calmed him for a second.

'How've you been working, then?' I studied a loose thread on the counterpane.

'We'll catch up,' Dirk said.

Stanley threw himself back on his pillows. 'What are you doing to my bastard business? First you don't turn up because you've no van, then you don't turn up cos you've no forge and now you don't turn up because you've no shoes, no nails and no bastard anvil!' He formed *Practical Performance Car* into a tube and started wringing it in his hands. 'Did you ring the council?'

'Ja.' Dirk's voice went quiet: 'They want a hundred and seventy-five dollar to get rid of that nest.'

'A hundred and seventy-five!' The silence swept in again. I could feel it roiling and seething round me. 'How can I pay that when you've not been fetching cash in?'

Dirk waited a few seconds before he spoke. 'With respect, Stan; we can't work with wasps in the forge.'

Stanley sat up. 'When can you work, eh? When can you

work? You've either no tools, or no van, or else no bastard idea!' Dirk bristled. 'In fact, why the fuck are you even here?'

'We were trying to cheer you up!'

'Piss off and earn me some brass if you want to cheer me up!'

Dirk stood and spread his hands. 'Money never made anybody happy, Stan.'

'Neither did bastard poverty – and I've given that a try!'

The following morning we made our first attempt to catch up on work, so when Mervyn announced that a three-year-old needed its first set of shoes, Dirk and I were less than delighted. It can take an entire morning to shoe a young racehorse for the first time. If it becomes stressed or upset, it'll cost more time – and possibly a kneecap – later on. We didn't have a morning, so we tried to persuade Mervyn to wait until Ewan was back, but he wouldn't have it. 'You'll have it done in an hour,' he argued.

Dirk shook his head.

'Honest! You wouldn't think it were a three-year-old! It's like that horse has been here before. In't that right, Jay?' Jay was crossing the yard with a saddle over his arm. He seemed to have forgiven me for Aintree and we were rubbing along again.

'Dinkum? Dream horse! Nothing fazes it.' I was sceptical.

'Suit yourself,' Mervyn said, pulling gently on Pig's ear. 'But if Stanley were here, he'd have it shod by ten o'clock.'

Dirk's pride had been pricked. I gave him a despairing glance but he was already unloading the van. Minutes later Jay was leading a sixteen-hand bay gelding into the shoeing bay and Mervyn had answered Dagmar's call to come back and finish his breakfast.

I approached the horse's head, chatting softly to it all the time as reassurance, then I ran my hand down its neck and shoulder and gently lifted a front foot. It didn't react – a good sign.

During my pre-farriery course at Warwick, there had been a tutor whose partypiece had been to name a horse from a picture of its foot. To me it was a trick worthy of Derren Brown. Nearly two years on, I was recognising it as an attainable skill.

'What do you reckon?' Dirk was musing, as he rummaged through the stock. 'A five or a five and a half?' I was still staring at the horse's foot when Dirk repeated his question. 'Will! A five, or a five and a half?'

'Dirk ...' I was still looking at the foot. 'I think this is Thwack It.'

He met my eyes, walked over, bent down and took the foot from me. He examined it, lifted its other front foot, examined that and placed it on the cobbles. 'Jay!' he bellowed. Jay ambled in carrying a curry comb. 'You've fetched us the wrong horse.' Jay looked at the calm bay gelding, then back at us.

'No, I haven't.'

'This isn't Dinkum.'

'It is.'

'This is Thwack It.'

'It can't be.' Then he must have realised that it could be, because the only indication that Jay had not turned to stone was the gradual stretching of his eyes. Slowly, his left hand came up and covered his mouth and one whispered word slithered between his fingers: 'Shit.'

'When did you bring it in?'

'May.' They stared at one another. 'It was grazing with Shebang. Fair Dinkum always grazes with Shebang!'

'Go and check its passport,' Dirk advised, but the magnitude of Jay's blunder was acting on him like glue.

'He'll kill me.'

Dirk wiped a hand over his face. 'Go on. Go and get its passport.'

'Dinkum's entered for a bumper in nine weeks ... It's never had a saddle on!'

'Passport!' Dirk urged. 'Before Mervyn finishes his breakfast.'

The mention of Mervyn spurred Jay towards the office. Within minutes, he was scurrying back with two Wetherby's passports. He was reading from Fair Dinkum's before he'd reached the shoeing bay: 'Whorl at upper eye level; mid-line.'

Dirk pushed the gelding's forelock aside, and Jay made desperate eye contact as he bowled in. Dirk shook his head.

'Tufted whorl at ventral lower third trachea?' Another glimpse, followed by another shake of Dirk's head. 'Left and right feathered flank?' They both knew this was futile.

'Pectoral whorls?'

Dirk didn't even bother answering. Jay closed the passport and Dirk took Thwack It's and opened it. 'Median whorls at base of forelock ...'

I lifted the horse's forelock. 'Yeah.' Jay put his head in his hands.

'... upper eye level, and muzzle.'

'Yeah and yeah.' Jay's knees buckled.

'Neck: left side crest whorl.'

I walked round the horse.'Yeah.'

Jay crumpled to the floor.

'Whorl on larynx.'

'Yep.'

His head was hidden behind his lower arms. 'He will kill me this time.'

He probably would. Mervyn's patience with Jay had been thinning for months, and there was no disguising this blunder. A horse who'd never been saddled was to race in nine weeks' time, and another who'd worked all season had missed its holiday. I picked up Dirk's toolbox, cast a glance at Jay's foetal position and headed for the van.

Dirk was sliding the anvil in when Mervyn shouted across the yard to him: 'Oi!' He was waddle-running. 'Where are you off to? What's job?'

Dirk slammed the van's back doors. 'You need to talk to Jay.'

Mervyn stared at Dirk who was heading for the driver's door, then, realising he'd get no more, he bellowed Jay's name. The silence was followed by a roar and the clang of a flying metal bucket. I climbed into the van, imagining the tightening of Jay's foetal position.

Chapter 39

At the top of Jennings' long drive, Caroline Jennings' Range Rover was gliding towards us. She slowed down and lowered her window. Dirk did the same and she addressed him over Lucky's yapping. 'There's an extra one to shoe, today.'

Dirk took his hands off the steering wheel and folded his arms. 'I think you might like to try that again, ja?' Her brow would have furrowed, had botox not been freezing it.

She sat back. 'Might I remind you that you are in our employ?'

Dirk leant forward. 'And might I remind you that manners cost nothing.' She drove off. So did Dirk.

Her husband was at the passenger door as soon as I stepped down from the cab. 'Where did you go last week? We looked round and you'd gone.'

'Oh, I took myself off,' I said, walking round the van. Jennings followed me.

'We never thanked you properly, so I'd like you to have this.' He handed me a weighty carrier bag. 'It was awarded with the prize money, so it seemed right you should have it.'

'Lucrative race, was it?' Dirk needled, as I slid a bottle of champagne from its wrapping, but Jennings was unabashed.

'Precipitant has a racing career now, thanks to this young man.' Then before he could be pressed further, he changed the subject. 'Look, I know you're short-handed,' he said, 'but if you could squeeze another one in today, I'd be really grateful.'

Dirk didn't take his head from the cavity of the van. 'Your wife said.'

'Ah.' Richard had heard Dirk's implication. 'I understand if you're too busy, and it's not a racehorse, so you might not have the right kit with you anyway.'

Dirk was interested now. 'Not a racehorse? What is it then?'

'It's a dressage horse. Dutch warmblood.' I was interested too. Why would Jennings have a Dutch warmblood? We followed him to the geldings' yard where a row of dainty thoroughbred heads was interrupted by the vast sculptural profile of the Dutch warmblood.

'Meet Vivacity,' Richard announced, opening the door.

All seventeen hands of Vivacity was restrained on a leather head collar, and crouched at his feet was Millie. I felt a pancake flip under my ribs.

'Millie's vetting him for me,' Jennings said, and when Millie smiled up in acknowledgement, I noticed the freckles speckling her nose. 'Toby thinks Pippa should give dressage a go,' Richard expanded, 'so she'll need the right horse.'

Millie caught my eye and the wry twist of her mouth said: *Just like that, on a whim – so he buys her a Dutch warmblood.* It was mischievous of her.

'Do you know how it's bred?' I asked.

'It's by Vivaldi.' I let out an involuntary whistle; according to *Horse and Hound*, Vivaldi's progeny was changing hands for six-figure sums. Jennings justified himself: 'If Pippa's serious, she'll need a schoolmaster to start her off.' I met Millie's eye again, and just before she raised it to the heavens, I noticed it was a cool jade green.

'I don't have the right shoes in my van,' Dirk said, 'but Ewan's back tomorrow. We'll shoe it then.'

Millie stood up and addressed herself to Dirk. 'Mr Jennings has had its feet X-rayed, so if you give me your number I can send the results on.'

'07896 123786,' I said quickly. She smiled cheekily and typed in my number.

'Or you could just send them to Will,' Dirk remarked, staring at me, not her.

I was walking towards the mare's yard, musing on Millie's green eyes and frothy curls, when Dirk's raised voice thumped into my thoughts. 'I said, how much do you think he's paid for that horse?'

'What? Sorry. I dunno. How old is it?'

He slid me a sidelong look. 'You were quick with that phone number.'

'Fifty grand, at least.' But Dirk hadn't listened to my answer; he was too busy laughing at me.

Back at the forge my phone rang. 'Yo!' It was a very cheerful Ewan. 'Have you finished?'

I asked Dirk. 'Half an hour!' he shouted.

'Great! I'll see you in the Fleece!'

We were thrilled to be seeing Ewan – but Maria was annoyed: 'Chicken with beans is ready *now*!' (It wouldn't have inclined me to stay.)

'I'll be half an hour,' Dirk insisted.

'I sick of this! I sick of not know when you in, when you out!'

'Maria! We're welcoming Ewan back, after his exams.'

'He gone four days! Four days!' She was holding four fingers up, then she threw her hands aloft. 'Is like you three gay boys!'

Dirk mimicked her all the way to the Fleece: '"Iss like yoo tree gay boyce!"' Ewan and Lee were at the bar; they'd got them in. 'Cheers!' Ewan grinned as we clashed glasses. 'It's good to be back!' He took a swig of longed for Yorkshire ale. 'How's Stanley?'

Lee gestured at his brother. 'This good mood of his has been freaking me out since Coventry. Tell 'em why, little bro.'

'I've finished my finals.'

'Bollocks!' Lee turned to us, gesturing with his thumb at Ewan. 'He has a lass.'

'No way!' It was out of my mouth before I'd thought about it. There was every reason for a girl to find Ewan attractive. He was tanned and muscular, and he was funny.

'What's so bloody strange about me having a lass?'

'Nothing! I'm just surprised.' It seemed remarkable that he would go to college to sit his exams, and come back with a girlfriend.

Dirk had been processing it. 'A girlfriend?'

'Yes! A lass! So?'

'No ... Great. Good on you, man.' There was still more wonder than congratulation in his voice.

Ewan put his pint glass down and stared at us both. 'Did you two think I was gay or summat?'

'No! It's just that ... well, you've never ...'

'I have!'

'When?'

'I fancied Pippa Jennings!'

'Everybody fancies Pippa Jennings!' Dirk appealed with his palms vertical.

'How did you meet her?' I asked, trying to sound genial.

'At college, duh.'

'What's she studying?'

'Farriery.'

'Farriery!' I hadn't meant for my voice to squeak.

Ewan glared at me. 'What's wrong with that?'

'Nothing. Nothing at all.' My hands were up in supplication.

'I'd have expected Crocodile Dundee here to be sexist, but not you.'

'Where I come from, man, she'd be a lesbian.'

'What's she called?' I pressed.

'What's it to you?'

'Jade,' Lee said, taking a sip of his pint. Ewan glared across the table at him.

270

'Did you see her then?' Lee was nodding at me and he would have said more but for Ewan's intervention.

'Why all the questions, eh? Why is my love life any of your business?'

'She must be a big girl,' Dirk said quietly. 'To be a farrier.'

'Stanley'll like her then.'

Ewan rounded on me. 'If you tell him, you're dead, Posh Lad.'

'He won't need to!' Dirk insisted. 'Stanley's juju will sniff it out. He'll be singing "Ring of Fire" within the week!'

I managed to change the subject and Dirk told Ewan how Millie had taken my number. By the time we'd recounted recovering Birdie's debt, Jay's precarious employment situation and whinged about the wasps in the forge, Ewan had relaxed. He went to get another round in and as soon as he'd gone, Dirk leaned across the table. 'What's she like then?'

Lee glanced over his shoulder. 'Massive.'

I snorted lager down my nose and Ewan shot us a glance. 'Listen,' he said, back at the table, 'Jade might not be in the same league as Pippa Jennings, but she's not spoilt, she's not up herself, and she's not afraid of a day's hard graft – and that'll last longer than a perky arse in a pair of jodhpurs!'

I was sucking froth from my half pint when my phone rang. Millie! I stood up. 'Hi, Millie.' Dirk almost choked on his lager. I turned and walked away from the table before the raucousness of their obscene gestures could travel down the phone line.

'I'm just about to send you the X-rays. There's nothing major. It could probably do with a bit of heel support, but it's short-backed – so I'll leave you with that dilemma.'

'Yes. Thanks.' My heart was racing. 'How old's the horse?' I wanted to keep the conversation going.

'Twelve, according to its papers.'

'In its prime, then.' That sounded professional enough.

'I would kill for that horse! And there's Princess Pippa

271

getting a horse by Vivaldi before she's even had a dressage lesson! Her dad must have more money than sense.'

'Richard's all right,' I said.

'You know the family then?'

'I ride work for her dad.'

'Really; I've never ridden a racehorse.' We were off! She was a keen dressage rider, twenty-four and qualified ten months. I was relaxing into the conversation when the pub's double doors banged on the wall and Maria blasted in.

'Chicken and beans is ruin!' Dirk cringed. The landlord turned to remonstrate, but Maria was off. 'One half, you said!' (she pronounced the 'l' in half) 'Is six big glasses on this table!'

'There're not all mine!' Dirk protested. A very amused Millie understood why I had to cut the conversation short and I returned to the table.

'Home!' Maria bellowed.

'I'll just finish this pint—'

'Now!'

Dirk stood, took a last gulp of his pint, and followed his wife like a spaniel. When the doors had closed behind them Ewan raised his pint glass. 'Jade likes a pint,' he said – and we toasted her for that.

Chapter 40

Ewan was running his finger down today's page in the diary. 'We've four to shoe at the maharaja's, four at Lofthouses, one at Mervyn's, and one at Jennings'!' He turned to Dirk. 'Why did you tell him we'd do that dressage horse?'

'Because last time Posh Lad upset the Jennings, Stanley nearly lost the whole bloody yard – remember!' Ewan launched a wet dishcloth at me as punishment. It arced past the wasps' nest which hummed like a temple at prayer, then disgorged a globe of whining wasps.

'Oh, well done!' I sneered, running for the door, but Dirk was pulsing with urgency.

'Get in here, man! We need to load the van if we want to finish before midnight!'

Grudgingly, I hunched inside my shirt and set about gathering shoes. Meanwhile, Ewan was protecting himself by wafting the dishcloth vaguely about his head, and Dirk carried on as if the wasps weren't there.

'A size three, do you think, for the warmblood, Dirk?' I scratched a tickle on the back of my neck, then swore and gripped my collar.

'Jeez, it's not a bloody scorpion,' Dirk scoffed. He must have forgotten how much a wasp sting hurts. I turned to Ewan and folded down my collar.

'Is the sting out?'

'Just get in the van, you big girl!' My neck throbbed and ached.

'I think you're meant to put vinegar on it,' I said.

'Van!' Dirk yelled. I half hoped for anaphylactic shock, just to prove my point.

Despite my disability, we completed the maharaja's four in three hours, which was good going, then it was straight on to Mervyn's.

I could hear the shouting from Mervyn's indoor school the moment I stepped out of the van.

'It said in t'catalogue that it had had a saddle on!'

'It might have had a saddle on its bloody stable door!'

'I've half a mind to put Ruudi on it,' Mervyn shouted as he emerged onto the yard complaining about Jay's uselessness.

'He's still here then?' I said.

'For now.' I raised my eyebrows and went to fill a bucket. 'There's more graft in Ruudi's little finger than in that useless beggar's body! And he's chirpy with it! His mother's the same. My house is spotless, t'meals on t'table six o'clock sharp every night.'

I would have questioned him about his plans for Ruudi, but Dirk's phone interrupted us. He covered the mouthpiece and mouthed *Stanley* at us.

'That's great news, but I've shipped the Hilux, man. Can't you ask them for an ambulance?' I heard Stanley's tinny rant on the other end, then Dirk agree to something and hang up. 'You're to fetch Stanley,' Dirk said. 'We'll finish this job, then I'll take you for your car.'

The collar of my polo shirt had been dragging over my wasp sting all afternoon. I hadn't complained for fear of cracks about crocodiles and African killer bees, but when Dirk dropped me off I was glad to find Maria at home. 'You should come this morning, Will,' she said, as she rubbed Anthisan into my sting. 'I sick and tired of this macho man.' For a proud second, I prickled with testosterone – then she clarified, 'Not you, Will,' and replaced the lid on the tube.

Stanley was sitting on his bed in ward B2, fully dressed and grinning. 'Right then, Posh Lad, let's get the hell out of Dodge.' I tried to take his bag, but macho man wouldn't allow it, so I walked ahead, empty-handed. 'What's to do with your neck, Posh Lad?'

'Wasp sting.'

'Wasp sting!' he sneered. 'They've just ripped me a new arsehole!'

I suspected they'd reinstated the one he already had, but it didn't do to argue with Stanley, so I changed the subject. 'Ewan's back.'

'I hope he's in a better mood.'

'He should be!' I'd activated Stanley's juju.

'How's that then?'

'Finishing his exams, I mean. I mean, it must be a relief, knowing they're all done.' I could feel his eyes. 'I don't know. I'm just going from how I'd feel ... Anyway, he seemed in a good mood when we took him to the Fleece ...'

'Has he gone and got himself a lass?' I should have denied it. I should have said, 'A lass! Ewan? You're joking!' but I pretended to be absorbed in scouring the car park for the Astra. 'Whey hey! Our Dolloper has himself a lass!' Stanley rubbed his hands and laughed. 'I can read you like the Yorkshire weather, Posh Lad!'

A welcoming party was waiting on the drive and when Stanley stepped out of my car Lucky almost turned herself inside out in Jack Russell joy. The greeting and back-slapping fired her into a volley of barking that made Maria cover her ears. Good wishes accepted, Stanley walked to the doorway of the forge and surveyed it, nodding approvingly and wafting at a couple of wasps. 'At least it's made you tidy up,' he said. Stanley had been denied the mundane pleasures and now he began to fill the kettle.

'We'd be better in the house,' I said, pointing at a droning pair of wasps now circling the sugar jar.

'Just fetch us some jam,' Stanley ordered.

'Are you joking?' I was considering the consequences of carrying jam into the forge.

'Just do as you're told, Posh Lad.'

I carried out his order, regardless of its lunacy, and Stanley took the lid off the jar, plonked it on the floor and handed me my brew. I watched as a dozen wasps congregated on the jam jar and we enjoyed a forge brew for the first time in weeks. Stanley asked about Aunty Dorothy, Dirk updated him on his plans for travelling home, Ewan reported on his exams, and Stanley asked Ewan if he intended to keep in touch with his college friends. 'You must have made some good pals, like, over t'years.'

'A few. Yeah.'

'Lads and lasses?'

'Mainly lads.'

'Did you not get to meet any lasses then?'

I knew exactly where this was going and despite being mesmerised by the growing globule of wasps on the jam jar, I was desperate to deflect him. 'Mervyn's been asking after you, Stan.'

It was as if I hadn't spoken. 'Is there a social club, like, where you can all mix in?' He was only moments away from Jade, and though I take no pleasure in animal suffering I was relieved when Lucky's ear-slicing yelp stopped all conversation and she streaked past, ears flat, tail tucked. She shot through the forge, crossed the garden, and buried herself in a hydrangea.

Stanley stood, but Dirk moved faster. He knelt on the lawn, stuck his head under the bush and tried to coax her out with a custard cream. She wouldn't come; if anything she buried herself deeper. Convinced she'd come out for him

Ewan reached in, then he roared, swore and snatched out his bloodied hand. The bush was emitting the gnashings of the van-devil and Stanley was becoming more and more agitated. Afraid he would try to get her himself, Dirk demanded the gardening gloves. Fully gauntleted, he plunged in and this time he dragged out a snarling, writhing shape-shifter which had completed the first stages of a mutation into Pete Burns.

'Jesus Christ!' Stanley yelled. 'I told you to sort these bastard wasps, Dirk!'

'I rang the council!'

'You should have got them shifted!'

'You wouldn't pay!'

'Look at my bastard dog!'

'What else could I do?'

'This dog needs a vet!'

'Calm down, ja?'

'Calm down? My bastard dog's turning into Jessica Rabbit!'

Ewan dashed across the lawn with the first aid kit. Stanley began rifling through it. A pack of gauze hit me on the shoulder. 'What bastard use is that?' A box of Elastoplast split and spilt on impact with the forge wall. Elastic bandages, TCP cream, eye pads and slings were flying across the garden, when Maria walked across the grass with a magnifying glass, a pair of gardening gloves and a tube of Anthisan. She placed them on the workbench, sighed and raised her eyes to the heavens.

Chapter 41

'Hey up, it's Hugh Heffner,' Ewan remarked when he saw Stanley on the drive in his dressing gown.

Stanley was jabbering through our open car window about not having slept a wink. 'I've been thinking about them wasps ...' It was too early to think about wasps, so neither of us took him on. 'And I've had a brainwave,' he said as I parked up and locked the car. He followed us into the forge chattering like an over enthusiastic five-year-old. 'Listen, listen to this ...' he was saying as he jogged alongside us. 'They only smoke them out, don't they, when you ring the council?'

I walked briskly towards the kettle. 'Do they?'

'Yeah, yeah – and then they charge you a hundred and seventy-five bastard quid for it.' I couldn't help noting the degree of consternation Lucky's wasp sting had created by contrast to mine. 'Well, I've got a weed burner, haven't I?'

Ewan had stopped in his tracks. 'No, Stanley.'

'What do you mean, "no"?'

'I mean, I'm having nothing to do with this.'

'You don't even know what I'm going to do!'

'I know that you, a weed burner and a nest full of wasps has got disaster written all over it.'

'Has it heck!' Ewan barged past him to put tea bags in the mugs. 'We'll get proper togged up so they can't sting us, and then we'll nuke 'em!' (The fact that Stanley was holding an imaginary semi-automatic as he spoke did nothing to reassure us.) 'Oh, come on! Maria's going out in ten minutes! We can just zap 'em!'

'I bloody aren't zapping nowt wi' you,' Ewan stated decisively.

'You'll do it, won't you, Dirk?' Dirk was sitting on a box of shoes and shaking his head like an exasperated parent. 'Come on! You've wrestled crocodiles and all that shit!'

Dirk looked him. 'I shot it.'

'What about you, Posh Lad?'

'No way!' Their solidarity had made me emphatic. 'I've only just recovered from the last wasp sting!'

'We won't get stung! We'll be proper togged up, like beekeepers!'

'And where are you going to get beekeepers' kits from?' Ewan asked.

'We'll improvise!'

'Bugger off.'

Stanley looked round. He took in Dirk on his box of shoes, Ewan with a teaspoon in his hand and me, leaning on the draining board. 'Is that it then?' We looked at one another to reaffirm our positions and nodded as one. 'Well, what a bunch of bastard nellies,' he said, and stomped into the house.

I was enjoying the final dregs of my Earl Grey on the garden bench, appreciating the cobalt sky and the insistent bird song that soared over the traffic on Hathersage Road, when Stanley made his entrance. 'Those striped suckers are gonna cop it now!' he drawled in a muffled accent that owed more to Bradford than to Baltimore. I turned to look at him.

Stanley was holding a propane torch in massive garden-gloved hands. A red scarf held an eye-slitted bed-sheet taut over his face and green wellies poked out at the bottom. He relaxed his gunman pose and swaggered a step. 'What d'ya reckon?' I'd already burst into laughter. 'There's nowt getting through this outfit though, is there?'

'You're out of your mind!' Ewan affirmed.

'Nellies!' Stanley shouted, and continued his swagger down the steps, though, unable to see, it soon degenerated into a tentative fumble. Dirk steadied him but Stanley shook him off, irritated. Slowly but determinedly he zombied a path towards the forge. We watched, then looked at one another in disbelief. The nuking of the wasps was imminent.

'Van!' Dirk commanded. Fishing the keys from his pocket, he headed for the driver's door. A panicked fumbling and he was in. He let me in and Ewan all but clambered over me. Dirk forced the windows up tight. Ewan pressed takeaway cartons over the pedals. I stuffed the air vents with tissues, sweet wrappers – anything, whilst thanking the gods that we never cleaned out the van.

Stanley was still plodding down the drive like a Hammer Horror extra. He passed through the door and into the forge. He lumbered to a stool and in three scraping lunges, had dragged it to the nest. We gaped through the windscreen as he climbed onto the stool and slowly raised the weed burner to shoulder height. He pointed the burner straight at the nest. I cringed in readiness.

Ewan started a countdown.

'Ten.' (Torch at arm's length). 'Nine.' (Nozzle touched nest). 'Eight.' (A click). 'Seven.' (Nozzle removed). 'Six.' (Lighter lifted to torch). 'Five.' (Torch sparked). 'Four. (Torch blazed). 'Three.' (Torch touched nest). 'Two' (Tongue of flame lashed forwards.) 'One.' (Tongue of flame lashed backwards.)

Stanley stumbled. He fell off the stool. His bed sheet was on fire and fifteen hundred wasps were loose. He scrambled up. He lurched away. Caspar the Friendly Ghost was blazing up the drive in a cloud of wasps. He banged on the bonnet.

'Fuck off!' Ewan shouted. The wasps were swarming like a single being.

'Let me in!'

'Sod off!'

Stanley staggered to Dirk's window. 'Help!'

'You're on fire, Stanley!'

'Open the door!'

'Look!' Stanley looked, saw it was true, and dropped to the drive. He rolled and groaned as wasps crunched inside his ghost costume. We were laughing with a brutality borne of disbelief.

'You bastards!' he shouted, as he staggered to his feet and plunged in the direction of Bling Manor. The haze of wasps was further obscuring his vision so he smashed into the French windows. He groaned, dragged them open, fell through, dragged them shut, slipped down the inside of the glass – and was still.

Time ticked. We looked at one another. 'At least he's inside,' I said.

'And the fire was out,' Dirk added. Stray wasps smacked the windows. Some stayed, sizzling on the glass. Dirk craned sideways, looking for movement from behind the French windows.

'Let him sing "Ring of Fire" at me now, eh?' Ewan said, and I laughed, half-heartedly.

'Do you think we should see if he's all right?' Dirk asked.

Ewan sighed and stirred in his seat. The wasps had thinned from a fog to a mist. Ewan dropped to the tarmac and swiped at the air. I raised the collar of my polo shirt. We crossed the patio.

We found Stanley puddled on the Axminster shagpile like a used Guy Fawkes. The bed sheet was taut as a drum skin across his gasping mouth and the buttermilk carpet around him was blackened with mud and cinders. Dirk dragged the remains of the sheet over Stanley's head and propped him against the glass. Stanley gasped and coughed. We waited whilst a spent, stung, singed scarecrow slowly reformed itself into Stanley.

Ewan folded his arms. 'They sell wasps' nest eliminator foam in B&Q. It's £4.99.'

After a moment's breathy silence the burnt rags stirred. 'Fuck off, Dolloper.' It was a raspy whisper, but it was recognisably Stanley.

Chapter 42

Ewan was at the window, pointing at a brown envelope and grinning like his smile would meet at the back. Ricky slipped round the door frame, tailwagging, and Ewan followed him onto the path waving the envelope. 'I've passed!'

Our meeting was a spontaneous embrace. 'Well done, mate! I knew you'd do it!' I followed him into the house, where his dad was preparing to celebrate with a fry-up. His face was glowing. 'What about that, eh? Triple As. There's nobody in our family gets As,' he said as he flipped a slice of bacon.

Lee spoke through a mouthful of sausage sandwich. 'If I'd have got an L in my GCSEs, I could have spelt "ugly".' Ewan furrowed his brow. 'U, G, E,' he explained, using three fingers.

Ewan's dad handed me a bacon butty. 'The U was in English.'

I walked into the forge ahead of Ewan, turned and pointed to him. 'Here he is! Ewan Grimshaw: Member of the Worshipful Company of Farriers!'

Dirk took two strides and lifted him clean off his feet. 'Good on you, mate!' he shouted, gave him a theatrical smacker then rubbed Ewan's scalp with enough vigour to burn his hair off.

Stanley was shaking his head. 'Bugger me, Dolloper! What about that?' He held out his hand for the brown envelope, but Dirk snatched it, whipped the headed paper from its envelope and read:

'Theory, A; Shoemaking, A; Shoe fitting, A!' He whistled

in admiration and went in for a shoulder hug. 'That's unheard of, man!'

'He had a shit-hot teacher,' Stanley observed, turning back to his workbench.

'Aye, Moneybags Morrison were a big help,' Ewan rejoindered, but Stanley was busy filing the end of a shoe.

'You've done all right, for a dolloper.'

Dirk wanted to book his flights. The three of us could easily have squeezed into the Old Van, but Ewan said he'd had enough of Lucky and insisted that I drove the Astra to Mervyn's.

'Not one word!' he fumed, as he climbed in. 'All I wanted was "Well done, Ewan".' My tyres crunched on the gravel drive. 'Would it have killed him, eh? Just once?'

'He's chuffed to bits,' I said as we joined the flow of traffic. 'Anyway, I'm the one who's stuck with him. You can work for anyone with grades like that!'

I felt Ewan turn to me. 'And live where?'

'I dunno. Rent a flat!'

'And I pay the deposit, how?'

'With what you've earned!'

'I can't earn without somewhere to live, and I can't get somewhere to live without earning!' His laugh was bitter. 'You've no idea, have you?

'Posh Lad' had been a joke, a tag, a nickname. I hadn't even seen myself as posh – but when it came to the workings of the world, it was true. Ewan had a street wisdom I'd take another lifetime to learn. He had just attained the best grades in the country, but his life would barely change.

'Come on,' I said, slapping his thigh. 'You've been aiming for this day since you were sixteen, and look at you! You've a face as long as a Pakistani wedding!'

He managed a weak smile, stared through the passenger window and started to tell me a story. 'When I was little – like, five or something – my gran used to pick me up from school, and on the way home she let me pick a cake. I always picked the meringue and I'd carry it home in its little white paper bag, really looking forward to it. I'd settle myself in front of the telly, and she'd fetch it out on a blue plate, and it looked like a cloud. I'd pick it up, put it to my lips, and bite – and d'you know what? It were nowt. Nowt. There was nothing to it. Just air.'

I didn't know what to say.

'It was like I couldn't believe it, because the following Friday, I'd pick the meringue again. I'd look forward to it again and I'd be disappointed again.' Silence filled the car. I hardly dared change gear. 'Nowt lives up to its promise.'

'It's just the anticlimax after the adrenalin,' I told him, but it was dawning on me that despite years of social reform, being a posh lad was more use than exam results. I pulled over and nipped into the newsagent's. The four Mars bars I bought were an apology for being middle class. 'Do you know how Jade got on?' I asked, back in the car.

'B and two Cs.' He swivelled his head to me. 'You haven't said owt to Stanley, have you?'

'Course I haven't!'

The first thing I heard on Mervyn's yard was Ruudi's voice: 'Will! Will! Ruudi pass jockey course!'

'That's great news!' I said. It was – for Ruudi – but Jay was a marked man now. Ruudi's grin showed the black slot where his teeth had once been and Stanley patted him on the back.

'Well done, lad.'

'Thank you, Mr Stanley.' I felt Ewan bristle.

'How long was your course then, Ruudi?'

'Four days!'

'Really? Mine was four years, wasn't it, Stanley?'

Stanley looked up from where he'd been sorting through nails. 'What do you want? A standing ovation?' He perched on the tailgate of the van whilst Ewan lit the forge. 'I suppose I'd better start thinking about a new van.' We both looked at him. 'Well, we're going to need one, aren't we? There's no point having two qualified farriers on one job.'

'Oh, so I do have a job then?'

'A job?' Stanley scowled. 'You'll be t'boss wi' Dirk goin'.' Ewan managed the first smile in an hour.

'So what model are you thinking of?' I asked, bracing myself for a description of a Corsa currently on bricks at a mate's house.

'Well, when I say *new* van, that'll be for me. Ewan'll be having the Old Van.'

'Fair enough.' Ewan shrugged, still quietly delighted.

'And when I say "having it", I mean during the day. I'm not having it parked on Cribbs Estate all night.' Ewan crumpled a bit, but he returned to his shoeing.

'And when I say during the day, Posh Lad will be driving it.'

Ewan stood up from under the horse he'd started to work on. 'Stan! I'll look a right berk being driven about by the apprentice!'

'You shouldn't have left lumps of my bastard vehicles all over Yorkshire then, should you!'

'Anyway, how can you train Posh Lad, if he's driving me about all day?' He'd played his trump card.

Stanley tossed an orange in the air and caught it in a downward sweep. 'All right, but if you inject this van into a bastard bus, you'll be buying the next one yourself.' Ewan winked at me. Stanley walked the length of the yard, then back again. He turned the standpipe on. Then he turned it off again. He wandered over to where Ewan was shoeing. 'You've taken a lot of hoof off there, Dolloper.' Ewan did not answer him. Stanley ambled back to the van and started cleaning his fingernails with a paring knife. 'You don't want to be putting the nails in too high either.' Ewan controlled an out breath. Stanley held the paring knife at arm's length. 'It's a clever design in't it, a paring knife? Somebody's thought about that.'

Ewan straightened from under his horse. 'Stanley, are you going to be coming out with us every day?'

He spread his hands. 'What else do you want me to do? Watch *Homes Under the* bastard *Hammer?*'

'I dunno! Go to see Mandy.'

'She'll be at work.'

I pretended not to notice when five minutes later rusty nails started pinging off my raised backside. 'Them nails look a bit high to me, Dolloper.'

'Stanley! I'm a qualified farrier!'

'You still know next to nowt.'

Ewan straightened up. 'What grades did you get in *your* exams, Stanley? Or were they still countin' on an abacus then?'

Nothing entertained Stanley like an argument and he'd have kept it going all morning if Mervyn hadn't slapped him on the back and shaken his arm like it was a football rattle. 'Good to have you back, lad. That bloody South African you've been sendin' has no idea.'

Stanley shook his head. 'He were all I could get, Mervyn.'

'He smashes their feet up! I've told him and told him about knockin' too many nails in. He's made a right bloody mess of 'em.'

'Aye, well, he's goin' next week.'

'Next week?' Mervyn looked concerned. 'Will you be fit to wrestle racehorses?'

'Dolloper's qualified now.'

'Is he?'

'Aye, he's going to be steppin' up. He only gone 'n' got the best bastard marks in his year!'

'Has he? I hope you're throwin' him a party.'

'Party!' Ewan scoffed. 'He's too tight to throw me a cricket ball!'

'Course I'm throwing him a party!' Stanley blurted.

Ewan stood up from under his horse. 'Are you?'

'Aye. Course I am. Saturday night at my house. You can come if you want, Mervyn.'

Mervyn winked at Ewan and walked away.

Chapter 43

'Right!' Stanley was leaning on the Old Van and counting on his fingers. 'Me, you, Dirk, Maria, Mervyn, Dagmar, Ruudi ...'

'Should we say Ruudi, plus one?' I asked.

Stanley looked up. 'No. He'll bring a bastard horse.' He was about to start counting again, then he stopped. 'Why? Do you want a plus one?'

'Me?' I shook my head. 'Your rules have scuppered my love life!'

'I think I might have a plus one,' Stanley mused.

Ewan poked his head round the back doors of the van. 'Who?'

'Mandy.'

'I don't even know Mandy!'

'You do!'

'I've met her twice!'

'Well you throw the bastard party, if you're going to start getting picky about the guest list!'

'I thought this was *my* party!'

'I've a brand new arsehole to celebrate, don't you forget!'

'And it is Dirk's leaving party,' I added.

'And Mervyn and Dagmar's engagement party ...'

'And Ruudi's jockey party ...'

Ewan threw his hands wide. 'Have I to bother coming at all?'

'Course you have! Fetch your plus one – and I'll fetch Mandy!'

'What plus one?' Stanley tapped the side of his nose and winked. Ewan glared at me. 'You've told him, haven't you!'

'No,' I said, 'but you just have!'

'Oh, just fetch the lass, Dolloper. Why the bastard cloak an' dagger?'

Ewan turned away. 'She's in Lincolnshire.'

'They have trains, don't they?'

'You'll just take the piss.'

Stanley chuckled and Ewan fell silent as he finished packing the van. I slid my toolbox in, held the door open for Lucky and jumped in after her. Dirk had cases to pack, Stanley had food to buy, balloons to fill, banners to hang and guests to ring, so Ewan and I would be working unhindered.

'You should ring her,' I said as Ewan closed the driver's door. It was a few moments before he answered me.

'She's not like Pippa Jennings, you know. She's not a perfect ten.'

'So?' Ewan slid the van off the drive and into the flow of traffic. 'Do you like her?'

'Course I do! She's a beltin' lass, but I can just hear Stanley: "By heck, she's etten all her puddings up. I'd have made two trips to Sainsbury's if you'd warned me ..."' I let the matter drop.

Ewan was the model of professional efficiency. The effect of the letters DipWCF was remarkable. He explained to the proprietor of Scorthwaite Livery Yard why he was rolling a cob's front shoes, he was patient with a shiverer and stood back to admire his perfectly aligned nails. Not once did he feign singeing me with a passing shoe or make a wanking sign behind the van door.

I was wondering how easily I'd adjust to the qualified Ewan when, instead of driving back to the forge, he pulled into a lay-by. 'What're you doing?'

'Chilling,' he answered, dragging on the handbrake. I clamped Lucky's jaws, tucked her under my arm and stepped onto the moor. 'He'll only pile more work on if we go back now.' I set Lucky down and she zigzagged joyously, snapping at insects. I followed Ewan up a meandering sheep path until he threw himself on the tussocky grass and lay with his hands behind his head. I crouched beside him and looked at the rumpled, ranging moor.

'Not a bad office to work in, is it?'

'I didn't think you'd stick at it, when you started.'

I laughed. 'I haven't yet.'

'You will though. You've fitted in.' I basked in the compliment and Lucky yapped at a distant stranger daring to walk his collie on the footpath half a mile below us.

'So, are you fetching Jade to this party, or what?'

'I dunno. It'd be different if you were fetching somebody.' I plucked at a handful of grass. 'Why don't you ring that vet?'

'Don't be daft. I've only met her three times.'

'She likes you though.'

'I hardly know her!'

'Go on! If you'll ring the vet, I'll ring Jade.' I watched a skylark rise and rinse the air with its bubbles of birdsong and remembered Millie's frothy giggles. 'What's the worst that can happen?' He was right; nothing ventured ... I took the phone from my pocket and stared at it. She'd probably pretend to be on call to spare my feelings. My throat was dry and my hands were sweating but I slid my finger across the screen.

She answered it quickly. 'Hi, Will.'

I stumbled and sputtered over a greeting then I gathered my mettle. 'Listen, I know you don't really know them, but Stanley's throwing a bit of a do for Ewan, the other apprentice – well, he's not an apprentice now. That's the point. You met him at Moneybags Morrison's. I know he's not really called Moneybags. His proper name's Michael, but we call him Moneybags. Well, anyway it's on Saturday night, and I was wondering if you fancied it. I understand if you're on call – I'll bet they always make the young ones do Saturday nights – so there's no hard feelings – but I thought I'd ask …' It was then I became aware that Millie was laughing.

'I said yes!'

'Did you?' I'd been so busy giving her exit clauses that I hadn't paused for her answer. 'So you'll come?'

'Yes!'

It was a date. I turned to Ewan, triumphant. 'You'd better hope that Jade can come or you'll be Billy No Mates!'

I collected Millie at eight on Saturday night. She'd looked pretty in the livery of Eckersley Vets, but tonight she looked beautiful. She wasn't classically good-looking; her nose turned up and her chin was sharp but her quirky attractiveness compelled me. My eyes only left her when Jade strode into the Fleece. She was between Ewan and Lee, and though Lee had The Belle of Cribbs Estate on his arm, (eyelash extensions, push-up bra, fake tan and scarlet lipstick) she was invisible next to Jade. Jade had charisma. She was wearing skintight leatherette leggings, a swinging red shirt and a studded biker jacket. Her black hair was swept up at the front, but tumbled in soft curls down her back. Her earrings were gold hoops, her heels were red stilettos and her smile lit up the public bar. When Ewan introduced us her rich voice seemed to smother us in molten chocolate and Ewan was transfixed. He watched her every move and when she sipped her drink, he sipped his own in synchronicity. I'd never seen him like this.

Before long we'd been joined by Stanley and Mandy. I'd built up a picture of a buxom farm girl in a checked shirt and tight jeans, but – aside from the buxom bit – I was wrong. Mandy was older than I'd imagined; easily as old as Stanley. She was wearing sensible shoes, a floral dress and a navy blue cardigan. (A degree or two colder and she'd have been in tweeds.) There was a brisk efficiency about her. 'Get the drinks in, Stanley,' and suddenly Stanley was fishing in his pocket. 'Where's that card we fetched him?' He patted himself in panic before remembering she'd put it in her handbag.

Ewan was opening his congratulations card when Mervyn and Dagmar walked in carrying balloons. The introductions were still going on when Flashman Freddie and Charmaine and Dirk and Maria arrived.

Bob Entwistle approached us from his usual table. 'Is it a party?'

'It is!' Ewan told him. 'And Stanley's in t'chair.'

'Mine's a whisky,' Bob announced, and settled himself in. Jay, Fintan, and Ewan's dad soon swelled the party and Ruudi arrived late, smelling of horses. The party spilled into the pub's backyard where three plastic tables stood on a carpet of tab ends – but it was too summery a night to be in the bar.

Like all Hathersage parties, Stanley's wouldn't start proper until the Fleece had stopped serving, so it was eleven o'clock when we crossed the road to Bling Manor, where we were joined by Sandra and several of the neighbours who'd fetched a basket of Yorkshire fare for Dirk to take back to Western Cape.

'Lekker!' he laughed, then fantasised out loud about eating parkin on a sun-soaked veranda. Maria dabbed her eyes and hugged all the neighbours in turn, and Sandra unveiled a cake in the shape of an aeroplane.

With Sandra's help, Stanley had hung lanterns in the trees, decked the dining room in balloons and festooned it with banners. Now he opened the French windows onto the patio which had become a makeshift stage, with microphone, iPod dock and karaoke machine. I explained Ewan's hospital performance to Millie and by popular demand (mine and Stanley's) Ewan kicked off the singing with 'Hot Stuff'. Jade's eyes were fixed on Ewan and his cheeky wink set her swooning. As the final note sounded he gestured to her and Jade bounded up the patio steps, took the microphone, and the opening notes of 'Summer Nights' sounded. She slithered her molten chocolate voice into a grinning, flirting duet with Ewan and they had found their element. It was clear what made them tick. I looked at Millie's profile as she smiled up at them in admiration. Meanwhile, Jade's rich voice seemed to soak the grass like dew as she began 'Leaving on a Jet Plane' for Dirk and Maria.

Stanley sidled over and handed me a can. 'I'll make a speech if ever we can shut Big Bird up.' I slid him a critical glance. 'Good singers are always big lasses, have you noticed?' I raised my eyes starwards as I opened my can. 'It's right! It's to do with ballast.' He took a swig. 'You couldn't choke her with bastard kerb stones, though, could you?'

Bob Entwistle shuffled past us with a bulging shopping bag. 'It'll keep me goin' all week, will this.' Stanley was protesting he wasn't running a bastard food bank when a strident voice cut across Jade's vocals.

'Stanley! How many cans is that?'

'Three, my flower.' It was at least his fifth. I was about to remark on it when the song came to a close, Stanley bashed his beer can on the wall for silence and took the microphone. 'Thank you, thank you.' The garden and the dining room dribbled to silence. 'Now, it's not so often you can say you're at a party with four qualified farriers ...'

Mervyn looked round. 'Four?' Ewan lifted his arm from Jade's shoulder and proudly pointed at the crown of her head. 'Hey up!' Mervyn said, and started a round of applause.

'There were a lot of reasons for this party,' Stanley went on. 'Dirk here is leaving us after cutting down my tree, half killing my favourite hen, overseeing the destruction of two of my vehicles and letting thieves in during the night, but I'll be sorry to see him go – not least because he'll be taking the lovely Maria with him.' Maria dabbed her eyes again, and the assembly raised a glass to Dirk and Maria. 'My old friend Mervyn has found true love with the beautiful Dagmar, who he's to marry next year ...' Dagmar twinkled her diamond solitaire in the lantern light. 'And Dagmar's lad, Ruudi, is Mervyn's newest apprentice jockey.'

'Bangor on Dee!' Ruudi slurred. 'Eight weeks!' And in

raising his can to toast himself he slid off the wall.

'The main reason for this party, though, is this lad here.' Ewan slid his arm from Jade's shoulder and joined Stanley on the patio steps where Stanley circled Ewan with his own arm. 'He's not only qualified as a farrier, but he got the top grades.' At this Jade put her fingers to her teeth and let rip a searing whistle. I stamped and cheered, Dirk yelled, 'Good on you!' and the rest of the party clapped politely. Stanley held up a hand for silence. 'Last week this lad got the best grades in the country, but,' he turned to Ewan, 'I want you to tell these folk what you knew when you came working for me four long years since.' Ewan shrugged. 'Go on, Dolloper – what did you know when you first come working for Stanley Lampitt, Registered Farrier?'

'Nowt.' Ewan shrugged.

'Correct answer! You knew nowt! And what do you know now?'

He shrugged again. 'Next to nowt?'

'Exactly! Next to nowt. But you're learnin' already, see?'

The group clapped, and Mandy appeared with another cake, this time in the shape of a horseshoe. After much cheering and singing of 'For He's a Jolly Good Fellow', Ewan cut into the cake, the speakers blasted 'Congratulations', he ambled down the steps and handed me a paper plate piled with cake.

'It's been a good night,' I said.

'It has,' Ewan answered through a mouthful of marzipan. 'Three more years and we'll be partying for you!'

'If I pass.'

'You'll walk it. Look how you've come on!' He glanced across at Jade who was piling her plate with fruit cake. 'You'd have been sat up in a corner this time last year.'

'Would I heck!'

'You wouldn't have said "would I heck" either! To our future, Posh Lad.'

I looked my new boss in the eye. 'To our future, Dolloper,' and we clinked cans.

295

Acknowledgements

This novel was inspired by the witty insights, tender observations and technical knowledge of my farrier son; thank you. Thanks are also due to my first readers, Elisabeth Bradshaw, Jackie Robinson and Pippa Taylor for their judgement and encouragement, and to my husband, John, whose patient rereading saved me many a gaffe. I continue to be grateful for the tenacious faith shown in me by Victoria Hobbs and Pippa McCarthy of A.M. Heath and Co, without whom I would most certainly have given up. My thanks are also due to Kate Mills of Orion for her advice, encouragement and shared sense of humour.